PRINCES OF SANDASTRE

Antony Swithin was born in England but now lives in Canada. While still a child, the mysterious Atlantic island of Rockall came to haunt his imagination; and it has done so ever since. Over the years, his concepts of the island have evolved into a whole imaginative tapestry, rich in detail — of its geography, its fauna and flora and the history of its peoples, so that the island emerges in his writing as a land as real as any to be found on our maps.

Princes of Sandastre is the first volume in a series of novels about Rockall. The second will be *The Lords of the Stoney Mountains*.

PRINCES OF SANDASTRE

The Perilous Quest for Lyonesse

BOOK ONE

Antony Swithin

FONTANA/Collins

First published by Fontana Paperbacks,
8 Grafton Street, London W1, 1990

Made and Printed in Great Britain by
William Collins Sons & Co. Ltd, Glasgow

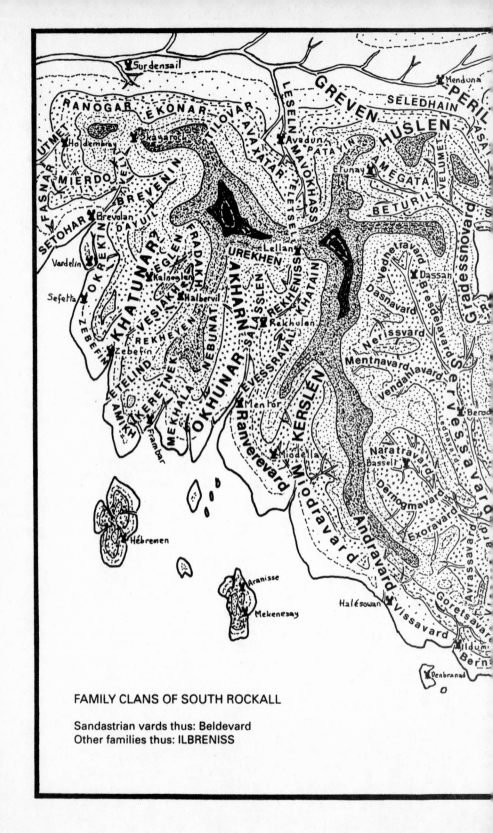

FAMILY CLANS OF SOUTH ROCKALL

Sandastrian vards thus: Beldevard
Other families thus: ILBRENISS

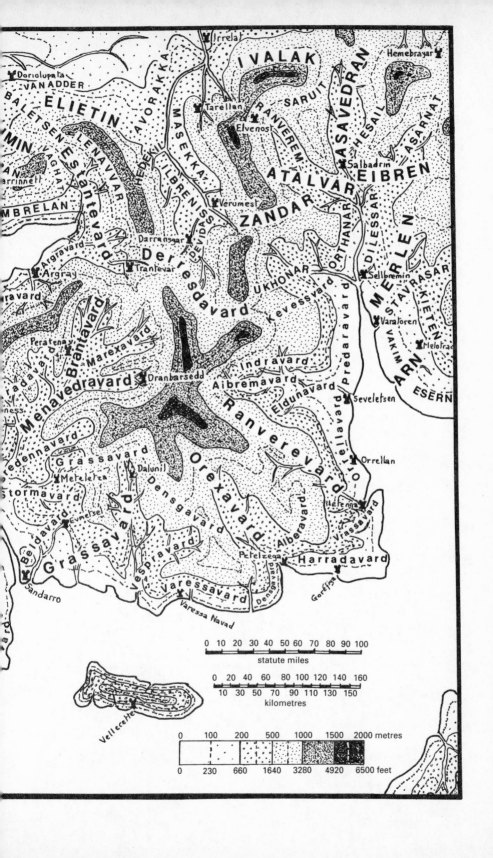

CONTENTS

ILLUSTRATIONS

I. Map showing the Family-Clans of Southern Rockall

II. Plan of Sandarro

FOREWORD

Though the immense riches of the mines of Reschora and Kelcestre have by now made it one of the wealthiest countries on earth, the Republic of Rockall remains remarkably little known. Its unique flora and fauna arouse profound interest among naturalists and its rocks condition the thinking of geologists about the structure of the whole North Atlantic basin; yet few naturalists or geologists have been fortunate enough to visit this sea-girt realm.

Indeed, Rockall is in many ways an unusual country. Its eight-house parliament is a model for study by political scientists, yet the operations of that parliament are little understood in other democracies and nowhere emulated. It continues to rely upon animal power and steam haulage for road and rail transportation and employs battery-powered helicopters for emergency services and for recreation. Petroleum is used only to power long-distance aeroplanes. Yet surely so wealthy a country could readily afford to import petroleum for surface transport also? Its refusal to do so has long been thought an inexplicable eccentricity. Only now, as world petroleum resources diminish, is that refusal coming to seem wise, even admirable.

Of all European countries, Rockall has the fewest roads, the most green countryside, the most benign and unspoiled shores, the least trodden and most challenging mountains; yet of all countries, it welcomes tourists from abroad least. Yes, exchange rates against the stable Rockalese currency are extremely high, but that is not the major problem. Rather it is that the Rockalese are so self-contained and so contented a people. They are not great travellers themselves, for they like their own land too well to feel obliged to visit others. Nor do they see any need to allow their land to be submerged by tourists. Why should they be subjected to the tiresome demands and unacceptable prejudices of foreigners, when they are wealthy enough to need neither Deutschmarks nor dollars to prop up their economy? Why allow their shores and mountains to be spoiled by high-rise hotels, constructed merely for the accommodation of strangers? Of all visas, that for Rockall is perhaps hardest to obtain; and thus is the peace of that land protected.

Geographically, Rockall is the farthest-flung of European countries, isolated by the turbulent Atlantic from the expansionist ambitions of kings and the greedy philosophies of clerics and republics. Even during the present century, Rockall has remained a country apart. The First World War certainly produced serious upheavals in the nascent republic, yet outside involvements were very largely avoided; and whilst, in the Second World War, Rockall did play a major role in the struggle against the fascist powers, afterwards it withdrew again within its own bounds. It gives financial support generously to United Nations projects; but Rockall is rarely active in that political arena and, indeed, keeps as much detached from world politics as can be contrived. Thus, whilst other Europeans, arriving as settlers or as fugitives, have played so prominent a role in the history of Rockall, the Rockalese scarcely figure at all in that of the rest of Europe. In consequence, in histories of the continent of which it is the westernmost part, Rockall receives scant attention.

Yet in the National Library of its capital, Rockall Peak, and in the ancient archives of the castle of Sandarro, there are to be found many dramatic and remarkable stories of heroism and adventure. Most of them, to be sure, are written in the difficult languages of that land and have not hitherto been translated into more familiar tongues. To those libraries, I am fortunate enough to have been granted access; and it is my aim, in this book and any that may come after, to retell some of those stories.

That which follows is taken from a lengthy manuscript appended to one of the Sandastrian *Books of the Years* — that long series of volumes spanning over fifteen hundred years and unrivalled, as a continuous record, by the archives of any other country. The manuscript was written by an Englishman, yet he wrote in the Sandastrian language and characters that had become familiar to him. To translate it into the English of his day would be as artificial as, and much more difficult than, rendering it in our modern tongue. Consequently I have adopted the latter course, though I have retained mediaeval words that have no close modern equivalents and have striven to avoid inappropriate images.

I have employed English equivalents to Rockalese words, wherever such exist; thus 'Rockalese' is used instead of *Rokalnen*, 'Sandastrian' and 'Baroddan' instead of *Sandastren* and *Baroddnen*, 'Fachane' and 'Fachnese' instead of *Fakhhayin* and *Fakhniis*, and so forth. I have done my translating informally and have at times inserted explanations or descriptions that the writer omitted; yet I shall tell the story in the first person, as he did, so that Rockall and his adventures there may be viewed through his eyes.

ANTONY SWITHIN, Chronicler.

Chapter One

THE WIND FROM THE EAST

News of the battle of Shrewsbury blew east with the wind — and that wind carried away for ever the life I had known. Soon I was to be whisked out of my quiet life and across the seas, to a land and into adventures stranger than the very wildest of my imaginings.

Mine had not been a bad sort of life, on the whole. It was true that my mother had died at my birth but, since I had never known her, I could not miss her. For my father, though, her memory was ever brought alive in me. Her family, the Watertons, who had been for so long seneschals of Pontefract Castle, were a small, dark, fervent race — some said, with Welsh blood in them — and she was a typical Waterton. My father treasured a portrait of her, painted for him on a roll of parchment by a wandering artist. He carried that portrait with him always and had shown it to me so often that I knew her features well. She had been as slim as I, with the same dark hair and brown eyes, even the same expression — an intent eagerness that was also shy. In contrast, my elder and only brother was as large-boned and blond as my father himself — the Branthwaites had always been big.

Since brother Richard was a true Branthwaite and would be his heir, my father had seen to it that he was fully trained for that part. When seven years old, Richard had been sent off to be a page to Lord Furnival in Sheffield Castle where, as well as learning the arts of courtesy and service, he had been given a good grounding in the martial arts. Afterwards he had constantly accompanied my father, be it to court or to camp. He had seen service in the marches of Wales, during the rising of Glendower. Following that campaign, Richard had been made armiger. Later, as one of the squires of the great Hotspur himself, he had fought the Scots at

1

Homildon Hill when Earl Douglas was taken. Richard could carry himself with the pride of a proven warrior and might hope soon to be knighted.

Very different had been my own upbringing. Perhaps because I reminded him so vividly of the wife he had loved so deeply, my father had kept me always by him — always, that is, save when he went off to the wars. Whenever father travelled to other manor houses or to court, I was allowed to act as page with the other boys of my age; but I had not been sent to live and learn away from home, as Richard and most of those other boys had been.

During those visits and at home, I had learned in some part the skills proper to a page; how to serve at table, to recognize and blazon coats of arms, to play backgammon and chess, to sing songs to citole and psaltery, to hawk and even to hunt. Yet I was not allowed even to begin upon that other and greater part of the training of a page — his training in the arts of war.

In falconry and in venery, yes, I had certain abilities that father could admire. There was my skill with animals, for instance. The most fractious falcon, the fiercest dog and the most rebellious stallion would alike respond to my voice and touch, becoming tranquil and obedient. As a result, I was an able falconer and a confident rider to hounds, out-racing and out-jumping all but the very ablest of the field. Father was very proud of this, even when he was anxious about my safety. Yet, despite my ability in riding, I was not permitted to try my skill with the wooden lance in the practice tourneys that the other pages so much enjoyed.

Father was proud also of my skill when hunting on foot. I had a quick eye for tracks and for those slighter disturbances of grass and plants that told of the passage of animals. Moreover, since I was light in build and quiet in movement, I could find and follow deer or wild boar and approach grouse or bustard with a facility that even John Stacey, father's huntsman on our rough upland demesne, could not surpass.

Yet certain of my attitudes puzzled both John and he; and perhaps these were additional reasons why I was not permitted to progress to that second stage of a page's training. Why was it that, when I went out hunting on foot alone, I brought home game so seldom? They did not understand and I felt unable to explain. The truth was that I had come to find pleasure in merely observing animals and birds and learning of their lives; in watching the hares cavorting under the March wind, the snipe drumming its bounds above the steep fields, the fox cubs rolling and playing at the mouth of their earth or the roebuck feeding in the coverts. I could not account, even to myself, for this abnormal attitude of preferring to watch creatures alive than to kill them — what, after all, was the purpose of animals and birds, save to provide sport for gentlemen? — so I did not try.

Why also was it that, having ridden in the front rank of the hunt till the very end, I seemed never in evidence at the finish? When the unfortunate quarry was being torn to pieces or given the *coup de grâce*, I seemed never to be there. This, father could not understand. Surely I must take pleasure, as a gentleman's son should, in such spectacles? Yet it seemed I did not; how odd!

From whatever causes — his lack of confidence in me, his over-protectiveness toward me — father would neither send me away from home to be trained in the techniques and strategies of combat nor, despite his own considerable skills, give such training to me himself. Even a basic instruction in swordsmanship was denied to me.

Moreover, as I grew older, my situation worsened; or so I considered. When father went off to fight in the border wars, I was left behind in the safety and boredom of our manor house of Holdworth, a boredom broken only by my daily ride to Sheffield Castle. There I was given instruction, not in the martial skills for which I yearned, but in manorial administration and accounting, the speaking and writing of Latin and the intricacies of religious doctrine. I was a reluctant pupil, but Lord Furnival's chaplain was a firm and formidable teacher. Despite my unenthusiasm, I learned much from him.

On his return my father, who was no sort of scholar, enthused over my abilities with book and pen in a fashion I found ominous. When I besought him once again to have me trained as a soldier he did not definitely refuse, but nor did he respond positively to my plea. He seemed unwilling to quench my ardour for such training, but equally unwilling to permit me to proceed with it, instead advancing reasons

3

for delaying any decision — reasons that were clearly quite specious. Uneasily I suspected that he was intending I should enter the Church — a common enough fate of second sons of gentlemen.

However, I was determined that it should not be my fate. Insofar as I could, I had long been striving to give myself the training that my father was denying me, the training proper to a knight's son. This was not easy. I had acquired an old sword but, having no-one with whom I could practise, I found it hard to improve my swordsmanship. To fence with one's shadow, and fiercely to attack bushes and trees, is not enough; I knew myself to be an execrable swordsman.

Nor did I fare much better in my attempts to train for tournaments. In one of our upland pastures, ringed by horse chestnut trees that both protected me from view and served as targets, I practised secretly with a long ash pole that I had fashioned into a lance. However, a tree is a very different thing from a mobile, mounted opponent and, for all my flourishes of horsemanship, I felt I was making little real progress.

So I taught myself other skills. I could throw a stone further and more accurately than most, by hand or with a sling. In addition, by standing long with heavy cross-stave in outstretched hand and by persistent exercising at the butts, I had made myself into a fair archer, able to outshoot most of the Hallamshire yeomen. My father knew of these abilities but, since they were not considered proper skills for a gentleman, he discounted them.

I had a third skill, learned from a Genoese traveller who had strayed into northern England and been engaged to tutor me in French; but that skill I kept secret, since I knew father would despise it also.

Nevertheless, though my oddities troubled my father and his over-protectiveness troubled me, our mutual affection did not diminish. Indeed — perhaps because of that deprivation brought to all three of us by my mother's death — there was a great love between my father, my brother and me.

My father had long been a close friend of Henry Percy, that handsome, forceful, passionate warrior whom men called 'Hotspur'. He had been at Henry Percy's side when Henry Bolingbroke was brought back to be king. The two had shared in the early triumphs of that monarchy, but they had shared also in the disillusionment that followed. As the rift between King Henry and the Percys grew ever wider, my father had of course given his support to his friend. Though father was no great noble but a mere knight, he spoke forcefully and well; and, because he was Hotspur's friend, he was listened to. In consequence, the King had marked him down as an enemy.

By spring of the year of our Lord 1403, the quarrel had become so bitter that Hotspur was gathering an army about him. It was inevitable that my father and Richard should ride west, with what levies they could recruit, to join Hotspur's camp.

The number of those levies, unfortunately, was few. Old Lord Furnival had no strong links with Hotspur, nor with the King for that matter; he was sitting tight in Sheffield Castle and showing no favour to either disputant. The iron-workers, smiths and knifegrinders of Hallamshire cared too little about what went on beyond their valleys to be involved in this conflict; they would not rally to such a cause. Though my father's renown as a warrior was great, our fief of Holdworth was not extensive and there were few who owed him fealty. Only thirty local men could be persuaded into following him.

My father's squire had been killed at Homildon, yet he would not accept me as his squire, preferring instead to promote John Stacey to that position. Nor would he permit me even to join that meagre band. Father was apologetic, but firm; I was too untrained a warrior and, since someone had to be left in charge of the demesne — who better than I, whom he could trust? However, as we both knew, he had accepted other, equally untrained soldiers into his following. The truth was that father could not bring himself to risk his beloved younger son in the bitter affrays of civil war.

So I watched them ride away, father and Richard in scarlet surcoats and bearing the scarlet shields with the three silver badgers of the Branthwaites, their followers in a motley collection of surcoats, some scarlet, some azure and hastily stitched with the Percy emblem (the five golden fusils joined in fess), most jacketed in leather or in cloth unadorned. Well, this might only be a small contribution to Hotspur's army, but many others would rally to his cause. Since that cause was just, it was sure to prevail! So I believed, as I watched them ride away that spring morning.

The weeks went slowly by and grew into months; spring burgeoned into summer; and the quarrel between Hotspur and the King ripened toward the civil war that all were expecting. A steady trickle of news flowed over the hills into Hallamshire. Sir Richard Venables of Kinderton and Sir Richard Vernon of Shipbrook, two worthy warriors, had rallied to Hotspur's standard; the Earl of Worcester had joined him also and Hotspur's father, the Earl of Northumberland, was raising a second army. The Welsh under Glendower had promised to rise against the King and Hotspur's former prisoner, Earl Douglas, was rallying the Scots to invade England yet again, this time in Hotspur's support. Some said even that the Prince of Wales, who had been Hotspur's friend, would side with the rebels against the King; but always I doubted that, for what would be the Prince's fate if his father were dethroned? Yet it did seem as if an irresistible tide was rising to overwhelm the Bolingbroke; and since I was sure Hotspur was invincible — and especially so when my beloved father was at his side — I had no fears about the outcome of the imminent conflict. Rather did I wish it might be swiftly over and my father and brother triumphantly home again.

There was, in truth, little for me to do during those weeks. Old Walter Tinsley, our steward, Peter the bailiff and Cerdic the reeve had the affairs of our demesne well under control. I would check the accounts with Walter once a week, ride around the manor each morning and discuss farming plans for the next day with Cerdic, and each evening dine at the high table with Walter and Peter to discuss the day's doings. It had been father's custom always to invite them to dine with him, except when he had guests; and, in father's absence I was glad of their company. However, I could have wished their concerns were less parochial and their conversation more stimulating.

In the afternoons, whatever the weather, I would exercise for an hour or more. First I would practise slashing with my heavy, blunt sword at an upright wooden post till my wrist and shoulder ached. Then I would shoot arrows at a 'saracen' cut from an old board. I did this from progressively greater distances, with, across or against the wind, to see how my arrows would behave in flight and with what force they would hit the target, so this exercise was more interesting. Only occasionally would I take my horse to that secluded pasture and practise with my 'lance'; I had become bored with that endeavour.

When my practising was done, I would wander off on most days into the woods that choked our Pennine valleys, up along the gritstone edges or across the bleak moors behind, to look for badgers or buzzards or whatever else I might sight. Though I took my bow, usually I returned empty-handed; and the servants would puzzledly shrug their shoulders yet again.

What was hardest during those weeks was being deprived of the company of my peers. There was indeed nowhere for me to go. Though I did once ride into Sheffield, it was to put in hand an order I wished executed privily, not to visit the castle. Until the coming conflict was resolved, I could expect no welcome there.

From my mother's family there had developed an estrangement so profound that I could not seek companionship at Pontefract Castle either. My uncle, Sir Hugo Waterton, was now its seneschal. He was a restless, discontented and land-greedy man whom I had never liked; even when I was small, father told me, I had bawled in dismay whenever I encountered him. Of late, however, he had given us good cause for a much stronger distaste. Sir Hugo had obtained or fabricated — we were not sure which — a document that, he claimed, gave him title to our feofdom. As he well knew, his claim had little justice. However, as he knew also, it would be settled, not in court but in the coming battle. If the King won, his malice would ensure that his judges granted Sir Hugo the title; if Hotspur won, the claim was assuredly lost. In the meantime Sir Hugo held Pontefract for the King. Had I tried to visit that castle — and I had no desire whatsoever to do so — I would have been turned from its gates.

July came and with it, at last, the news of the proclamation of revolt. Men said that Hotspur had rallied an army of fifteen thousand already. He was advancing on Shrewsbury and the Prince, who held that town, must soon capitulate. Meantime, Northumberland's army was marching south and the Scots also. The climactic battle must be at hand, surely? Yet the days passed and it did not happen. My restlessness became ever more extreme, as I became ever more impatient for the good news that I was confident must come. Our demesne received little of my attention in those weeks.

Then came the tiding that the special order I had placed had been fulfilled; and, one bright Monday morning, I mounted my horse to ride into Sheffield again. There had been no rain for a week or more, yet the day was humid. Moreover, there seemed a tension, an expectancy, in the air. Was there a storm coming, or was this tension merely a product of my own thoughts?

My horse was a handsome white stallion, a full fourteen hands high — a big horse for one so small as I, and of such uncertain temper that he had been named Firebrand. For that reason, father had left him behind; but I knew I could trust Firebrand and was proud to ride him. I had put on a surcoat of scarlet silk from Genoa, which had been carefully emblazoned with the three silver badgers of the Branthwaites. It was much the most expensive garment that I possessed and more suited to a tourney than to a country ride. However, when I would be riding so close to Sheffield Castle and the vacillating Lord Furnival, somehow I felt it necessary not just to indicate, but to stress, my family identity.

Because that ride, in a sense, marked the end of my childhood, I remember it well. Eastward I headed, out of our demesne lands; through the hamlet of Holdworth where were clustered the cottages of our villeins, the children calling merrily to me as I passed and exclaiming at my bright cloak; then down among the dappled light and shade of Loxley Chase, to follow the banks of the little River Loxley till it tumbled into the Rivelin. After so dry a spell, even their combined waters were shallow; Firebrand was only fetlock-deep when we forded the river, to follow the well-beaten track along the west bank of the Don into Sheffield.

It was Fair Day. I lingered in the shade of the castle walls, examining the stalls of velvet, wool, ribbons and furs; harking to the cheapjacks as they pattered to the crowds about medicaments which, they claimed, would cure all ills; watching a juggler as he tossed more and more balls ever higher and higher; and listening with pleasure to a group of goliards who were making music on shawm, pibcorn and psaltery.

Since this was such a small fair, I was startled to encounter a man bearing a square frame about his shoulders, on each corner of which a hooded hawk was perched. I bargained with him a while for a splendid goshawk, but its price was too high for me.

Lord Furnival's steward was hovering nearby, eager to buy yet unwilling to be seen in my company. Mischievously I bowed ceremoniously to him and was much cheered by his evident embarrassment. Then I bought bread from a pestour and, after eating it and sampling the wares of a buxom alewife, went on my way.

I had only a few miles farther to ride, up the valley of the Sheaf to where a wooden wheel was trundling its waters to foam. Here was a little forge where knifegrinders worked, under the supervision of one Adam of Heeley. Men said he was the best craftsman in all Hallamshire; and it was to him, a few weeks before, that I had entrusted my commission.

He was a short, square man with a brusque manner and little time for civilities. 'Well, Master Simon,' he said, 'Ah've done some funny jobs in my time, but none so rum as this. It took three tries to get 'em cast, with all thy fuss about *weight* and *balance* and all; and Ah'm none so sure they're reet yet. Any'ow, Ah'll fetch 'em so tha can see for thiself.'

He brought out for me a shallow wooden box lined with lambswool. In it were packed the special items I had ordered him to make: twelve small, shining knives, each with heft bound in leather, with heavy curving blade and pointed tip. These were throwing-knives, made to the model of a single Italian knife left for me by that Genoese traveller two years earlier. I had practised often with that knife and knew it to be quite as dangerous a weapon, at short range, as any arrow from a crossbow. However, one such knife was not enough, for it might all too soon be lost. I had needed more and my father's prolonged absence, though so much regretted, had at least afforded me the opportunity to have them made.

I picked up one of the knives and tested its balance, then

touched its blade against my finger, wincing as it cut into my skin.

'Aye, they're sharp enough,' Adam laughed. 'Tha mun take care! And they'll cost thee a pretty penny. Three castings, it took . . . A groat apiece they'll be; and Ah hope tha can think the money well spent, for it seems a reet waste to me! What does tha want wi' knives with such little blades? Ah can see no use in 'em.'

I grinned at him, picked up one of the knives and, with a quick flick, threw it at a tree stump. The blade buried itself so deeply into the wood that it took quite a pull to release it.

Adam nodded slowly. 'Aye, so that's thi idea; Ah see now . . . Sharp enough they are; keep them so and they'll serve thee well. And tha'd better have t'original knife, too, while Ah think on.'

He went again into the forge and returned with the little Florentine blade, putting it into the box and wrapping the box in sacking. I handed Adam four florins, plus an extra groat for luck. He gave me a quick word of thanks and a brief salute, then disappeared back into the forge; time was not to be wasted on further civilities!

As I rode away, I wondered if he'd ever again receive such an order; somehow I doubted it. I was glad to have those throwing-knives at last and I whistled as I rode back into Sheffield. That was to prove the last thoroughly happy hour I would enjoy for many days.

Even as I drew near to the fair, I was aware that something had happened. The people were no longer straggling about the stalls and the goliards' music had ceased. Instead, the crowd had coagulated into little clots, talking avidly and in hushed voices. Recognizing one of the yeomen from Bradfield, I hailed him: 'Hey, Robin, what's the news?'

He looked at me solemnly and shook his head. 'Why, Master Simon! There's word come east of a battle — a big battle. Ah reckon it's bad news for the Branthwaites: for they say Hotspur's army has been broken by the King and the Percy himself slain.'

Hotspur's army defeated? Hotspur himself fallen? No, it could not be; surely it could not be . . .

Yet, though none knew how the news had come, it seemed

10

dishearteningly definite. King Henry had marched across England faster than any had believed possible, to relieve his son the Prince in Shrewsbury. He had challenged battle with the rebels before the Earl of Northumberland and his troops had arrived, before even the Welsh had rallied. With profound unwisdom, Hotspur had accepted the challenge — and lost. There were no real details yet as to who had lived and who had died, save only that Hotspur himself was dead. That indeed was enough, for without his leadership the revolt must collapse.

While I asked anxious questions, cloud was spreading to blanket out the sun. As I rode home there came rain, steady, soaking rain, as if the very heavens were weeping at the downfall of a hero and a cause.

During the next two days, more news drifted across the Pennines as the first soldiers from the broken army fled homeward. It seemed Hotspur had been infected with madness. He had given battle to the King when there was no need to give battle; and he and the Douglas had led a charge when there was no good reason to charge. They had seemed irresistible at first. The Earl of Stafford and Sir Walter Blount had been slain and the Prince of Wales sorely wounded; even the royal standard had been beaten down. Yet that charge brought disaster, for Hotspur was struck by an arrow and died almost instantly.

After that, the rebel army disintegrated. The Earl of Worcester, Sir Richard Venables and Sir Richard Vernon had been taken. Two days later — on the very Monday of my ride into Sheffield — they had been executed at the High Cross in Shrewsbury. Yet this did not sufficiently assuage the King's fury; he vented it further by having the dead body of his one-time friend Hotspur crushed between two millstones and afterwards beheaded and quartered.

If that was the King's mood, there could be no mercy for my father and brother; but of them I could gain no news. Surely they must have been involved in that charge, yet they were not named among the slain. If they had been captured, Richard might have been forgiven but my father would assuredly have died at the High Cross. They had not been taken, then . . . Was there hope that they might yet escape the King's wrath? Might they be fleeing homeward to Hallamshire? Might they be seeking refuge in the Welsh mountains with Glendower, or going to exile in Scotland, perhaps, or France? I could not guess; and, as you may imagine, those were restless days.

Sometimes I waited for tidings in or about the manor house; sometimes I ranged the moors and woods, always on horseback now, looking out for fugitives; and twice I rode into Bradfield, to offer frantic prayers in its little church. At dinner I would talk gustily with Peter the bailiff and old Walter, then fall silent. Those were difficult times for them also, for all three of us knew the days of the Branthwaites at Holdworth Manor to be numbered and our futures uncertain.

It was on Saturday that, at last, the word came — on another day of rain, with mists clinging to the hillsides and the paths ankle-deep in clay. Out of the rain and into the courtyard came a solitary, mud-bespattered horseman — John Stacey, my father's erstwhile huntsman and squire. Surely he would not have left my father; did this mean my father was dead?

Before even the groom had seen John and run out to take his horse, I was by his side. As he dismounted, I seized him by the shoulders. He was so weary that he swayed in my grasp.

'John, I'm blithe that you're back — but my father, and Richard? Are they dead? What has happened?'

He looked at me and sighed. 'Nay, they're not dead. Your father was wounded right enough, but he could ride. After the battle, we got him away, Richard and I . . . But he's gone; Richard and he, they're both gone — gone to Rockall — gone to Lyonesse!'

Chapter Two

RAIN IN THE HILLS

This was enough for the moment; John was weary and clearly famished also. I led him inside, helped him off with his cloak and boots — a service at which he protested, but which I insisted on performing — and found a drier cloak for him.

While the butler set out food and drink for John in the solar, I gathered the other servants in the hall and told them briefly that their master, Sir William, and his son were alive but in flight — news which set them chattering like a tiding of magpies. Well, fair enough; I understood their excitement and accepted their hesitant expressions of sympathy. However, I knew also that, with a change of masters in prospect, most of them were no longer to be trusted. Consequently I asked old Walter to guard the door while John talked further.

With food and good ale inside him, my father's squire soon brightened. He told me more of the combat — how, in the charge, my father had slain Sir Walter Blount before being himself wounded; how Richard had been at the Percy's side when that stray arrow had stricken him down; and how, with Hotspur beyond his aid, Richard had joined my father in further hard fighting before the rebel army finally broke.

With the battle lost, they had ridden from the field and found concealment in a thicket. While John tended to my father's wounds, they had hastily reviewed their situation and found it desperate. That no forgiveness could be expected from King Henry, they knew well. Where then, might they go? That there was no refuge to be found in Wales, they were sure; Glendower might have received them kindly, but the Welsh had betrayed their own leaders too frequently to be trusted by any Englishman. My father had fought the Scots so often that to venture himself in their country would have been madness; and the shifting politics of France and the Low Countries made them uncertain refuges. So the three had ridden southward without any clear aim in mind, save to evade the King's reach.

By Monday noon they had reached Bristol. There the news of Shrewsbury was already in the streets, but fortunately my father was not recognized. They had made their way to the quays, still without clear plans. As it chanced, a ship from Rockall was in port. Deciding quickly that so distant a land would furnish them with a safe refuge and fresh opportunities, father and Richard had approached its captain and secured for themselves passages to Lyonesse.

However, John would not go with them; he knew himself to be in no particular danger and was too distrustful of foreigners to wish to leave England. So he had been entrusted with the sale of the horses and with a farewell message for me — a verbal message, since that was felt to be safer.

'Tell Simon,' my father had said, 'that since God has not chosen to favour our cause, there can be no life for Richard and me in England. The memory of the King is long and his wrath bitter, as all know. Our fief of Holdworth is surely forfeit and, were we to stay, our lives also would be forfeit. So we accept exile; we shall sail to Lyonesse and there find a new home. Tell Simon that he may seek mercy from the King if he so wishes, for the King's anger may not reach out at him; or perhaps Simon might take up holy orders, for the strong arm of the Church would surely protect him. Yet, if he desires to do neither thing and if his soul be brave, then he must follow us to Lyonesse. Whatever be his choice, Simon has my blessing and his brother's.'

So those were my father's words; the last, perhaps, that might ever come to me from him. They showed equally his pride and his doubt in me, yet also they portrayed his love for me and his gentleness. First came the suggestion that I might choose to seek the King's pardon; surely he knew well that I could never do so? Next, his old idea of holy orders. Yes, the Church would indeed furnish for me a sanctuary, but I had no ambition to seek such sanctuary. Only in third place came his other suggestion, that I might follow my brother and he to Lyonesse; but that, surely, must be what he desired, in view of his love for me. Yet, regardless of my choice, his message ended with his assurance of that love — an assurance without condition.

At last I had the challenge for which I had been so long seeking, the challenge to adventure. Of course I would follow him! My decision was instant; yet little could I foresee the length of that road, or its perils.

After bidding a reluctant and affectionate farewell to his master, John had ridden away from the quay, leading the other two horses. He had been fortunate to find buyers for them immediately for, with the revolt crushed and many knights slain, there would soon be a plethora of warhorses on the market and few purchasers. John had lodged overnight in the back room of a Bristol alehouse. Understandably after two exhausting days, he had slept long and late. When he went down to the quay next day, it was to learn that the ship to Rockall had already sailed on the early-morning tide.

In the ensuing days, John had made his way northeastward across England through the backwash that followed the breaking of the storm-wave of battle. It had been no easy journey. The King's officers were busy seeking out those of Hotspur's principal supporters who had not been killed or captured at Shrewsbury. Though John himself did not figure in their list, his master was at its head, especially now that the Earl of Northumberland had been taken. Because of this, the towns were not safe. Moreover, since the rougher of Hotspur's defeated followers had already taken to ambush and robbery, to seize what gold they could before Henry regained full control of his kingdom, the countryside was little safer. John had slept wherever he could find shelter, beside his never-unsaddled horse and with his cloak as pillow; and, during the daytime, he had been ceaselessly vigilant. There had been two narrow escapes from robbers in the forest rides, when only his quick eye had saved him from ambush . . . Yes, it had been a hard journey, but it was behind him. With evident relief, he pulled out a leather purse and counted into my palm the twenty nobles that the sale of those horses had brought.

I congratulated John on his valour and honesty, entreated him to say nothing of my father's destination and message, and sent him off to his cottage to rest for a few hours. He undertook to return before dinner. I was glad of that, for I knew I would need more of his advice, but I was glad also that there would be a few hours alone, for I needed urgently to make plans. Thinking was impossible in the disturbed ant's nest that our manor had become, upon receipt of the morning's news; so I saddled my horse and, donning the scarlet surcoat more, as a sort of defiance than because it would provide real protection against the rain, I sallied forth.

I took a path northeast, up on to Onesmoor where the wet wind would be refreshing and there would be none to disturb my thoughts. I rode slowly, allowing Firebrand to pick his own way over the stones and through the tussocks, and tried to remember all I could about Rockall. Lyonesse — yes, that had been the legendary realm of the father of Tristan, a realm overwhelmed and drowned by a great sea-wave. Yet it had also come to have a reality, and that through a knight from these very Pennines in which I lived.

Arthur Thurlstone was his name. His mother and father had died, while he was yet an infant, in the Black Death of 1369, and he had grown up in the charge of a maiden aunt. She was a wise soul and proud, by nature a warrior yet prohibited by her sex from such a life. Consequently Arthur had become the focus for her unattained ambitions. She had crammed him full of history and legend. He had come not only to know thoroughly, but also to accept as veritable truth, the legend of Tristan and the stories of his own namesake, King Arthur.

In their image and at his aunt's urging he had made himself into a knight, valorous in tourney and in battle. He had been befriended by another young Yorkshire knight, Sir John Warren of Mytholmroyd, and somehow had persuaded his friend to participate in a quest of truly Arthurian character — for that Isle of Avallon to which, according to Geoffrey of Monmouth's *History*, the wounded King Arthur had gone to recover his health, never yet to return to Britain.

Nor was their idea so wild as it sounded. As all knew, there *was* an island out in the Atlantic, where the old traditions of chivalry persisted and where weird beasts roamed the forests and mountains. To that island of Rockall many an English, Scottish and Gascon knight had gone during the last few turbulent centuries, to seek sanctuary or honourable adventure. Sir Arthur was sure that Rockall was none other than King Arthur's Avallon. There, maybe, the King had died; or maybe he had formed another Round Table and was awaiting England's overweening need before returning.

According to my father, Sir John Warren never put much faith in his friend's theories and never truly believed that Rockall could be the lost isle of Avallon. However, since Rockall was a real island, he had been willing enough to accompany Sir Arthur in his quest. Nor had it been hard for the two to find other followers. Fifteen years ago, frustration at the misdoings of King Richard II had been at its height; there were plenty of other valiant young warriors eager to join in any quest that offered fresh prospects and new horizons. The band of adventurers had bought a ship and sailed west. And, indeed, they had carved out for themselves their own realm, somewhere on that distant island. Yet they had named it, not Avallon, but Lyonesse — quite why, no-one seemed to know.

Three years after they had first sailed, Sir Arthur had returned to cajole more men into following him. Since that time, there had come no further news of Lyonesse. However, stories enough about it were told in the Pennine villages — of creatures so fell and happenings so wondrous that I put little trust in those tales.

Yet Lyonesse must still exist, for had not my father gone there? And other ships from Rockall did put into Bristol from time to time; that much I knew. Well, I must go to Bristol and find my own passage to Rockall, to Lyonesse. I would prove to my father that his younger son was also valorous!

Good enough; I would leave Holdworth soon — tomorrow, perhaps, or the next day. No doubt the Watertons would seize it; their lawsuit would surely succeed now! Old Walter, our steward, would never willingly enter their service; well, I could give him enough gold from my father's store to see out his days in comfort. Peter the bailiff and Cerdic the reeve were wedded more to the lands of Holdworth than to any master; they and our other servants would accept the Watertons readily enough. As for John Stacey, there was a farm up among the limestone hills near Malham to which my father owned title and of which the Watertons knew nothing; I would give him the deeds to it. I rather thought he'd be taking a girl from Penistone up there with him, for he'd found many reasons in the past year to visit that village . . . For me, Holdworth had long been home, but recently it had come to seem like a prison; I could part from it without regret.

As I rode and pondered, the rain had slackened and ceased. Now a watery sun was emerging from behind the clouds, as hesitantly as a badger emerging from his sett at dusk. That image heartened me; badgers were the emblem of the Branthwaites and sunshine always brought cheer. Yes, I had been too long pent up in these Pennine uplands by the clouds of doubt and despondency: it was time for me to go forth into the wide world beyond. I turned Firebrand's head and rode back towards Holdworth.

This time I followed a different path which, as it chanced, brought me through the cluster of cottages in which our yeomen lived. Few people were abroad; the women had stayed indoors because of the rain, the men were still out working their lands. However, as I passed the first cottage, John Stacey ran out and called to me urgently.

'Master Simon! Master Simon! Wait on; there's news — bad news!' As I reined up, he ran to my side. 'You mind young Ralph — old Watkyn's son? He fought with us at Shrewsbury. Well, he's back; he's in the cottage now. He came through Ashbourne and met up with some King's officers. Seemingly you're on their list for arrest! The King is angry as a bear that he's missed catching Sir William and says "If I can't take the hawk, then I'll have the eyas." So they're coming to Holdworth to arrest you! They'll be here in the morning, Ralph reckons. What shall you do?'

This news had set my pulse racing; events were surely crowding in on me today! However, I summoned up a smile for John. 'It looks like I'm going to have to leave, doesn't it?'

'Aye, but there's another problem. Guess who's at t'manor just now? That popinjay Hector Waterton, Sir Hugo's son! Come on a cousinly visit, no doubt, or maybe to survey his future property.' John snorted in disgust.

'Well, of course I must welcome my cousin, mustn't I?' I responded lightly. Yet John was right; I must return at least briefly to Holdworth and, if dear cousin Hector were there — not that there was, or ever had been, any affection between

18

us! — my departing would surely be rendered more complicated.

It was late afternoon already; Hector was sure to expect to be accommodated overnight. It would be hard for me to find any excuse not to entertain him; despite the lawsuit, our relations with the Watertons had remained at surface civil. Moreover, though Hector was presumably not yet aware that I was under threat of arrest, I could scarcely leave the manor while he was there without my departure being most carefully observed.

John walked beside me as I rode back to the manor. He spoke no more, for he knew I was thinking furiously.

Hector was still in the courtyard when we arrived, elaborately instructing the groom concerning the proper care of his horse. This was a black stallion with a hammer head, inferior indeed to Firebrand, as I noted with amusement. Hector himself strove to be at the height of fashion; his garb had surely been chosen to impress rather than for practicality. He wore a green houppelande of the 'bastard' calf-length but slit at front and back to make riding, if not easy, at least possible; it was high-collared, ornately embroidered and had full sleeves with elaborate dagging. His legs were enclosed in tight yellow hose and his calves in fawn boots, pointed-toed and buckled at the sides. On his head was a turban-like hat from which two curling feathers sprang — or rather, trailed, for the wet weather had not done them good. Indeed, his whole appearance was bedraggled; he looked not so much a leader of fashion, but rather like a court jester too long shut out in the rain.

Hector pretended not to notice me as I rode in, but I was sure he did, for he ended his instructions in words pitched loud enough for me to hear: 'I realize you have no good stabling here, fellow, but do the best you can and you shall be rewarded.' Then he turned, affected to notice me for the first time and said in tones of the most ineffable condescension, 'Ah! Cousin Simon!'

I dismounted and, hastening up to him, took the limp hand he offered. Not without irony I responded: 'Cousin Hector! What an unexpected pleasure — and what an honour!'

As we embraced with a maximum of courtesy and a minimum of affection, I took hasty stock of him. It was many months since last we had met and I had forgotten how very alike we were in appearance. Both of us were small and dark, slim and brown-eyed. We might easily have been taken, if not for twins, certainly for brothers; though Hector had a quality of effeminacy which, I trusted, I lacked. Hector was eyeing me with equal interest. I could see that my silk cloak had impressed him, for his own, although so elaborately embroidered, was only of wool; and I could see also that he envied me of Firebrand. At that moment, a plan began to burgeon in my mind . . . I signalled John to wait, conducted Hector inside and ordered my butler to see to his wet clothes. Then, excusing myself, I slipped outside again to talk to John.

When I joined Hector in the solar an hour later, I found that he had shed that wet houppelande and set aside his hat; both indeed had been taken away by the butler to be dried. Instead he had borrowed from my wardrobe a loose-sleeved scarlet jupon which, with his yellow hose, gave him an even greater vividness of colour. He was sitting relaxedly on a padded stool, a flagon of sherris sack on the chest beside him and a goblet in his hand.

'You've been the devil of a time, Simon,' he observed discontentedly.

'I'm sorry,' I answered meekly. 'As you'll understand, cousin, I had to ensure that a fitting meal would be prepared, properly to mark your visit. Normally, of course, we would be eating much more simply.'

This was only in part true. I had indeed arranged a banquet, but I had also been busy with other matters. To old Walter I had confided the news of my imminent departure, passing on to him the gold that would ensure his own future comfort — the old man had been afraid of that future and was deeply grateful — and arranging that the deeds of the Malham farm be given privily to John Stacey. I had also made a few other covert and hasty arrangements, about which I had no intention of telling Hector.

My reply, and its tone, pleased him. 'Yes, yes; very proper. Well, cousin, I need hardly say how grieved we were when your father chose to side with those damned rebels. Fore-doomed, of course; we all knew that His Majesty King Henry would soon settle Hotspur's hash.'

Odd, then, I thought to myself, that you chose to hole up in Pontefract Castle instead of riding to the King's aid! However, I said nothing and Hector continued: 'Have you had news of my uncle your father and my *dear* cousin Richard? I trust most sincerely that they did not fall on Shrewsbury field?'

Liar, I thought to myself; you'd be happy to know that they were safely dead! But I replied sweetly: 'Your concern is most creditable, cousin. I am happy to say that I have had news that my father and Richard both survived the battle almost unscathed.'

Hector's brows contracted at this, but I went on: 'However, I understand that they are fled from this country. I am not sure whither; somewhere across the Narrow Seas, I doubt not.' No, I would not tell him where they had gone.

At the news that they were fled, Hector drew in breath and relaxed visibly. He observed portentously: 'Very wise . . . very wise. I fear King Henry is wrathful indeed. And of course, that ridiculous judicial dispute between your father and mine need trouble the justices no more. Under these changed circumstances, our right to these lands of Holdworth surely needs no further demonstration.'

No indeed, I thought bitterly; that cause was tried in battle — but not by you! — and lost irrevocably. Yet I said nothing, merely nodding gravely.

'Had your father been wise enough to admit the justice of our claim from the outset, much time could have been saved; and I am sure my father would have appointed him seneschal, to hold these lands for us. But under these circumstances — these unhappy circumstances' — he coughed — 'we cannot, of course, make the same offer to his son. You will understand that, with the King so justly wrathful with the Branthwaites, we dare not be so generous.'

Hector paused, striving to look magisterial, sympathetic, yet firm. He did not succeed, for his underlying glee at our downfall was too apparent.

'I understand, cousin,' I responded neutrally; and he continued with what was obviously a prepared peroration.

'Naturally you must throw yourself upon the King's mercy. My father Sir Hugo trusts that, since you did not take up arms in this *most unhappy* rebellion' — his sententiousness was excruciating — 'such mercy will be granted. I am hastening tomorrow to the King's court. You may rely upon it, cousin Simon, that I shall speak in your cause when I have opportunity. If all goes well, perhaps we may retain you in our household — not as seneschal, of course; that would not be fitting; but as our accountant, perhaps? They tell me you have more use for the pen than for the sword, that you can read well in both Latin and French, and that you are a pretty singer to the citole. With such accomplishments, you might do well in our service!'

So you would like me both to work for my keep *and* sing for my supper, I reflected bitterly; and assuredly it would be satisfying for you, after so long a quarrel, to know that a Branthwaite had become your dependant! My wrath was rising at Hector's pretences and condescensions, yet somehow I contrived to contain it.

'You make overmuch of my skills, cousin,' I responded. 'Yet it is true that Lord Furnival's chaplain has taught me well. And of course, it would mean much to me if you were to speak to the King on my behalf.'

He smirked with satisfaction at my apparent capitulation, quaffed heartily from the goblet and set it down on the chest. I hastened to refill it. For my own good reasons, I intended that Hector should drink deeply that night!

'Yes, I trust that King Henry may listen to me and withhold his hand from you; and I am pleased, cousin, that you recognize the courtesy of my father Sir Hugo in his dealings with you. What a *pity* your father chose to be so foolish . . . Well, well; you may be sure that I, at least, have your interests at heart!' He quaffed again from the glass. 'Now tell me something of this demesne.'

Thereafter I was subjected to a surprisingly detailed cross-questioning about the holdings of our manor of Holdworth; the extent of demesne and glebe, of commonland and Lammasland, the number of our vassals and villeins, the details of their service, the productivity of the fields, the size of our cattle herds, and much else. Though Hector might seem so affected in his dress and his manner, he had inherited his father's solid grasp for matters of money; and Sir Hugo had always seemed to me better fitted to be a moneylender than a knight. By the time we were summoned down to the hall for dinner, Hector had not only exhausted the flagon of wine but also, with his questioning, just about exhausted me.

Normally old Walter Tinsley, Peter the bailiff and Cerdic the reeve would have dined with me at the table on the raised dais at the head of the hall; and I would certainly have invited John Stacey to join us also. Unfortunately, such company would have been unacceptable to Hector. Had he been made to sit with them, he would either have ignored them or insulted them in other ways. So that night, only Hector and I sat at the high table.

Nevertheless, I had made sure that the table settings should be at their most magnificent. I had set before him the great silver saltcellar, fashioned in simulation of a castle keep, and beside him the silver nef made in Italy, shaped like a Genoese sailing-vessel and loaded with spices. I knew he would normally eat from silver platters; tonight, instead, there were plates of the beautiful iridescent Moorish pottery (a gift to my father from Henry Hotspur, though I did not tell Hector this!). The knives were elaborately wrought from silver and had ivory handles. For the dessert we had been set forks in the new fashion, likewise wrought of silver and ivory. All in all I had made every effort, not only to impress Hector but also to convince him that he was an honoured guest.

When he started in surprise at the table furnishings, then drew himself up, laid his hand upon his breast and smirked with satisfaction, I knew that I had succeeded. Hector was further pleased when I asked him to say grace. He did so at length, and not in Latin but in French, though I was probably the only one in the hall to realize the difference! Then, at last, we sat down to our banquet.

As I knew well, this would be my last dinner in my old home. As course succeeded course, infinitely would I have preferred to have been enjoying the homely conversation of John and old Walter rather than enduring the high, affected voice of Hector and his secondhand recountings of fashionable doings or amorous adventures at court. Yet I smiled and nodded, asked artless questions in simulated admiration whenever there was opportunity, and kept plying him with more wine — a dark malmsey now, much more potent than the sherris sack had been.

Since this was a feast for our vassals and villeins also, the hall was crowded with them and their families. Plenty of beer was provided; a good monastic barley brew, stronger than that to which they were accustomed. Soon the hall was loud with talk and song.

I had thought Hector might be discountenanced to see such profligate supplying of food and drink to the 'lower orders'. However, he had drunk much wine by then and, perhaps for that reason, seemed to approve of this general festivity. Indeed, his high voice was faltering a little by the time the seventh course was removed.

When Hector pushed away unsampled the pewter plate with the gingerbreads, I felt it was time to proceed with the next act of that evening. I rose to my feet, hammered on the table for silence, and spoke.

'Good people all, this evening is both a happy occasion and a sad one. Glad we are to welcome our honoured guest, my fair cousin Hector, the son of our respected neighbour Sir Hugo Waterton.' I paused and, when Hector had nodded his approval of what he considered a very proper sentiment, went on: 'It is sad, though, that my father, who has been for so long your master, and my brother cannot be here to welcome Hector. As you will all know, they have been caught in the wreck of the fortunes of Sir Henry Percy. I am sorry to say there is little hope that they will ever again return to this manor of Holdworth.'

At this there were cries of consternation and a buzz of conversation, hastily suppressed as I continued to speak. 'You will all realize that this will mean great changes here at Holdworth. It is likely — it is virtually certain — that your future liege lord will be our good neighbour Sir Hugo. Sir Hugo himself is not here, but we are fortunate in having his worthy son to represent him. So let us now pledge a toast to Sir Hugo, the future master of this manor, and to his son Sir Hector. Cousin Hector, please rise!'

Hector rose to his feet in readiness thus to be pledged. His smile was smug but his eyes were looking a little glazed; the wine was taking effect. However, as I raised my glass and surveyed the hall, I saw no signs of enthusiasm for that toast. Instead there was a shuffling of feet and muttering of dismay, for Sir Hugo was known to be a hard and ungenerous master; I sympathized deeply with our people.

Nevertheless, since the servants were busy recharging the earthenware beakers with ale, maybe the toast might have been drunk, albeit reluctantly. However, this was not to happen. As I was about to pledge it, John Stacey rose also. Though his charged beaker was clutched in his massive right hand, he had no toast in mind. He was as angry as a bear at a baiting.

'Master Simon and people all,' he growled, 'hearken to me! I've followed our good master Sir William for nigh on twenty years, and well he's treated me. Whether in the fighting field or at home here in Holdworth, he's always been kind and generous — you all know that.'

There was a chorus of agreement; and John went on: 'Gladly I'd have followed his fine son Richard also; or, for that matter, you yourself, Master Simon. But not a skulking coward like Sir Hugo, afraid to fight either for the good cause of Hotspur or the bad one of King Henry and instead hiding away like a frightened cur in his castle of Pontefract! Now that the battle's over, I don't doubt he'll be sticking his nose out again and come sniffing out after the moneybags, like a jackal picking up scraps when the lions have gone. I'd rather face eternal damnation than follow such a creature; for "man" I will not call him! And as for this pretty scarlet popinjay, this son of his — *that* is what I think of him!' He flung the ale straight in the face of the unfortunate Hector.

There was a silence of shock, and then laughter and shouts of approval. Yet I, who was of course delighted by this scene, must simulate anger.

'John Stacey!' I shouted over the din, 'John Stacey, you have insulted my cousin and our guest. You will pay dearly for this. Peter, Walter, Cerdic — seize him!'

I leapt over the table to go to their aid; but Hector made no attempt to do so. He was wiping his face and trembling, quite as much from fear as from fury.

Nor did we have an easy task, for there were many indeed that were prepared to stand with John. If they had had weapons, their subduing would have been a bloody business.

There were some, however, whose urge for self-preservation was undulled by ale. The days of the Branthwaites were done at Holdworth. Whether or not Sir Hugo would be a good master, he would *be* their master, so why fight in a lost cause? Others were loyally inclined to follow my orders, however unwelcome. With aid from men of these two groups, John was secured and his supporters subdued or bundled out into the rain.

I returned to Hector's side. His elaborately curled hair had been turned into rat's tails by the ale and his face was white; the scarlet jupon was irretrievably stained. I contrived to look properly sympathetic and said fawningly: 'Cousin, I am appalled by this unhappy scene; I am grieved that your worthy father and yourself were thus insulted. Be sure that the insult will be avenged!'

John was now brought before me by two stalwart yeomen. His hands had been tied behind his back, but even so they were not finding him easy to handle. I turned upon him in pretended fury.

'John Stacey, you have long been my father's servant; yet such outrageous behaviour is beyond toleration. Your holding here is forfeit; you are expelled forthwith from this hall and this demesne. You will be locked in the barn tonight. Tomorrow you will be taken to Sheffield Castle, to be imprisoned till it is time for you to face the King's justices. Take him away!'

As the yeomen strove to hustle him out John turned his gaze upon Hector, who cowered back fearfully in his chair. 'I've not done with you yet, popinjay!' John shouted. 'You and yours have not heard the last of me, be sure of that!'

Hector watched with relief as John was taken forth from the hall, then rose and said shakily: 'Cousin, I — I don't feel well . . . I think I must retire to bed; you must excuse me . . . No, I don't feel well at all . . .'

With appropriate noises of sympathy I escorted him up the stone stairs to the solar, where my father's bed had been made up for Hector. My pretences of concern were so effective, and my assurances of a harsh retribution for John so convincingly fervent, that by the time I left him Hector was somewhat soothed in spirit. He paled, however, and refused very firmly when I offered him more wine. I thought it prudent to place a large wooden bowl within easy reach of his bed.

For my own part, when I had done what other things I must that night, I rolled myself in blankets in the hall, beside old Walter and among our servants. For the few short hours I might, I slept soundly.

Chapter Three

THE LAST HOURS AT HOLDWORTH

By the first light of another grey morning, I was standing beside Hector's bed and shaking him into reluctant wakefulness. 'Cousin! Cousin! Wake up! Bad news — terrible news!'

He stared up at me pallidly, fearfully, and his lips trembled when he spoke: 'What, Simon, what's afoot? Why so early? I don't feel well . . . What's the matter?'

'It's John Stacey!' I said urgently. 'He's escaped! Someone must have freed him from his bonds and the barn; I fear he has too many friends here . . . Worse yet; he and his friends have stolen your fine horse from the stable! They have stolen also your beautiful houppelande from where it was drying by the fire, and your good boots. And John — they say that John was vowing to hie him to the greenwood. Some others are gone with him, and they say he is threatening dire vengeance on you and yours!'

Hector had sat up in startlement, but now he shrank back against the bedhead. He had looked pale at awakening, but now he was yellow with fear. 'Oh, Simon, cousin Simon, I must get away from here; but Simon, how shall I go, when that villain has seized my horse? And my fine houppelande . . . Oh, I would that I had never come to Holdworth!'

I spoke slowly, hesitantly, but as if seriously: 'Yes, indeed; greatly though it pains me to say so, you are not safe here. There is an old woman in the village who they say is a witch. I don't believe she can work magic, but she is known to see far into the future. She has prophesied that if a Waterton comes to Holdworth, a dire doom will fall upon him and his . . . Yet you and I, why, we're too sensible to heed such nonsense! Even so, you'll need to go quickly to the King, for both our sakes. When as roused and angry as now he is, John is capable of any violence!'

Hector looked positively green. He licked dry lips and asked urgently: 'Yes, I must away; but how shall it be managed? I have no horse . . . no cloak . . .'

I pretended to ponder. 'Well, as for a horse; we can surely find you a horse . . . Ah, I have it! You and I are much alike, you know. It is a blessing that, in my shaping, there was so much of my mother, of the Watertons. Why should you not borrow my horse, my good Firebrand; and why should you not borrow my scarlet surcoat? They are well known here in Hallamshire and even in the county of Derby. If you are thus mounted and thus clad, with a pair of my boots also — why, you'll be taken for me and neither John nor his friends will trouble you!'

He brightened at this idea, seized on it and worried at it. 'Aye . . . but your servants? And my voice, it is of a higher pitch — a finer pitch — than yours . . .'

'Old Walter is awake and two others, but most of our servants are sleeping deeply after their carousal. And it is a grey, wet day again; you see how feeble the light is. Few will be abroad. If you depart soon and ride swiftly, none will see you or trouble you. You need not go out through the hall; there is a smaller door for servants just below the stairs, behind an arras. If you put on my cloak and if Walter brings round the horse, your leaving will not be noted. Yet you must be swift!'

'Yes, you are right — yes indeed!' said Hector; and he almost leapt from the bed. There was a copper bowl of water on a stand nearby and a good linen cloth set beside it. Normally Hector's toilet would have been prolonged and painstaking. That day it was of the hastiest, for he was in too much of a fright to care about the niceties of his appearance. As I descended to give instructions to Walter, Hector was already dressing.

I had thought Hector would run down the stairs after me; but no, he was too nervous for that. Instead, he waited for me to take the scarlet surcoat and boots up to him. After donning them he followed me down hesitantly, hugging the shadows. He slipped through the little door after me with the furtive speed of a mouse evading a watchful cat.

Once outside, we perceived that the rain had ceased for a while. Indeed, though the air was heavy with moisture and the clouds dark and turbulent, there was even an early shaft of sunshine coming pale out of the east and causing the puddles to sparkle with light.

Walter was waiting already with Firebrand; and Hector, after a last anxious look round, mounted hastily. Thus assured of escape, Hector relaxed perceptibly. He seemed suddenly to become aware of the splendour of his scarlet garb and the excellence of his mount, wriggling his shoulders so as to cause the cloak to drape more picturesquely and smoothing back his hair carefully, before grasping the reins with self-conscious negligence. Somehow he reminded me of a cock sparrow preening himself after a dustbath — and indeed, he still looked so tousled that the comparison was apt. He gave a self-satisfied smirk and became condescending, chiding.

'Well, cousin Simon, really I cannot congratulate you on your turbulent household. Things will be very different, I assure you, when my father Sir Hugo takes control here — *very* different . . . However, I will trust you may yet seize that rogue John and retrieve my horse and cloak; I am sure you recognize your duty and will make every endeavour to do so. In the meantime, I thank you for the loan of your horse and this surcoat. They'll do well enough, till I have my own again; and of course they will be returned to you at the *earliest* opportunity. Be sure also that I will speak in your favour when I have the ear of the King!'

I doubted both of these promises. Whatever the Watertons had, they held on to; and, in the unlikely eventuality of Hector's gaining the ear of the King, it would be in Sir Hugo's interest or his own that he would speak, not mine.

Instead of responding, I said urgently: 'Then, for both our sakes, you must hasten, Hector! The King must by now be returning toward London; you must hurry south to meet him. And remember: if you are challenged in the next fifty miles, give my name and not your own. Say only that you are riding southward; do not say you are riding to the King, for that would give you away. Remember also that John must be in hiding nearby. He is a fierce man and dangerous, as you know. Watch out wherever an ambush might be set; watch for pursuers also, for John may yet perceive our deception. Your life depends on your watchfulness! Ride swiftly, and Godspeed!'

At this reminding of possible dangers, Hector paled anew. He turned Firebrand about, drove in his spurs and, with the most perfunctory of farewells, rode away as if the Devil himself were at his heels.

We watched him go from sight, then I turned to smile at Walter. I found that he was already laughing heartily.

'My, what a scare you've put into him!' he chuckled. 'I hardly believe he'll stop till he's in Cheapside! Indeed, Master Simon, your schemes are working well! Yet you must take care also. You must hasten directly to meet John in Loxley Chase, ere Cerdic and the others see you, for I trust them not at all! I'll follow when I can. You must not return to the hall, even for your sword. I'll bring that and your gold, trust me! Go now, for I hear sounds of awakening!'

Thus, though Hector had left on horseback and I did so afoot, for us both the setting forth from Holdworth was covert and swift. There was such need to beware of being seen that, as I followed the field paths away toward Loxley Chase, I took no thought to gaze back toward the home I was leaving. In any case, the rain was again coming down so heavily as to deter any sentimental lingerings.

Our rendezvous was an abandoned charcoal-burner's hut, set among trees by the banks of the little River Loxley. Two horses were tethered outside it, John's own grey and the black stallion on which Hector had yesterday arrived at Holdworth. Within I found John, relaxing by a little fire. As I entered he rose, grinning from ear to ear.

I threw my arms about him and hugged him. 'John, John, you were magnificent! My father would have been proud of you!'

'Nay, Master Simon, it was a pleasure. Yon Hector looked proper taken aback — we've put a right good scare into that young coxcomb! First time since Shrewsbury that Ah've had a real good laugh! Well, if that Sir Hugo is to have this land, Ah'll be leaving Holdworth without more ado; and there's a few other lads will be riding north with me. They'd sooner work for my girl and me up at Malham than swink for that mean old devil!'

I laughed. 'Excellent! It'll all help convince poor Hector

that you're somewhere in the greenwood, waiting for him!' And I told him the story of the witch's curse that I'd so hastily invented.

To my surprise, John took it seriously. 'You know, Master Simon, I don't reckon the Watertons *are* going to be so glad, in the years to come, that they've seized this manor. Curse or no curse, they'll find no content here, you'll see. Ah'm no witch nor warlock neither, but Ah'm sure of that. Well, time will tell.'

We breakfasted together on some hunks of wheaten bread and a crumbly Dales cheese. Between bites, John spoke consideringly. 'Mayhap I'd best change my name, as well as my residence; and I'd best urge those that go with me to do likewise. I doubt whether Sir Hugo's arm can reach so far as Malham; they're good folk up there and won't relish interference from such as he! Still, 'tis best not to put ourselves at hazard without good cause!'

'Aye, you're right, John: and the more mysterious your vanishing, the more anxious Hector and Sir Hugo will be!'

We laughed again together at the prospect of their further disquietude. Then John, eager to be gone before the rain ceased and the fields became busy, said an affectionate farewell. As I waved a last salute and watched him ride away, I must confess that my eyes were moist; such friends as he are rare and to be treasured.

Another hour had gone by, and the morning was well advanced, before old Walter came to the hut. He was carrying over his arm an old brown leather gambeson, such as a mercenary soldier might wear, and over his shoulder was slung a satchel. By that time I was becoming tense and anxious, so that his arrival was a relief.

'Walter, at last! I was beginning to fear matters had gone wrong.'

He smiled. 'Aye, well, it wasn't so easy. First of all, t'hall and village are like an ant hill that someone's stirred with a foot, all comings and goings and rushings about! Our folk, they've excitement enough and more — John's performance last night; the news about old Sir Hugo and his grabbing of Holdworth; and young Hector's riding away so early! They all think that was you, off to join Sir William somewhere. Yon guest of yours away too — they think *he's* scuttled back to Pontefract, being so scared last night — they're all chuckling about that. Then, to top it all, a troop of soldiers come to try to arrest you!'

I whistled. 'What, so soon? They must have ridden early from Ashbourne.'

'Aye, they rose early; and they cut across t'moors, thinking to catch you. But you were earlier yet!' He laughed heartily, joyously. 'And now they're off riding lickety-split after yon Hector — and he as scared as a rabbit already, and travelling so fast that they won't be catching him today, nor yet tomorrow neither! It's a right caper, it is indeed!'

Walter had brought a leather purse clinking with gold coins — nobles, half-nobles and florins. He insisted that I count them, though I had no least doubt of his honesty. There was more money, by far, than I would require — or, indeed, than I dared carry. I returned much of it to him, directing that he use it covertly to aid those of our people who fell into need.

'Aye, I'll do that and gladly,' he answered. 'But some of it I might use in other ways . . . Happen Ah can help t'Watertons into thinking John and his men are on t'moors or in t'woods, waiting to get at 'em. It'll do 'em good to stay scared!'

Soon I had exchanged my wet cloak for the leather gambeson and fastened my belt about it, attaching the scabbard to one side and tucking the leather purse, now much lighter, beneath it at the other. The sword gave to my appearance a formidability that was impressive, albeit quite false when I was so poor a swordsman. A flat steel helmet, acquired for me by Walter from some returned soldier in the village, enhanced my guise. As a horseman I could scarcely carry a bow and arrows; so, for my defence in need, I must rely instead on the throwing-knives. Four of these were in sheaths attached to a cloth belt about my shoulders under my jupon; three others were hidden elsewhere in my clothing; but six were in sheaths affixed to my belt and would be readily available at need. Walter eyed these curiously, for he had no concept of their purpose; but he made no comment.

That was a day of partings. Saying farewell to old Walter was as difficult as the farewell to John had been. He walked down with me to the Loxley's bank. Its waters were in spate and swift; the rain was again falling heavily. After my horse had forded the little river, I turned to wave a last salute to him. The greyness of the sky, the pouring rain, and that elderly figure waving back from among the trees combine to furnish my final memory of the home I was forever leaving.

Many years were to pass before I learned, from a chance traveller from Hallamshire, anything concerning the fate of Holdworth and the Watertons. We had frightened poor Hector so thoroughly that his precipitate flight continued for three whole days! He seems to have imagined himself unsafe until he had left, not only the Pennine valleys and moorlands, but even the bosky recesses of Sherwood Forest — so renowned a haunt of outlaws — far behind.

Hector must have been a better rider than I supposed, to keep Firebrand at such a pace for so long! Yet the King's officers found it no problem to follow Hector's trail, for the big white stallion and his scarlet-cloaked rider attracted attention everywhere. Eventually, four days after my last sight of him, they caught up with him. It was near a village called Clophill, south of Bedford. He was found sitting forlornly by the roadside. Firebrand had at last rebelled, thrown him and bolted; and poor Hector was bruised and weary.

When set upon a horse and told he was to be taken to the King, Hector was at first surprised and flattered, calling the officers 'fine fellows' and commending their 'proper courtesy to a gentleman'. Only when the order of arrest was read to him did he realize his situation. He was in succession incredulous, indignant, and frightened. His protestation that he was not Simon Branthwaite, but Hector Waterton, did him no good; the King's officers were not north-country men and had never heard even of Sir Hugo, let alone of any son of his. Was Hector not wearing the surcoat of the Branthwaites? Had he not fled south before them? What nonsense; of course he was the man they sought!

King Henry was pleased by the arrest, but not much interested. In truth it was my father whom he desired to have in his vengeful hands, not a mere Branthwaite sibling. Now that he was calmer, the King knew he would attain little satisfaction, and politically might lose much credit, by wreaking public vengeance upon one who had not taken up arms against him. Instead the supposed Simon Branthwaite was discreetly tucked away out of view in a prison cell. In consequence, poor Hector had no chance to make his pleas in court, where someone might have recognized him. Indeed, several uncomfortable months passed before Sir Hugo learned of Hector's predicament and took action to save his son.

When King Henry realized he had been tricked, his anger was great; so *all* the Branthwaites had evaded him! Yes, Hector was reluctantly released; but only to find his former friends laughing at him behind their hands because of the fashion in which I had fooled him.

Moreover, the amusement of the court was adding fuel to the King's smouldering wrath. Under such conditions the Watertons could expect no favours from King Henry; instead, they must hasten away from court and lie low till his anger had subsided.

Yet they *did* gain Holdworth. With no Branthwaite to contest it, the justices inevitably found in favour of their claim.

However, the legend that John Stacey and his men were waiting vengefully in the greenwood was by then universally accepted. Old Walter did as he had promised. There were a series of 'incidents' — the burning of a barn, the raiding of a few grain stores, the vanishing of a few Waterton cattle (eaten, I doubt not, by hungry villagers!) — that combined to suggest a watchful, hostile presence in the lands about. Moreover, since any mischances — the crushing of a cart by a falling tree, an unexplained death, even unexpected failures of crops — were laid to the account of 'John of the Moors', the legend grew steadily even without Walter's guileful help.

My story of the curse seemed to have sunk deep into Hector's mind and to have been effectively transmitted by him to his father. As a result, it was long ere Sir Hugo would even venture near Holdworth. The clerk he appointed to take charge of our former demesne seems to have been of dubious morals, but timorous. Under his uncertain and lax rule, the villeins fared well but the Watertons profited little. Yet almost five years were allowed to slip by before Sir Hugo summoned up the courage personally to investigate why his pickings from Holdworth were so meagre.

At that juncture, chance stepped in to enhance the legend. When the old man was dismounting in the courtyard of the manor, he did so clumsily, catching his foot in the stirrup and falling heavily on to the stones. His arm was broken and he was badly shaken. Moreover, the incident frightened him, for he was superstitious and it seemed symbolic. There must indeed be a curse on Holdworth!

To underscore Sir Hugo's apprehensions, that night there came a summer storm of considerable magnitude. The manor's granary went up in flames. Had it been struck by lightning or was this the work of 'John of the Moors'? No-one seemed to know and the latter theory found favour.

Next morning it was discovered that Sir Hugo's clerk had fled during the storm, taking with him much gold — or so it was believed. Had he gone to join John's band? So it was rumoured. The clerk was not apprehended, for heavy rain had caused the River Don and its tributaries to rise overnight; even the little Loxley had become impassable.

For a week Sir Hugo, his arm painful in splints, was pent up fuming in Holdworth. Then it was discovered that his horse had mysteriously gone lame; the curse again, or the work of John's men?

Whatever the truth of the matter, Sir Hugo was deeply alarmed. He appointed our old bailiff, Peter, to the charge of the manor and was carried back to Pontefract in a cart. Within a year Sir Hugo was dead — poisoned, some said; the curse, said others.

By then cousin Hector had been accepted back at court. He was not eager to be reminded of his flight on that wet summer morning or of the humiliations that preceded and followed it. The imagined threat of 'John of the Moors' long haunted him and the very mention of Holdworth was anathema. Upon Sir Hugo's death, Hector sold the demesne immediately to old Lord Furnival for what was, considering the Watertons' avidity for gold, a remarkably trivial sum. Never again did he venture into Hallamshire.

Thus John's prophecy proved correct; the Watertons found no content in, and little profit from, the seizing of

Holdworth. About John himself, legends aside, I heard no more; yet the memory of his strength, devotion and affection remains alive in me. I can only trust that, with wife, children and friends about him, he lived contentedly and long in his upland farm.

Chapter Four

THE ORANGE CLOAK

My ride across England was all through country unfamiliar to me. It took nine whole hard days, for I had no map and must take care always when asking my way. Yet it has left few memories.

One reason was the weather. Though this was high summer, there was little sunshine and much rain throughout that journey. Day followed sweaty day in the saddle, with the rain running off that accursed steel helmet, dripping down on to my arms and legs and trickling down my back. That equally accursed gambeson was much too hot to wear in such weather, yet so vital to my protection and disguise that I dared not shed it. Stream after stream, river after river had to be forded; rutted and puddled paths and lanes innumerable to be followed; woods and copses, green and dripping, to be skirted or traversed with care in case of ambush. And always there was mud — mud splashing up my horse's legs, mud on my boots, mud everywhere . . .

Indeed, my disguise *did* help. After the brief storm of civil war England seemed awash with soldiers, as a river is awash with branches after a rainstorm. In such circumstances I attracted no particular attention. I was especially watchful when passing through villages and preferred to skirt past towns, yet little enough notice was taken of me when I did ride reluctantly along streets. I was just another soldier from a defeated army, men thought, and there were all too many soldiers roving around the Midlands in those days, singly or in bands. Nor was any attempt made to rob me; I did not look rich and, however falsely, I *did* look forbiddingly formidable.

However, a few recollections do persist. I recall the relief of climbing from the slippery, shaley paths of the gritstone dales up into the limestone country of Peak Forest, where the green grass was drier and the gusty winds between the showers were refreshing. I spent my first night in a lead-miner's cottage near Hartington, where I was at first regarded dubiously as a foreigner. Yet once it was realized that I had visited Peak villages before and knew the miners' special jargon, I was made very welcome. Indeed, I was so overwhelmed by a spate of talk on winzes, rakes, adits and headings, the inadequacies of the local barmaster and the iniquities of church tithing, that my comprehension was strained to its limit and I began almost to wish I *had* been a foreigner!

Most other nights were lonelier. Often, indeed, I slept huddled up in my gambeson in the best shelter I could find among wet bushes, wishing I were as wise and as warm as a fox in his earth. My meals were mostly of bread, cheese or pasty, with draughts of ale, much of it flat and as flavourless as muddy stream-water, taken in such villages as I felt it safe to visit. And always there were the rain, the sweat and the mud, and a horse so brutish in his unhappiness at the long ride that neither of us developed any least affection for the other. One Midland village name remains in my memory — Draycott in the Clay. Somehow that name epitomized that whole wet, sticky journey.

I avoided busy Gloucester, threading my way instead along the western edges of the Cotswolds. Though its villages had names that seemed strange to my ears — Uley, Wickwar, Pucklechurch, even Chipping Sodbury — that was a green countryside in which I would have liked to linger, had my journey been less urgent and the weather less vile.

At long last, I found myself riding one morning over the bridge and under the arch of Frome Gate into Bristol. I followed Broad Street down to the great High Cross at the centre of the city. There, regardless of the stares of the passers-by, I dismounted and knelt awhile to say a prayer of thankfulness that my journey was over.

I sold my horse to a Wynch Street dealer and parted from him without regret. The dealer also bought the steel helmet and the gambeson I had come so much to hate. He gave me little enough for them but, since they had cost me nothing, I was not disposed to complain.

Having rid myself of that unloved mount and that irksome garb, I felt curiously lighthearted. Moreover the sun came out at last, as if to beam approval of my new freedom from sweat and from mud. Really I should have gone straight to the quays, to enquire about a passage to Rockall. Instead I wandered about, admiring the fine stone churches — St Stephen, St Warbors, St Alphius, All Hallows, St Maryport — and poking among the stalls clustered in the shadow of the old inner wall of the city.

On the proceeds of my horse-trading, I ate a good meal and acquired for myself some new clothes — a chestnut-brown jupon with lighter-coloured sleeves and a dark brown pelican. The latter garment was rather old-fashioned in cut — Hector would have hated it, I reflected with amusement — but well made and of good cloth. Also I bought two pairs of knee-length boots in a flexible brown leather and waited while the cobbler, surprised but compliant, made modifications to them on my request and for my particular purposes. Thus I looked smart enough and yet not conspicuous; not like a soldier (despite my sword), certainly not like a courtier or man of fashion, yet respectable and, despite the satchel slung over my shoulder, reasonably well-to-do.

It was pleasant to be among a crowd again, for I had not been in one since that market under Sheffield Castle walls. I had been too much alone and too unhappy in the intervening days; it was good to lose myself and my cares for a while in that press of people. There was the fun also of trying to make out what was being said, for the burring bumblebee voices of these Somerset and Devon folk were utterly different from the abrupt phrases of Hallamshire and the gusty talk of the Pennine miners.

I dined early, seated at a trestle table in a Corn Street eatinghouse, and found lodgings nearby that seemed clean, cheap and secure. But I did not retire early. Instead I rambled around, watching the street life and listening to the music of goliards and minstrels, till even the long summer day was drawing to its end. It was good to be dry, warm and safe again; I slept excellently and long.

Morning was well advanced when I rose. I was annoyed with myself for sleeping so late, especially when I saw that the sun was bright and the sky blue and clear. I knew little enough of ships and the sea, but I *was* aware of the importance of tides; why, in such benign weather, a ship to Lyonesse might already have set sail that very day! Yet a cheery greeting from the bright-eyed little woman who kept the lodging house made me feel better. The excellent breakfast she provided — of sliced cold beef, onions and cresses, with a small ale of better quality than I had tasted since leaving Holdworth — quite restored my spirits.

It was too warm a day for wearing the pelican, so I rolled it up and strapped it to the satchel before setting forth. The old woman knew nothing about what ships were in port, but she was able to tell me where I should enquire — at a little tavern close to St Peter's Cross in Dolphin Street, where the sea captains gathered to do business with the merchants of Bristol. To it I made my way.

The tavern was crowded, mugs of ale and trayfuls of curious wrapped-over pasties called 'oggies' being energetically consumed amid a roar of conversation. I was too young and looked insufficiently wealthy to warrant attention from the company. Thus it was some time before I persuaded a friendly, bearded sea-captain — from London, by his sharp accent — to listen to my enquiry. His response was disheartening.

'You're seeking a passage to *where*, young sir? Lyonesse? Never 'eard of it, in all me born days. Here, Jem, can you aid the young gentleman?'

Thus adjured, the Bristol seaman did indeed respond; but he was unable to be helpful. He did recollect that there'd been a vessel from that place, oh, maybe a couple of weeks since — first one for years — but she'd sailed. Would there be another? Well, he couldn't rightly say. Didn't seem likely, though; first one for years, that'd been. Other men joined in the discussion, but all shook their heads. Well, no; didn't seem likely, didn't seem likely at all that there'd be another ship going to Lyonesse. For a while I was the focus of the sympathetic attention of the whole tavern; friendly people, these were, but they could not assist me.

My London friend made one suggestion, perhaps from continued beneficence, perhaps to be rid of me and return to his drinking. 'You should talk to Ben Emery. Quaymaster, he is; knows more about Bristol shipping than anyone, he does. He don't drink here, though, mind; he stays closer to the Backs, where the big ships discharge cargo. There's a tavern down on Back Street, the Trident; maybe you'll chance to find him there. Walk along St Maryport Street and it's not far from the bridge.'

Disappointed though I was, I managed to smile and express thanks before leaving the tavern. It was in no good heart that I went onward. If ships from Lyonesse came in so rarely, why, it might be years before I found a passage there! When the King discovered my deceptions, there'd be a hue and cry after me; and, if His Regrettable Majesty chanced to have learned where my father and brother had gone, my very enquiries today might give me away.

The directions I'd been given seemed clear till I reached the bridge, but then I got lost among narrow streets backing the wharves. A full hour had passed before I found the Trident tavern. It was past noon by then and most folk had eaten. A serving maid was polishing plates in the back and the only other person visible was a squat, rumpled man, wearing a faded blue cyclas over a scruffy brown tunic and with a bristling fringe of black beard all about his face. He was sitting at a bench just inside the tavern. Before him were the scanty remains of what had clearly been a huge meal and by his elbow was an immense ale-jug, which he drained just as I entered. In no way did he fit my concept of so important an official as a quaymaster — only later did I learn that the quaymaster was not truly an official, but merely the strongest and most masterful of the men who unloaded and loaded the ships — so I was surprised at his answer to my hesitant enquiry.

'Seeking Ben Emery, be you? Well, then, you've found him. What can I do for you, young man?'

His voice was a surging roar, like the sound of waves breaking on an offshore reef. He signalled me to sit down and then thumped his jug for more ale. For this, naturally, I paid. When we had been served, I put my question once more.

'Wanting passage to Lyonesse, are you? Well, well . . . And just a week or so since, we had a ship put in from there; first time in many years, that was . . . No, Jem Shenfield was right — can't say when there'll be another — *if* there'll be another; you'll be mebbe raising your grandchildren by then!'

He took a pull at the jug, set it down and considered me reflectively. Pretty dejected I must have looked by then, for his mouth buckled up in a wry sort of smile, causing the fringe of beard to stand out like the prickles of a hedgehog, before he continued.

'No, there's been few enough sailings to Lyonesse in the twenty summers I've worked on these quays. Yet they do say as Lyonesse is in Rockall — and there are boats enough to Rockall! Mentonese boats they are that come here; and, though I've heard tell that there are other ships sailing from Rockall to London, English ships don't seem welcome in Rockall's harbours.'

I had perked up considerably at this news. The quaymaster gave me another beard-prickling smile before continuing.

'Quite a trade there is with those Mentonese nowadays, for they bring many a thing that our English gentry like and will pay good gold nobles for. What do they bring? Why, a fancy red spice — teymery, they call it; and a perfume the ladies splash about themselves, called vodime. Then there's cakes made of pressed yellow berries, sindleberries; sweeter than honey, they are. And great rolls of white parchment; the bishops buy that, to scribe church accounts on I doubt not. There's candles, too, that them bishops like for their masses; they burn bright, ice-blue. And a stuff called jenoxiam, that's used for embalming. What do they take in exchange? Why, not gold, as you'd think; they're not interested in gold, though they'll use it, mind, in their dealings ashore. No, they want good English woollens and broadcloth, dyed in bright colours — red, yellow, blue — and they'll buy silks and velvets from France and Flanders, and wine from Gascony. Aye, that's what they're after.'

He took another long pull from the jug, then went on: 'Funny they be to deal with, though, these Mentonese. Big men they are, with tow-coloured hair like Danes; but they don't speak no sort of language that *I've* ever heard. Odd sort of a noise, it is! I doubt not they're some sort of unbeliever; there's always a little fire burning on their ships and strange chants being sung around it. But they're as astute as Jews in their dealings and quick enough at learning our tongue. Could you travel with them? Well, not to Mentone; not to Angmering, which seems to be their chief town. They

44

won't allow that; I know, for enough of our merchants have tried, thinking to make a tidy profit.'

He paused and, at my renewed expression of dismay, gave me a third time that hedgehog smile. 'Yet maybe, if you could pay, they'd take you and set you ashore *somewhere* in Rockall. Yes, they'd accept your gold; they'd spend it in Bristol before they sailed maybe, or maybe keep it till their next coming. And I doubt not they'd treat you fair enough; they hold to their bargains, that I will say. Not many of 'em come on shore; you won't find 'em in the taverns or stews. Yet the captain'll always be ashore, of course, to do his dealings. Those Mentonese captains like doing their bargaining late in the afternoon. Strange ideas they have; they think good fortune only comes when the sun's past his prime, they won't willingly trade earlier in the day. Why yes, I *will* take another drink' — for indeed, he'd emptied the jug already.

When it had been refilled, at my expense of course, he continued: 'And you've come to Bristol just right, for there's a craft from Mentone on the river now. Her captain's been doing business ashore these last three days. Yesterday she loaded and I did think she'd sail last night, but no, she's still on the river.'

Involuntarily I heaved a sigh of relief. Ben cocked an eye at me and grinned knowingly: 'Aye, there's a good many folk lost their fortune in battle and gone to seek another in Rockall; some not so long ago, I hear tell . . . Since his ship's still in harbour, the captain'll be coming ashore this day as ever. You'd best seek him and see about a passage.'

He broke off, gazing past me, his mouth dropping open; and he said: 'Well, now just look at that!'

I turned about, my eyes following his. Indeed, the sight was startling. Out on the street, walking past the tavern, was a young man with the reddest hair and beard I had ever seen. There was a sword at his belt and he was carrying over his shoulder a whole bundle of staves for long-bows, made from a variety of woods. That was strange enough, for he was clearly neither of the labouring nor of the merchant class; but what was truly startling was his garb. Over a tunic of the brightest yellow he was wearing a cloak of a colour I had never seen hitherto in cloth, only in the marigolds

45

clustering round cottage doors — a rich, bright orange, echoed somewhat by the russet leather of his boots. In that dingy Bristol backstreet he seemed as out of place as a tropical bird.

A cluster of ragged children was following him and calling to him. As we watched he turned, laughed at them with an affectionate gaiety that quite warmed my heart, and dug into a leather purse at his waist for some coins to throw to them. While the children scrambled with noisy delight among the cobbles, he passed from our view.

Ben drank deep, then said: 'Did you ever see the likes of that? I wonder what dyestuff they used? Of course, if it's good, it'll come to Bristol; everything good comes to Bristol . . . Well, now, yond ship from Mentone. These Rockalese won't bring their ships up to the quays. Maybe their ships can't sail in close, or more likely they don't trust us — and I can't blame them, at that, for there's ruffians enough on these quays. So they anchor downriver, seaward of the last of the quays, out by the marsh. We have to load and unload from boats — a proper caper *that* can be, too, with the boats pitching and them Mentonese jabbering away at us in their heathen magpie-talk . . . The captain'll land on the first quay, just this side of the city wall where there's a stack of old barrels; you can't miss the place. You must wait for him there, but you've time enough — it'll be an hour or more ere he comes ashore.'

He drank once more, then went on: 'Don't let him take too much gold off you for the passage; you can be sure he'll try it on . . . Have I sailed to Rockall? Never, young man, never; and never will. I've never left Bristol and never shall. You ever been on a ship? No? Well, now, that's a pleasure to come — and you're *most* welcome to it!'

For a third time, the quaymaster drained his jug. Then he scattered some coins on the table in payment for his meal and, waving an amiable arm in response to my thanks, shambled away down the street.

I sat at the bench a little longer, sipping my own ale at more leisure and thinking. I felt much more cheerful now. Perhaps I could not find passage directly to Lyonesse, but at least I could travel to Rockall; and once there, surely I would find my way to Lyonesse quickly enough! Rockall was only an island, after all; the distance could not be great. These Mentonese sounded to be strange people, but clearly Ben respected them and, up to a point, trusted them . . . In any case, if I could be aboard soon, at least I would be safe from King Henry's men!

I procured some bread and cheese from the serving maid, a dark and silent girl whom I guessed to be Welsh, and ate it slowly while I finished the ale. Then, when a crowd of sailors poured in and began to clamour for beer, I paid my bill and left also.

Most of the smaller coastal craft trading into Bristol sail up the lesser of that city's two rivers, the Frome, and unload their cargoes on the quays on the northwest side of the city, close to St Augustine's Abbey. Only a few ships come in at the Backs seaward of the Avon bridge — the bigger vessels, from France, Flanders and the Hanseatic ports. That day only two were in. There was a cog from Danzig, with a great square sail striped vertically in red, blue and gold and an after-castle blazoned with arms in many bright colours. Sailors and labourers were swarming about it, under the attentive eyes of a group of portly and portentous merchants in furred robes. I watched for a while, then walked on. Beyond was a bigger, two-masted vessel with sails furled. From her name, *Santa Catarina*, I guessed her to be from Castile or Portugal. All her sailors seemed to be ashore and all her cargo already stowed or disposed of, for she appeared quite deserted. I walked on past her and out towards the city wall.

Here, behind the quay, there was a triangle of meadowland. Once it must have been an attractive place, but now it looked pretty desolate, for it had become a sort of dumping ground for rubbish from the quays. There were broken crates, heaps of straw, broken jars and flasks, knotted lengths of decaying twine and rope, torn fragments of faded cloth and the rotting remains of sacks, all amid a tangle of brambles and wild flowers. Two old coracles had been dragged ashore and overturned, looking like immense brown beetles among the weeds; and there were piles of beams apparently salvaged from wrecks of much bigger ships, so long ago that blackthorn bushes had taken root among them. Only the part of the quay closest to the water's edge had been kept clear of rubbish.

At the western end of this wasteland, on the inner side of the high city wall, there had been assembled by some industrious merchant, for purposes inscrutable to me, a vast accumulation of old barrels. There were piles of them, hillocks of them, ranging in size from quite tiny rundlets to huge casks big enough, I felt, to contain a pickled oliphant. Many were in poor shape, the staves starting out and the iron hoops corroded or rusted; these were strewn higgledy-piggledy, some upright, most lying on their sides among the weeds. In contrast, the ones in better condition had been stacked close by the edge of the quay, in careful piles up to six barrels deep. No-one was about.

This, surely, must be the place described by Ben Emery, the place where the Mentonese captain would come ashore. Here, then, I must wait.

There was shade to be found among the forest of barrels, but it was too dank down there. After so many days of rain I had an urge to enjoy more sunshine. Maybe, if I were up on top, I might be able to spot the Mentonese vessel? Well, anyway, it would be fun to try climbing the barrel mound!

With much difficulty I ascended the highest stack; but it was no use, the city wall blocked off my view downriver. The wall itself could not be climbed here and, though there was a tower not far away which surely must contain a stairway, I was disinclined to leave the quayside. My first sight of the ship must come later. As I cogitated, the barrel on which I was perched shifted under my feet and the whole stack swayed ominously. Hastily I descended.

In the heart of the barrel stacks was an immense cask, fully eight feet in height and hemmed in on three sides by piles of smaller barrels. To this perilously I scrambled and on it I sat, shrugging the satchel from my shoulders and arranging my rolled cloak to make a back-rest. This would make a good place for waiting, for there was a clear riverward view and I could even look for some distance along the quay. It was very quiet in the afternoon sunshine; even the activity about the Hanseatic cog had diminished. I dozed.

It must have been half an hour later when I awoke with a start. Stupid to fall asleep anywhere in a town, where one might so easily be robbed; particularly stupid to drowse when one was waiting for a boat to come ashore! However, no boat had moored; I sighed with relief. Yet something had awakened me, some person, some movement. I looked about me carefully.

Yes, that was it; there were men close by me, four men huddled in the shade of the barrel pile, *hiding* there . . . They were in a sort of alcove between high stacks of small barrels, quite close to my perch atop the huge cask. Three had the air of petty criminals. They were small, wiry men, two of them in ragged tunics and armed with rusty-looking shortswords, the third in plumed hat and padded jupon, carrying a bow as well. The fourth, though; now *he* was of quite a different class. He was wearing a coat of mail under a green surcoat; his legs were encased in stockings of good quality and his feet in boots with fashionably pointed toes, boots of which even cousin Hector would not have been ashamed. The sword hanging by his side was thrust into a scabbard chased with silver. Altogether, he was an unlikely figure in such disreputable company.

Evidently they had not spotted me, perched high above their heads as I was. For that I was grateful, since I knew they would have given me short shrift and knew also that I was not enough of a fighter successfully to battle even one, let alone four, assailants. Moreover, I was intrigued. Clearly they were lying in wait for someone. Were they waiting to ambush the Mentonese captain when he came ashore? No, surely not; they were looking, not seaward, but along the quay towards the bridge.

Their leader turned toward me a little; I saw now that he was lean, dark-haired and bearded. He started, whispered something to his companions — I could not catch the words — and pointed. I looked also.

To my surprise, I recognized their intended victim. There, walking along the quay in our direction, was the young man in the orange cloak that had so startled Ben Emery. As he drew closer, I saw he was still carrying that bundle of bowstaves over one shoulder; but he was doubly burdened now, for he was also carrying a satchel much like mine. Evidently he was not anticipating trouble, for he was walking along jauntily and whistling. A sword hung by his side but I realized sickly that, thus encumbered, he would be given no time to draw it. Already the man in the padded jupon was fitting an arrow to his bow.

No, the young stranger was certainly not aware he was in any danger; the men were too well concealed among the barrel stacks. He was coming close now and they were tensing; predators about to leap upon their prey. The man with the bow was drawing back his string . . .

Whatever the risk to myself, I could not let this murder happen. Quietly I rose to my feet; they were looking away from me, they would not perceive me now. I drew one of the little knives from my belt, pivoted it between my fingers and threw. Almost at the same moment, I yelled with all my might: 'Ware ambush, stranger!'

The throw was good, better indeed than I could have hoped. Not only did the knife cut across the knuckles of the hand holding the bowstring but also, being needle-sharp, it severed the string itself just before the arrow was released. The bowman gave a sort of double howl of pain, the second coming as the broken bowstring clipped him smartly on the cheek. Bow and arrow clattered to the ground.

His three companions were almost as startled. One of them leapt backward so forcibly against the stack of barrels that it toppled and collapsed thunderously, an avalanche of casks rolling out on to the quay. The bowman and the man who had set the barrels moving both had their feet knocked from under them and were carried along the barrel tide, yelling with fright, till they sank amongst it. They were very definitely out of the fight, for a while at least. However, the lean man and his remaining companion somehow contrived to leap clear. Then, with drawn swords, they advanced upon their intended victim.

By this time, the man in orange had thrown down both of his bundles and likewise drawn his sword. It was very quickly apparent that he was more than a match for his two assailants. A swift feint at the smaller man was followed by a backward flick which sent that man's sword flying into the waters of the Avon. It was enough for him; he scuttled away like a rat among the barrels. His two companions, winded and battered by the rolling casks, picked themselves up and fled also.

Their leader was already retreating before the superior sword play of the man in orange. As I scrambled down to join the fray, drawing my own sword from its scabbard, the attention of the lean man was momentarily distracted. In that moment, the sword of the man in orange thrust powerfully past his guard and into his body. His mail-coat did not save him, for the sword had been driven upward beneath it. He gave a gulping gasp and crumpled backward on to the stones of the quay, staining them with his blood as he died.

Chapter Five

THE MENTONESE CAPTAIN

T he man in orange withdrew his sword and stood back, eyeing his dead opponent grimly. Then he turned to me and said: 'I thank you for your warning, friend. Without it, I think my own blood would have been spilled. But how did you disarm the archer and how' — he grinned suddenly — 'did you arrange that so-convenient rolling of barrels?' His English was good but his intonation was unfamiliar; evidently he was some sort of foreigner.

Without immediately replying I sheathed my sword and, delving among the barrels, found the bow, with its severed string, and the arrow. Beside it was my little knife. I picked up both bow and knife and said simply: 'I threw this; they're useful little weapons at close range. It startled him quite a bit, didn't it? As for the barrels; well, it was when one of his friends jumped in surprise that *they* started falling!'

The man in orange took the knife from me and balanced it in his hand, then returned it to me. 'There is blood: you did more than cut the string, I see . . . I am deeply grateful; I shall not forget this.'

He turned and bent over the dead man. 'I wonder who . . .? The others were rabble, but this one was different . . . I think he was from Barodda; he has the look; but I cannot be sure . . .' His voice trailed off; then he said crisply: 'Well, he is dead, and only God or the Devil can question him henceforward. Now, friend, let me introduce myself: Avran Estantesec of Sandastre, eternally at your service!'

With an exaggerated flourish of the orange cloak about his shoulders, he bowed deeply; then looked up at me and smiled mischievously. 'Under such circumstance, that is the proper response, is it not?'

I laughed outright. 'Well, it's very splendid! As for me, I'm Simon Branthwaite, presently of nowhere in particular.'

He smiled again at this. 'Well, there is much to be said for having so wide a fief! I am honoured to know you. Yet allow me a moment before we talk. I am sure that the good citizens of Bristol will not want to see their fine quayside cluttered up with corpses. My late assailant came out from among the barrels; I think he should go back among them!'

Then, as he bent to lift the body of the bearded man, he paused and looked up at me. 'Your sword — it is, I am sure, a venerable weapon, hallowed by the use of distinguished ancestors in many famous campaigns?'

I laughed again. The courtesies of the man in orange might be cumbrous, but they concealed a bubbling humour that was altogether engaging. 'No, I am afraid it has no noteworthy history, it's just an old sword.'

'In that case, why not effect an exchange? Assuredly our bearded friend will have no further use for *his* sword; and it is a good blade, an Arctorran blade. The swordsmiths of Andressellar are quite as skilled as those of Toledo. The scabbard also is attractive; the patterning in silver marks it, I think, as Dupratan. Please take them. I have my own good blade and you deserve the honours of that combat.'

'Thank you; I'll welcome the exchange, though I confess I'm a poor swordsman.'

I unbuckled the scabbard from my belt and, when we concealed the body of the bearded man among the tumbled barrels, it was my old sword that was cast down by his side.

Then Avran turned to me again. 'I would like to entertain you, if not to dinner, at least to a tankard of ale over which we might properly pledge our friendship. Unfortunately, I am leaving this city too soon for any such celebration. Indeed, I now await the return of the captain of the vessel on which I am to travel homeward. He is due shortly and our ship is to sail at high tide. Under such circumstances . . .'

'Are you sailing for Rockall, then? Is the captain already ashore?'

'Why yes, I'm travelling to Sandarro; and the captain, he came ashore a full half-hour ago!'

'Yet his boat — it isn't here?'

'No indeed; it returned to the ship and I, after arranging

my passage, to my inn for these burdensome objects!' He gestured at the satchel and the bundle of bows.

I cursed myself. By so stupidly falling asleep, I might have missed the chance of the passage I sought; yet . . . 'You say the captain will be returning soon?'

'Very soon; for, as you may mark, he is coming now!'

Avran gestured back along the quay. There, approaching us, was a group of three men. Two of them were young and burly, wearing simple blue tunics and with long yellow hair tied back by twisted braids. Battle-axes were strapped at their waists — a bodyguard, clearly. The third was shorter, more elderly, but more richly attired. Though his tunic was blue also, it was elaborately embroidered in floral patterns with gold thread. Clearly this must be the captain I sought.

I hesitated. 'You see, I want to make the voyage to Rockall. I was waiting to see him, to try to arrange it, and — well, I fell asleep in the sunshine.'

Avran laughed joyously. 'So *that* was why you were so fortunately there, ready to act as my saviour from death! I am grateful indeed for your sleeping! And to what part of Rockall would you voyage? This vessel sails first to Sandarro, then to Brevolan in Fachane, and after that only to Angmering — and they will not take you to Angmering.'

Both other names were equally unknown to me. 'Well, I don't know,' I responded hesitantly. For some reason, I was reluctant to disclose my ultimate destination.

'Then you must travel to Sandarro with me. Please permit me the pleasure of negotiating for you. It will prove less expensive, for I know these Mentonese.'

The three seamen were almost upon us as I nodded assent. Avran stepped forward and, as the men halted, began to speak rapidly in a language quite unfamiliar to me. When he paused, the captain gazed at me with eyes as bright and expressionless as those of a lizard; then he replied abruptly in the same language. They exchanged a few brisk sentences and I understood that they were bargaining. Quite soon the captain uttered a single, abrupt word and held out his cupped hands. This was in Rockall, as I discovered later, a signification of the acceptance of a bargain.

Avran turned to me. 'You are fortunate,' he said. 'The captain is in a hurry to make the tide; usually these deals take much longer. I have told him you are my comrade, which perhaps has helped also. He will take you for ten nobles; and, er' — he hesitated — 'if you have not so much gold, I would be pleased to, er, advance it.'

I smiled with relief. 'No, that's fine; I can pay that amount easily.'

I fetched out the leather purse and paid the ten coins into the waiting palms of the Mentonese captain. He scrutinized them carefully, inclined his head in acceptance of the deal, and handed them to one of the seamen, who stowed them away in a leather pouch at his belt.

While this negotiating was in progress a dory, manned by two blue-tunicked sailors, had drawn up at the quay behind us. As Avran picked up his bundles preparatory to boarding it, I remembered my own satchel and pelican.

By the time I had scrambled up and retrieved them from the top of the big barrel, Avran and the three Mentonese had dropped down into the little boat. It was bucking so erratically on the rising tide that, when I followed suit, instantly I lost balance and tumbled forward almost into the lap of the captain. He drew back disdainfully; but Avran, sitting by him, smiled, and the sailors laughed. Thus undecorously did I leave my native shore forever.

The dory seemed to spin away from the quay as the four sailors, two from the ship and two from the shore, pulled on the oars they had already taken up. Down-river we went, past the city wall to the sea. I was facing back toward Bristol and, watching its spires at first diminish behind the wall and then come into view again as we floated farther down-river, was not aware of the ship till we were almost at its bows.

Very different it was, even to my eyes, from the two ships I had seen drawn up at the Backs. It was broader in the hull and more spacious, with a square foresail, a much huger square mainsail and a triangular mizzen sail over the stern, where a greater depth of the hull and a series of portholes revealed the presence of cabins below deck. (Such ships were then unique to Mentone, but the design was later to be borrowed by many European peoples, the Portuguese in particular.) All three sails were green, of all unlucky colours, and bore a saltire — a St Andrew's cross — in white.

As we approached the ship, one of the sailors blew on a strangely shaped horn. In response, a rope ladder was lowered over the side. Its ascent was accomplished with speed and ease by the Mentonese sailors, even the one who had shouldered Avran's bundle of bowstaves. (I wondered again what they were for.) Avran, with his satchel, climbed up more slowly; and, as for me, I found the ascent altogether alarming, the ladder seeming to bob around like a tassel at the belt of a running footman.

Once we were aboard, the dory was secured by ropes and drawn up from the water, to be inverted and tied in place at one side of the mid deck; another dory, similarly secured, lay on the further side. In between, just abeam of the main mast, was a recess in the deck from which smoke was rising. The captain, ignoring us, went straight to that recess and descended some steps out of my view. A series of four throbbing notes was blown on a horn — an instrument twisted and ribbed like a goat's horn, but amber in colour and quite translucent. At this sound, all the sailors began to gather. The smoke billowed and turned to flame.

'Come forward,' said Avran in an urgent undertone. 'This is their ceremony before setting out from land. They do not like it to be watched by outsiders.'

We stepped under the shelter of the foremast. Two other men were there, passengers like ourselves on this vessel; a plump, amply befurred merchant who, by his accent, was from the Low Countries, and a lean, dark-haired man with a thin face. The latter gentleman gave only the curtest of acknowledgements to our greeting before striding away brusquely.

'Another Baroddan, I think,' Avran whispered to me. 'Many of them have no love for we of Sandastre. Well, I suppose it is understandable, even after a hundred years.'

Whilst the ceremony was in progress, Avran engaged the Fleming in conversation. The merchant was voyaging to Fachane in an attempt to set up new trading arrangements that might bypass 'these accursed Mentonese' — a sharp nod forward — who were, it seemed, expensive middlemen. As for me, I had no knowledge whatsoever of Mentone or Fachane — and little of the Low Countries, for that matter — so their conversation did not hold my attention. My concerns were becoming more personal, for my stomach, as I was increasingly aware, was *not* adjusting well to the slow heave of the anchored vessel.

The conversation ended when a roar and flare of flame from near the main mast, followed by another braying of the horn, indicated that the ceremony was over. With a rattle, the anchor was drawn up. The Fleming hurried sternward and disappeared from view into the recesses of the ship. Since the presumed Baroddan had already gone below, I looked at Avran questioningly.

'No, we don't follow,' he said. 'They have only two small cabins for the passengers; we must remain on deck, I'm afraid. They'll bring blankets for us, and food when we need it — *if* we need it . . . But now, I fear our troubles are just commencing!'

I noticed that his cheeks were pale, so I guessed that he was beginning to feel as unwell as — yes, as I was myself. The sailors were heaving upon ropes now; the ship was swinging out into the tide. I watched as Bristol's spires receded from view; it was becoming desirable only to watch, not to converse. How this wretched deck did shift about — why, the ship was like a live thing! And how curious; apart from its heaving, the ship seemed to be still and the land to be moving away from us. Moreover, after so much rain there was a hanging haze. As the Severn took us downstream, the haze obscured the green banks increasingly behind a silvery veil through which a pale sun shone yellow. My last views of England seemed blurred, dreamlike, altogether unreal.

They were, in any case, unpleasantly terminated. As we sailed out into the Bristol Channel, I felt a new motion, a sort of transverse bucketing as the hull of the ship responded to the swell. This was too much for me; I sought the side and was very, very sick. Now I knew what Ben Emery had meant — a pleasure to come, indeed . . .

Chapter Six

THE ASSASSIN

A vertical yellow line of light, bright as a newly-lit candle in a dark room, appeared on the eastern horizon. The light spread laterally till the whole edge of sea against sky glowed gold, and vertically till the wave crests were tinged with brightness and the clouds edged with shining silver. Then the sun itself rose, as intolerably bright as molten metal poured from an ironmaster's crucible. It seemed as if the very radiance of the new day was subduing the sea for, as the light increased, so did the height of the waves dwindle till they became little more than wrinkles on its broad face.

Their diminishing was welcome. Before even the shores of England were fading from view behind us, the Mentonese vessel had begun to encounter heavy seas. By the first night we had run into a squall, with driving winds. The ship had pitched with the concentrated ferocity of a bucking horse at a fair, trying to dislodge its rider before two minutes were up and a prize obtained.

I would surely have gone overboard had not one of the sailors rolled me under the lea of one of the overturned dories and, bundled in blankets as I already was, roped me to the ship's rails. Indeed, so miserable was I by then that I resisted his attention, feeling it preferable to be tipped into the sea than to endure this appalling physical discomfort. Again and again Ben Emery's words came to mind; fully did I understand, now, why he preferred to be a longshoreman than a sailor! And yet, not only did these Mentonese endure the motion but they seemed almost to revel in it. To see them hurrying up aloft on those swaying, pitching masts and spars was a dizzying spectacle, especially to one feeling so ill as I. Those four days had been, beyond question, the most utterly wretched in my entire life.

Had been . . . Why yes indeed, I was beginning to feel better! I had woken, still feeling miserably unwell, when it was still dark and the ship still rolling abominably; yet I had not been sick. While watching the sunrise, I had not even been conscious of my own inward feelings; it was the first time in four days that anything had distracted me from my sufferings. (*Mal-de-mer*, the French called it; what a mild term for such an appalling experience!) And now — yes, I was definitely better. Not to the point of welcoming food — I recoiled from the very thought — yet it *did* begin to seem possible that soon I might unhitch myself, stretch and rise!

Suddenly I remembered Avran. He had been in little better condition than I and, throughout those four days, we had scarcely exchanged either word or look. Despite the weather, he had refused to be moved under the lee of the dory. Instead he had remained on the open deck, swathed in his orange cloak and covered by a tarpaulin provided by one of the sailors. I could see him now, lying as inert and enwrapped as a chrysalis by the rail only fifteen feet or so from me. From his stillness he must surely be asleep, reasonably enough at such an hour and after such afflictions.

As the light of the rising sun showed me more of the deck, I realized that Avran was the only person in sight. The sailors, no doubt exhausted after so long a fight with the storm, must be below and sleeping; the helmsman was not within my view. Overhead the mainsail was dark against a sky that was paling now to grey. A random sunbeam highlighted Avran's red head and an edge of the orange cloak wrapped about him. I smiled when I saw him hunch and shift away from its light; it was my first smile since I had set foot on the ship.

Yet, what was that? Surely I had seen a movement, in the shadow under the main mast. Yes, there *was* someone, someone emerging from the recess in the deck that contained the Mentonese shrine. It was not one of the seamen, for all of them, even the ship's officers, wore blue tunics and all were fair. No, this was a dark-haired man, dark-cloaked also.

Ah, now, I had it! This was that fourth passenger, the one whom Avran had called a Baroddan, the one who had turned away from our greeting. I remembered Avran saying that many Baroddans hated the men of his own nation — what was it called? Oh yes, Sandastre. At that memory, I felt a sudden disquiet which jolted me into full attention.

I tried to sit up but, with the blankets and rope so tight about me, could only manage a half crouch. The man had not seen me, concealed as I was under the boat. He had moved forward a little, still keeping within the shadow of the sail. I saw him glance hurriedly up and down the deck; it was still empty. Evidently reassured, he stepped out from the shadow, not boldly even now, but watchfully — like a rat that, although seeing some helpless prey before it, is yet conscious that cats might be about. Indeed, lean and dark-coloured as he was, he looked curiously ratlike. Nor could there be any question that his prey was to be Avran.

I strove again to sit upright, but could not. Only my right arm was free, and there was nothing within reach which I could use, one-handed, to pull myself loose from the swathing blankets. Moreover, as I realized with increased anxiety, the rope was too tight about my shoulders for me to reach any of my throwing-knives. Nor would a shout avail much. Avran's sword was not to hand, for it was tucked away somewhere inside his tarpaulin; and, in any event, he was too deeply asleep to respond quickly.

The Baroddan, if such indeed he was, was edging forward. His mouth must be drawn up into some sort of smile, for there was a gleam of white teeth. Appalledly I perceived that something else was gleaming — a long dagger, held in semi-concealment against his chest but ready for use, for murder.

Still there were no sailors in sight or even, I presumed, readily within hail. Only I might save my friend; but I was almost as swathed and helpless as a fly cobweb-enwrapped by a spider. Yet not quite, for I did have one free arm. What might I do? Was there any stone to hand, any lump of metal — anything I could throw, to startle the would-be assassin and save Avran?

The ratlike man was advancing more quickly now, his attention wholly concentrated upon my sleeping friend. Close by though I was, he had not perceived me. And supposing he did, I thought dismally, it would mean a second murder . . .

Yes, after all there *was* something to hand — a coarse,

heavy earthenware bowl. It had been placed to receive my vomit but, though all too frequently utilized, presently was empty. An awkward missile indeed this would be, especially for a one-handed throw, but it was all I had! I grasped the bowl by its rim and swung it out from my body. Then, as the dark-haired man ran forward with dagger drawn back, I hurled the bowl at him with all my might.

It was not a good throw, yet it served. I had aimed for the assassin's shoulders, but the bowl was too heavy to be thrown so high; it hit him in the legs instead. Yet the shock proved enough. He staggered, stumbled and, as the ship dipped into the trough of a wave, fell forward. A gap had been left in the rails so that the dory might be drawn aboard or lowered. Into that gap he plunged and, with a despairing wail, fell from my sight into the sea.

Feverishly I freed myself from the rope and struggled out of the blankets, to run to Avran. The assassin's cry had aroused him; he turned and sat up, looking about him disturbedly.

'*Varatie* — Simon, what happened? Why so hasty? What awakened me?'

'The dark man — your Baroddan . . . He had a dagger — he tried to kill you . . .' I was breathless and shuddering with reaction, the words tumbling forth.

'But where . . .? Calm yourself, friend, and tell me what happened.' Avran was fully awake now.

My legs seemed wobbly — as, indeed, they were, after so many days of unpleasant semi-inertia. I sat down beside him, swallowed hard, and then told him what had transpired, shuddering as I realized how close he had been to death.

Avran listened intently, then sighed, smiled at me and said: 'How very valuable it is, Simon, that so often you observe, yet are not observed. And how truly excellently you throw! Twice now you have saved my life. Already I was deeply in your debt. What now can I say, save that I shall strive to repay that debt somehow, in some fashion. And that you are forever my friend. You said that, in England, you are of "nowhere in particular". Be sure that you will always have a place in Sandastre!'

Those words caused me to blush with pleasure. Moreover, they were uttered in so regal a tone — not a tone of condescension, but rather one of pride and assurance — that, for the first time, I realized Avran must be of high rank in his own country. That there had been two assassination attempts on him in so short a time also showed him, as I realized now, to be a person of consequence.

Avran had been looking serious, as well he might after so close a brush with death. However, while I was hesitating as to how I should respond, he laughed suddenly. 'How very humiliating for our late acquaintance, to die, not from sword or lance, but from the blow of an earthenware pot. It is surely unprecedented in the annals of errantry! And see, there is the pot, unbroken, ready for re-use if the occasion warrants!'

I turned and looked. Yes indeed, there was the bowl; it had rolled into the scuppers and become wedged. A little hesitantly at first, then more wholeheartedly, I began to laugh also. As I laughed, I knew suddenly that I had left my seasickness completely behind me. Moreover, the sun was rising higher and the day was surely going to be a glorious one.

I strove to be serious. 'Thank you for your kind words, Avran. Yet I must ask you to please tell me — and please forgive the ignorance that makes me ask this — where and what is Sandastre? And — if you'll again forgive the question — just who are you? I mean, what is your own rank?'

'You ask large questions, friend! To tell all about Sandastre, why that would take many days! Let me say merely that it is a land — a beautiful land, to my eyes — in the south of our island of Rockall. As for me, I am of the gard, its ruling house — its present ruling house. My father is eslef — ruling prince, in your language. As one of his sons — the third — I am indreslef, a sort of secondary prince I suppose. Helburnet, my eldest brother, will be eslef some day — if he lives; for already they have murdered my second brother and it is clear that they are trying hard to murder me also. If we both die, the Estantesecs will cease to be gard; and then, *then* there will be trouble!'

'But who is trying to murder you — who are "they"?'

'I cannot be sure, but I think the Grassads are behind it. Always they prefer to make others wield weapons in their cause, so as to further, but yet to mask, their own purpose — their long purpose, to turn Grassavard into Grassagard!'

63

I was becoming confused by now and Avran realized it. 'I apologize; I must explain more lucidly. It is early in the day to speak of history and of politics, yet I must strive to do so. Where, then, shall I begin?'

'At the very beginning, please. I know nothing of Rockall. If, as it seems, I am to live there, I shall need to know much.'

'The beginning . . . Well, I shall try. Long ago, Rockall was but the northern part, the mountainous part, of a great empire. A great and rich empire that was, rich in gold and copper and a lost red metal which we call evragar; I have been told that it was called orichalcum, in the ancient writings of Greece. The peoples of that empire built great cities, fine roads to speed their armies, and temples with stepped sides, dedicated to the sun they worshipped. My own people lived in the mountains north of their realm. We were conquered by them, but never wholly subdued; we paid tribute reluctantly and supplied victims unwillingly to their temples. For they were very evil, those people of that empire. Their many slaves groaned under their rule and the stink of their sacrifices rose to offend the heavens.'

Avran paused, his brow shadowed by the envisioning of his ancestors' sufferings, but then continued: 'In the end there came retribution. Great earthquakes threw down their temples. The waters of the oceans rose and overwhelmed their land, drowning fields, mines and cities. Only our high land of Rockall remained and a few lesser hills to the southward, left now as islands.'

'When was this?'

'Oh, long ago. Two thousand years ago, perhaps.'

Well, that was clear enough. I understood now that Avran must be talking of the great flood to which the Bible refers, though I was surprised Noah had not encountered these islanders during his voyage. 'Please go on.'

'Our tribes rose and overpowered the rulers, the governors, that had been imposed upon us. Many of them were killed, but some were not. Those survivors might well have been enslaved, men, women and children alike, as my ancestors had been; it would have seemed just. However, there was a great leader of my people, Selvar Dragat Indren. He said: "God has extirpated our oppressors, because they were evil.

We have been spared, but we must not imitate their wrong-doing. We must neither murder nor enslave those over whom we now have dominion. There are islands off our new shore; let them go to those islands and live as they wish!" And so that remnant of the people of the empire was permitted to make boats and to sail away to those islands. No further blood was shed and, in our realm and those about it, slavery has been forever forbidden.'

'What happened to those people?'

'Oh, they live yet on the islands; on the five islands off the south coast of Rockall and on Vragansarat and its lesser islands — a whole string of islands. We have no contact or trade with them and they have never troubled us; no, not in all these long years. Sometimes we glimpse their ships at a distance; that is all. With our oppressors gone, we peoples of Rockall resumed our old lives in freedom. New realms arose — Barodda and Fachane to the west of us, Arcturus and Salastre to the east, and a tangle of little kingdoms to the north, some eventually giving birth to the greater kingdom of Temecula. When we are in Sandarro I will chart them for you.'

'Yes, I'd welcome that,' I responded. 'My tutor showed me maps of High and Low Germany and of the Holy Land, so I have some skill in reading them.'

'Yes indeed,' Avran responded seriously. 'You must learn how our lands relate to each other, but you must learn also about how my own land came to attain its particular governance. For indeed, even in Rockall Sandastre is unique.'

'Please do,' I responded bravely; though, as Avran said, it was early in the day for such concentrated instruction.

'Now, in Sandastre when the empire collapsed,' Avran resumed, 'there were forty-five vardai, forty-five great families of persons sharing a common kinship and name. The question was, which should rule? Well, Selvar Dragat Indren was certainly our greatest leader. He might have established a kingdom for Indravard in perpetuity, but he would not. Instead, he would take only the title of eslef, of prince; and he ordered that the title should pass through his sons and their descendants only while the direct male line lasted.'

'But what happened when that line *did* end? Were there not great arguments?'

'Not at all. Selvar Dragat had set up a Ruling Council, made up of the leaders of the forty-five vardai. Its tasks were to advise him and, when his line failed, to choose which vard should become the next gard — the next Royal house. When the line of Selvar Dragat ended, the Orexins were chosen, Orexavard becoming Orexagard; when Orexagard failed, the Lednarens were voted the throne — Lednagard. And so the rule has passed from family to family, with no vard permitted to hold the throne twice until that distant time shall come when all forty-five families have, in their turn, ruled.'

All this sounded admirable indeed, but I could not see how it had been made to work. 'But Avran, what would happen if a ruler decided that he wanted to change the system? If he had royal power, how would you stop him?'

'Simon, you must understand that an eslef is not a king. He governs only with the consent of the Ruling Council. That Council makes the laws; the eslef must govern within the laws. Your king has a parliament, but he may call it or dismiss it at his will; his power is absolute. And so it is in Fachane and Temecula, for they have a dakheslef, a king with great powers. So it was in Barodda. Yet never has it been so in Sandastre. In our land, the authority of the ruler is strictly circumscribed. If he should turn to evil, his reign, and the rule of his gard, would be ended. When the Marrecs turned to evil ways, Marexagard was deposed. Thus it should always be.'

'It seems an excellent system,' I said seriously, remembering the wars of succession that had torn England asunder, family against family and brother against brother, for so long.

'So I think; yet there are those that wish to subvert it. The Ranverems, for example. They are the most powerful vard, with many relatives inside and outside Sandastre. Ranverems hold the throne of Temecula and there are many of that vard in Barodda. Yet it chanced that, when Ranverevard became gard, they held power for two years only. Breldnett Ranverem and his sons rashly took ship together — we Sandastrians distrust the sea, and how wisely! — and, when their ship was wrecked on a rock, all were drowned. So now the Ranverems urge that the laws be altered, so their vard might again rule. Yet I do not think the Ranverems would conspire with the Baroddans.'

Avran paused again; but by then I was deeply interested. 'Please go on,' I urged him. 'Are the Ranverems not the only threat to your family's rule?'

'Not so. The Ranverems are a numerous clan, but the Grassads are yet more numerous in Sandastre — indeed, they are the largest of the vardai. Yet Grassavard has never ruled, for it is distrusted. Properly so, in my view, for its leaders desire to be, not eslevei, but dakheslevei; not princes with limited powers, but kings with absolute powers. They argue: "We are many, while some vardai — Lednavard, Argravard — are few. It is not right that great Grassavard should hold only one position in the Ruling Council, when even tiny Lednavard holds as many!" And their claim is persuasive; many believe it just. They do not perceive the wisdom of Selvar Dragat's design, that the power and greed of large vardai should be counter-weighted by the votes of the smaller ones.'

'And where does Barodda fit in?'

'Well, that story is long also, so I shall tell it only in part. If one is successful, it is often one's nearest neighbours who are most envious and most likely to be one's enemies. So it is with Sandastre. Our realm has been strong; never has it been conquered since the empire fell. Throughout that long time, our most constant enemies have been the Arctorrans, to the east, and the Baroddans to the west. Our wars with each have been many and, with both together, several. Yet, though again and again we have been victorious in those wars, we did not try to seize either land or even to exact indemnity or tribute from them in defeat.'

'Why not?' I asked surprisedly. 'Surely, to the victor go the spoils!'

'Ah, but we have remembered always the wisdom of Selvar Dragat. If it is wrong to enslave a man, then it is quite as wrong to conquer or pillage a realm.'

'So that, even when unjustly attacked, your people have never felt need for vengeance? That is remarkable.'

Avran sighed. 'Never did we do so till just a century ago: and the wrong done to us then was beyond even our forgiveness. The King of Barodda, Saiondar III of cursed memory, invited Prince Laidnar IV Vesprassad and his fine sons to a feast and, although their host, murdered them. He thought he might conquer Sandastre by this infamy and by invading without declaration of war; but he did not. Swiftly the Ruling Council chose my own vard, the Estantesecs, as gard. My great-grandfather Vindicon I Estantesec, helped by the King of Fachane who was properly appalled by such treacherous slaying of guests, defeated him and led their armies into Barodda. The northern Baroddan faraslevatai or, as you would style them, earldoms of Aldagard and Darrinnett were annexed to Fachane. South Barodda, which we call Breveg, became a new faraslevat and was entrusted to Vindicon's eldest son, my grandfather. Thereafter each eldest son has been Earl of Breveg before succeeding as Prince of Sandastre; my eldest brother is now its ruler. In the same fashion, I understand, the son of your King of England is made Prince of Wales. Be sure that Breveg is quite as difficult to rule as Wales!'

'But I don't understand. If the Baroddans hate Sandastre so much, would *they* not try to kill you? Why need they be prompted by others? Why are you so sure the Grassads are involved — or the Ranverems, maybe, if they also want to see the rule of your family ended?'

'Well, of course their idea is that we should blame the Baroddans. But you see' — he grinned — 'in Baroddan eyes, I'm not an important person. Not so important that they would send assassins after me, so expensively and so far, all the way across these dreadful seas to England. My father, now, as ruling prince — yes, the Baroddans might like to kill *him*, if they could; or my brother, who rules Breveg presently. Yes, brother Helburnet is a just ruler and kind, but he is not Baroddan; there are many who would like to see him die. Indeed, when my other brother was murdered, he was travelling in Barodda.'

Avran stopped and sighed: quite evidently, the memory was still grievous to him. When he spoke again, however, it was with an attempt at lightness.

'But little me — why should I concern them so much that they pursue me so far? Neither do I have power, nor am I seeking it; and certainly I am no great or famous warrior. Were I in Barodda — yes, they might seek to slay me; and indeed, if my father and brother and I were all to die, then Estantegard would lose the throne. Yet there are plenty of other vardai to provide successors. To a Baroddan, one Sandastrian ruler is just as undesirable as another. Only the Grassads or the Ranverems would truly gain from a change in the ruling family, unless . . .'

He paused. 'I had not thought of that. Why, of course . . . I was thinking that our two late friends were merely hired killers . . . But you are right; either the Grassads or the Ranverems — not both vardai, for they would not work in double harness — may have made some deal with the Baroddans. Freedom for Breveg, perhaps, in exchange for help in gaining the throne of Sandastre. If the Grassads gained power, or if the Ranverems seized power again, they would never relinquish it; no, not they! Sandastre would become just a kingdom, like Fachane or Temecula; all our freedoms would be lost . . .' His voice dwindled away. His usually merry face had become solemn. Clearly he was thinking hard and anxiously.

I was too interested to let the conversation end thus. 'Yet how were they able to arrange these attempts on your life? How did the assassins find you? And, if I might ask the question without embarrassment — don't answer if you'd rather not — why *did* you travel all the way across these stormy seas to England anyway? You do not seem to me altogether a joyful sailor — you've been quite as ill as I, these last few days!'

He grimaced, then replied wrily: 'You are correct, friend Simon — painfully correct. No doubt others might find such voyaging delightful and healthful, but not I! Once I am again safe on the good, stable shores of Rockall, be sure I shall never more cross these dreadful seas that forever pitch, and toss, and heave!'

I laughed at this and Avran smiled in response. Then he continued: 'As for my purpose, it need not be secret from you. Indeed, having seen my burden, you may have guessed it. You English have won many wars in the last hundred years, in part because of courage and good leaders, I doubt not, but also because of your particular weapon — the long-bow — and the skill of those who wield it. We of Rockall have bows and arrows, yes, but only smaller ones. Our arrows are suitable for the shooting of birds and small animals for food, but they will not pierce the armour of a

69

warrior. We did not know how to make long-bows, what wood to use, how best to string or how to wield so powerful a weapon.

'So, at my suggestion, the Ruling Council sent me to England. My particular task was to learn how long-bows are constructed and to bring back examples, fabricated from different woods, for examination. The decision was taken suddenly, while a vessel from Mentone was actually moored at our quays. It was not noised abroad, but since Draklin Grassad and Seld Ranverem are both members of the Council, their vardai would be informed immediately of my voyage. Indeed, I recall now my father's surprise when Draklin Grassad spoke in favour of my idea; the Grassads usually oppose his schemes.'

'So the Grassads are likeliest to have set those assassins on your trail,' I interjected.

'Yes indeed, though I cannot be certain. Mayhap it is fortunate the ship was sailing so soon. My fellow travellers on that voyage were all from Fachane; there were none from Sandastre or from Barodda. If any enemies *had* been voyaging with me, I might never have reached your city of Bristol, for I was very sick and as helpless as a child, with no obliging Englishman to watch over me! Yet of course there have been other ships from Rockall since, two at least from Mentone and one from some other land not known to me. It must have been on one of those ships that the Baroddans came to Bristol in pursuit of me.'

'Yet, if they came on later ships, how did they contrive to find you in England?'

'Why, that was not difficult. Wherever I might go, I had to return to Sandastre on a Mentonese ship, and their ships sail only from Bristol. The man whose sword you keep had ample time to hire those three dock-rats and set them to watch for me. That second assassin, perhaps even now swimming back to England, must have been ready to act if the first should fail.'

'Well, both did fail,' I commented comfortingly, for my friend was evidently disturbed at the recollection of how greatly he had been in peril. 'What of your quest, though?'

'It went well enough. I spent more than a month in travelling around England and learning the art of the long-bow.

Of course, most of your young men were off to fight for the King or for the rebel Henry Percy — and, against such a king, who would not rebel? Yet I found many bowyers and fletchers, willing to show me the woods that could be used and how the bows and arrows were constructed; and I encountered many old archers, happy to earn their ale by teaching me to shoot with the bows I had made.'

He sighed. 'Yet, in an important way, I failed. I know how to make such bows now, and the arrows also, but I am not sufficiently skilled in the use of the long-bow to teach it. I had hoped to find some archer who would travel back to Sandarro with me; but I did not succeed. All the archers whom I approached were wedded and settled or, if single, fearing the ocean even more than I! Some sons of nobles proved more venturesome but alas! they were not archers.'

I cocked my head and looked at Avran hesitantly. 'Well, as for using a bow, I'm reasonably sound at that; and I believe I might train archers. However, you see, I'm on — well, a sort of a quest . . .' I hesitated again and stopped.

Avran looked at me alertly. 'Ah, indeed!' he said. 'I had thought you were merely in flight — a fugitive, perhaps, after the Percy's fall, or a victim of the anger of your King Henry.'

'Well, yes; in a way I am — a fugitive from the King, I mean. Yet that is not the whole reason . . .' So long had I been keeping my purpose to myself that, even now, I was finding it hard to divulge.

Avran reached out his right arm and clasped me about the shoulder. 'Simon, I have said already that I am deeply in your debt and forever your friend. I shall be glad, indeed I am eager, to assist you in any way that is within my power. Please trust me. Please tell me what it is that you desire to do, what you aim to attain, in our land of Rockall.'

At his warmth, my heart responded in a fashion that I had not experienced hitherto, save in the company of my father and brother. I had found pleasure in the affection with which, as I knew, John Stacey and old Walter regarded me and had done my best to repay it; but I had never enjoyed a close friendship with anyone of my own age and class. Now I knew that I had at last found such a friend. That knowledge gave me great joy.

'I'm sorry — I've been keeping my own counsel for so long that it has become a habit. Well, matters transpired like this — ' and forthwith I plunged into an account of my recent doings. Once I had begun, words tumbled out at such a pace that poor Avran must have had trouble in following my story. Yet he managed well, laughing aloud at the tale of my cousin's discomfiture and smiling sympathetically when I told of my relief at being rid of horse, helmet and gambeson. Nevertheless, at the end of my story, he appeared very much disquieted.

'Of course you must seek your father and brother,' he said. 'You have accepted your father's challenge and you must prove to him your quality — a quality of which I have no doubt. Yet, my friend, how shall you set about it? Rockall is large — much larger than Britain, I think. And it forms not one kingdom, as does England all the way to the Scottish border, but many smaller realms — and with wild lands between. This land that you seek; what was it? Ah yes, Lyonesse . . . Of it I have never heard, though perhaps my father or his advisers may be better informed. However, since I know nothing of it, Lyonesse cannot be at all close to Sandastre — or to Fachane, where this vessel will stop also. Perhaps it might be close to Angmering, the capital of these Mentonese, but they will not carry you to Angmering.'

'Then what *must* I do?' I asked rather helplessly. 'Where *should* I go?' That Rockall might be a greater island than Britain, I had never even guessed. Hitherto I had thought my task would be easy, once I had crossed the ocean to Rockall; but Avran's words forced me to a recognition of the true magnitude of my quest.

'Well, I am quite sure that, from Sandarro, you must travel northward. North and west, perhaps; north and east, maybe; but certainly northward. Beyond the southern hills of our land and beyond the plains where the Montariotan riders roam, there are said to be great forests. I have heard that, in their glades, many English and French knights have built castles and set up little realms. Perhaps, somewhere in those forests, you will find that land of Lyonesse — I do not know.'

These further words cheered me considerably. 'Then my task may not be so great, after all!'

'Yet it will assuredly prove hazardous. Even in crossing those mountains and those plains, you will face many perils; and there will be perils also amid the forests. How will you survive on such a journey if, as you say, you are not expert with the sword? With bow and knives, yes; but how will you withstand the sudden ambush, the onrush of attackers? Moreover, you do not know any of our languages. I can speak English, yes, but the only others able to do so, even in Sandastre, are my elder brother, my sister and four, perhaps five others. Between Sandarro and the forests you will meet none that speak it, unless you are very fortunate. How will you ask your way? How will you obtain food and drink, even?'

These further observations were depressing indeed and, unfortunately, I had to recognize them as entirely apposite. My face must have again fallen, for Avran gave me another brief hug, this time of encouragement.

'I think you will need a companion on your adventure,' he said, 'and me, I shall be blithe to go with you. I have not seen enough of our island. It will gratify me greatly to have good cause for travelling northward and seeing the grasslands and the great forests. Merely to hang around the castle of Sandarro, awaiting a Grassad dagger between my shoulders and without the defence of your well-aimed missiles, would be tiresome and tedious . . . Yes, if you will accept me as your companion, I shall go with you!'

I was overwhelmed. 'Oh, Avran, I would be truly delighted to have your company. Yet your father the Prince, your family; will they permit you to venture into such danger?'

He grinned. 'They do not usually prevent me from doing what I wish — though sometimes they try! Yet I think that, by your leave, we should not propose the matter to them immediately. It would be well if you learned something, at least, of our language. Sandastrian is not the only Rockalese tongue, by any means, but it is widely spoken. Moreover, you should learn our ways a little. Our food and drink, our customs and our courtesies, they are very different from those of England. You must learn also to ride the sevdru and fight with the sasayin. So many things will be new for you! The hospitality of the Estantesecs is yours; assuredly you must be our guest while you prepare properly for your quest. When you are ready to set forth, *then* I shall discuss the matter with my father and family!'

I could perceive how very sensible were these proposals. Moreover, they would afford me a welcome respite. Now that I had learned so much from my new friend, I was beginning to understand how ill-equipped I was for the venture upon which I had embarked. Indeed, the thought of that vast, unknown island was forbidding. Even though it might take time, it was essential that I be better prepared. A knight who enters a tourney, knowing neither its rules nor even how to wield his weapons properly, may be valiant, but certainly he is very foolish.

'Very well, Avran. I am sure that you're right. I shall accept your hospitality with pleasure, though I fear you'll need to be very patient with me. Thank you; and, for my part, mayhap I shall be able to lend aid with your bowmanship.'

'Excellent! We will prove fine partners, I am sure. Ah! now I see we have some sailors on deck at last! After so many days of enforced fasting, I am very hungry. You also, friend? Good — then we'll seek some breakfast!'

We ate well and amply. Small honey-flavoured cakes, slices of a dried and spiced meat that Avran called varas, rather wizened English apples — the last apples I was to taste in many months — and beakers of a sweetened milk-like drink were set before us and dealt with swiftly. After that, pleasantly replete and bathed in the warmth of a bright sun, we both drowsed away the morning.

Our departed assailant was not missed for several hours. Both he and the Fleming had, it seemed, been almost as seasick as Avran and me during those days of the storm; and, indeed, the Fleming did not emerge from his cabin even on that bright morning. It was only toward noon that a flurry of excitement among the sailors, and the arrival of the captain from the foredeck to investigate, indicated that the vanishing of the Baroddan had at last been noticed.

Through Avran, we were both asked if we knew the missing man's whereabouts. If we had been asked whether we had seen him, we would have been made to choose between telling the truth or a falsehood. With the question phrased thus, no such choice was forced upon us. Avran, solemn and straight-faced, assured the captain that we did not know where he might be — which, by then, was true enough!

After that, the two of us walked about the decks awhile. For the first time, I began dimly to understand how a sailing ship operated; how the ropes controlled the sails, how the rudder was worked, how the ship was steered. The captain had withdrawn again from our view, but the other Mentonese sailors seemed friendly enough. The problem was that their native language was very different from Avran's and their Sandastrian vocabulary was not extensive — a few basic words only. As for Avran, he seemed unwilling to talk more about Rockall, preferring instead to cross-question me about my Hallamshire home, my father and brother and the sad debacle of Hotspur's rebellion.

Toward the afternoon's end, the breeze stiffened and the waves became choppier. The Fleming, who had briefly emerged pale-faced from his cabin, precipitately fled back again. However, the rougher seas did not trouble Avran and me. We ate a second, larger meal with enthusiastic appetite, watched the sun go down and, rolled up again in our blankets, slept well. Neither during that night nor thereafter was the earthenware pot again used, for either of its purposes!

Chapter Seven

THE ENDING OF THE VOYAGE

Next morning when I awakened, the sun was high in the sky and the sea tranquil; but where exactly *was* the sun? Why, almost behind the ship; the shadows of the sails were making long, narrow lines forward toward the bow. What did that mean? The sun must be southeast of us; then we must be sailing more or less northwestward! As I laboriously worked this out, the mental effort and my realization of the strangeness of our course brought me fully awake.

Avran had awakened earlier and, indeed, had already found breakfast for us. There were hunks of the curious crusty bread the Mentonese favoured (surely not made from wheat?); two crescents of a reddish cheese that, by its flavour, came from Somerset; and, best of all, two cakes made of crushed yellow berries. These must be the sindleberries which Ben Emery had mentioned as an item in Bristol's trade with Mentone. When I tasted them, I knew why they were desired; their flavour was wholly beguiling, bitter-sweet, as if one were eating bilberries spiced with almond. A stone crock of a dark red, sweet wine completed the repast. I wondered what fruit it was made from — neither grapes nor elderberries, of that I was sure. Yesterday I had been so hungry that I would have wolfed anything; today I noticed, and enjoyed, the strangeness of my meal.

Avran could not tell me about the wine, for it was strange to him also, but he *was* able to explain our course. Driven first by the storm and then by yesterday's gentler following wind, our ship had travelled at a good pace. At first we had sailed more or less westward, till we were out beyond Ireland, then southwestward till we were south of the latitude of Portugal and Castile. By then we were south also of Rockall, yet still east of it. Now we were heading in a more northerly direction and might expect quite soon to make landfall.

Indeed, when in mid-morning a stir of excitement among the sailors aroused our attention, there was land far away ahead of us on the starboard side — a dark splinter on the horizon which, Avran said, was the southwesternmost tip of an island called Sayangadek. This island, it seemed, was a part of the residual realm of the people of the vanished empire, one of the five principal islands along the south coast of Rockall on which they lived. Varaldek, off the coast of Fachane, was the westernmost; then there were Skayadek and Aranadek, with a few smaller islands between, offshore from Breveg; Vasadek south of Sandastre; and, largest and easternmost, this island of Sayangadek off the southern coast of Arcturus. Further off from Rockall's shores, away to the south and east, other islands were held by them, the biggest called 'Lesser Rockall' by English sailors but properly named Vragansarat. However, beyond their names, Avran seemed to know little of these islands. After so many years, the descendants of the exiled rulers of long ago seemed to him of no importance.

Instead, during that morning and afternoon, he instructed me concerning the way of life and the manners of his own people, the Sandastrians. Since much of what he taught me will transpire naturally as my story progresses, I shall not recount it all here. However, two matters on which he laid especial stress deserve immediate mention.

First of all, it seemed that most of the peoples of southern Rockall were Christians — or at least nominally so. They had an ancient belief in one God and a prophecy of revelation from across the seas. This had been fulfilled seven hundred years before, when holy men came to Rockall from Ireland to preach the true gospel; the Time of the Saints, Avran called it. In contrast, when Irish holy men like St Aidan and St Colman brought Christianity to my own north country, they had had no prophecy to aid them. I was well aware not only that my own ancestors had been pagans but also that, in some parts of northern England, the ancient Norse gods still attracted furtive worshippers. In southern Rockall, seemingly, the conversion had proved a much easier business and religious wars were unknown.

78

What startled me, though, was to learn that Sandastre had no monasteries or nunneries to provide refuges for scholarship and prayer, nor any churches even. Its priests were not celibate but married, living in the community and often performing tasks additional to their religious duties. They conducted services in hall or house or even in the open air, not in specially consecrated buildings. Moreover the Bible, instead of being read only in Latin by priests and a few educated men, had long since been translated into Sandastrian and was copied and read by everyone.

Well, I had heard its translation into English advocated, if only hesitantly and furtively; and I remembered how vehemently Lord Furnival's chaplain had denounced such 'heresy', as he called it. At the time I had wondered why it *could* be wrong, to be able to read and properly understand the word of God. Consequently, though surprised by this information from Avran, I was not much disturbed.

I learned also that the authority of the Pope had not yet come to be recognized in Rockall, even though Ireland itself had long since submitted to Rome. Again this surprised but did not discountenance me. After centuries when there had been two popes, one in Rome and one in Avignon, with neither showing much love for England, my compatriots' acknowledgement of papal authority had for long been a matter of token only.

The second principal matter which Avran raised was that of the Sandastrians' attitudes to animals and to hunting. He had been greatly shocked, I learned, by the casual cruelties of the English — the cock fights and dog fights, the belling of cats, the baiting of bulls and badgers. He had been almost equally shocked by our methods of hunting. The pursuit of one fox, one otter or one deer by a whole pack of hounds and a great troop of huntsmen and followers seemed to him grossly unfair.

The Sandastrians did hunt, of course, for they had no distaste for any equal contest. Falconry was a respected occupation and Sandastrians would hunt larger animals alone, or in small groups, when food was wanted or when there was need to destroy a dangerous predator. The use of hounds was foreign to them, however. Nor could they ever stomach any cruelty to a helpless, cornered prey;

instead, the animal would be dispatched as swiftly and mercifully as possible.

Avran put these points before me very hesitantly, quite evidently anticipating that I would disagree wholeheartedly with him and defend vigorously my countrymen's attitudes. He was visibly relieved and heartened when I did not. Indeed, for years I had cherished very similar ideas. I had not dared to express the revulsion I had so often felt, fearing the scorn of my father and my peers. Now I was delighted to learn of a land where my personal prejudices were not considered freakish, but universally held.

While we talked, the splinter of land remained long in view; but we did not approach closer to Sayangadek and eventually it vanished beneath the horizon. By midday our course was becoming more easterly and by mid-afternoon, land was again glimpsed. This time it was ahead and to port, a high hump of an island which Avran said was Vasadek. Soon we were entering the Sandevrin Channel, one of a series of straits separating the offshore islands from the mainland of Rockall.

As the afternoon progressed, Vasadek elongated and transformed into a high mass of hills, dark against the bright southern sky. Avran gave it little attention. Instead he looked ever and again to the northward, anxious for a first glimpse of his homeland; but to the north, all was veiled in haze.

By late afternoon we were past Vasadek and once more there was open sea to the south of us. A sailor brought us what was to be our last meal on board. Again there were hunks of bread and crescents of cheese, with another crock of the sweet red wine but, disappointingly, no more sindleberry cakes.

Up to that time we had seen nothing of the Fleming, but the warm afternoon sunshine at last beguiled him from his cabin. He came to sit beside us on the deck.

'Due in Sandarro this evening, they tell me,' he rumbled. 'On to Brevolan tomorrow, with luck. Shan't be sorry to see the end of *this* voyage. Since that other accursed fellow disappeared — an unsociable, curmudgeonly being though he was, and no loss — I must say I don't feel safe. I'm not sure whether these Mentonese threw him overboard themselves, or whether they think that *I* did, but they're watching me all the time. I trust I'll find good trade in Fachane, to compensate for all these hardships and risks.'

We murmured polite echoes of this hope and Avran asked, as if idly: 'Did you ever discover his name, or where he was going?'

'Some barbarous name — oh yes, I have it! Akharn — Asd Akharn; and, like me, he was voyaging to Brevolan, though he would not say why. Seemed to resent my very questions, he did; no manners, no manners at all.'

'Was he trading, do you think? Any goods with him?'

'No, none; only a small satchel. Ah yes, I *will* have some of that wine — thank you.'

We pledged him and wished him success in his trading. He ate with us, but as soon as the meal was done he returned to his cabin, to check his goods and his gold before the landing in Sandarro.

After he had left us, Avran said quietly: 'The Akharns are a Baroddan clan. They live in the hill country above Rekhulan, on the Sekheyin River in northern Breveg. That won't mean anything to you, but it means much to me. Of all the Brevegens, these people of the north are the ones most fiercely resentful of Sandastrian rule. Well, that supports our ideas but it tells us nothing new. Would that I could examine the contents of his satchel!'

Almost as he finished speaking, the ship's course was again altered, to the north and across the wind. This was a manoeuvre involving much activity, as the mast heads were reset. Avran's eyes were eager now and, at his beckoning, I went with him to the bows. As the sun sank, the haze was at last lifting. Suddenly we saw Rockall — a line of green hills above the horizon.

'Sandastre, praise God!' crowed Avran in a sort of subdued ecstasy. 'Never again shall I voyage across those horrible, perilous seas to your land — or indeed, to any other! Once ashore, it will be long ere I can be persuaded again to set foot on shipboard. If perchance I *must* again put out to sea, be sure I shall make my ship hug Rockall's coasts as closely as it may!'

Within minutes a second line of green hills had come into view on the port — the west — side. 'The Bernevren Hills,' murmured Avran. 'The lands of Bernavard and

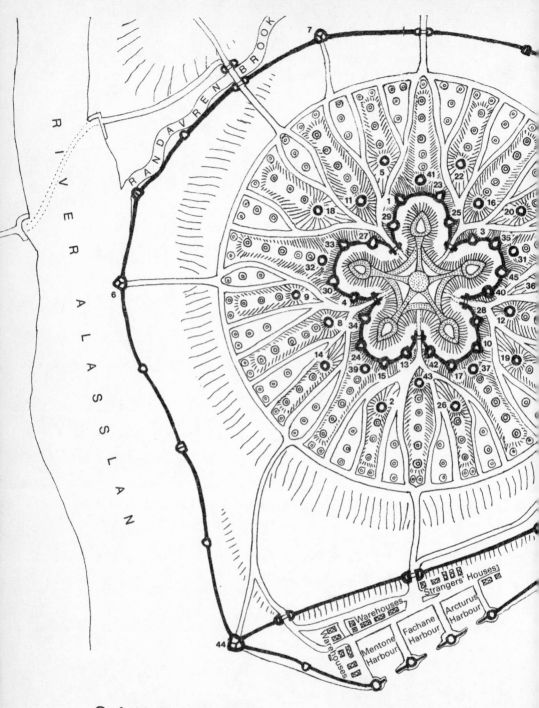

RIVER ALASSLAN

RANDAVREN BROOK

Strangers' Houses

Warehouses

Warehouses

Warehouses

Mentone
Harbour

Fachane
Harbour

Arcturus
Harbour

SANDARRO

TOWERS OF INNER BAILEY
 1 Aibremavard (Aibremen)
 3 Andravard (Andracanth)
 4 Aradavard (Aradar)
10 Bredennavard (Bredennar)
13 Densgavard (Denesgar)
15 Derresdavard (Derresdem)
17 Estantevard (Estantesec)
23 Indragard (Indren)
24 Kevessvard (Kevess)
25 Lednavard (Lednaren)
27 Menavedravard (Menavedra)
28 Mentnavard (Mentlidd)
29 Miodravard (Miodren)
30 Naratravard (Naratren)
33 Orexavard (Orexin)
34 Predaravard (Predaren)
35 Ranverevard (Ranverem)
40 Vednetravard (Vednetren)
42 Vespravard (Vesprassad)
45 Vrassavard (Vrassan)

STRONGPOINTS
 2 Alberavard (Alberim)
 5 Argravard (Argray)
 8 Bernavard (Bernut)
 9 Brantavard (Brantvut)
11 Bresdelavard (Bresdeln)
12 Dasnavard (Dasnar)
14 Dernogmavard (Dernogme)
16 Eldunavard (Eldunar)
18 Exoravard (Exor)
19 Goretsavard (Goretsad)
20 Gradessnovard (Gradessnovar)
22 Harradavard (Harradas)
26 Marexavard (Marrec. Malladec)
31 Nerisnavard (Neriss)
32 Orellavard (Orellan)
36 Redvravard (Redvud)
37 Servessavard (Servessil)
39 Varessavard (Varess)
41 Vendahlavard (Vendahl)
43 Vissavard (Vissavant)

FORTS OF OUTER BAILEY
 6 Avrassavard (Avrassan)
 7 Beldevard (Beldevil)
21 Grassavard (Grassad)
38 Stormavard (Stormassad)
44 Vragaravard (Vragar)

KEY

◎ Houses of wood and brick

⚙ Fortifications of red sandstone

◈ Fortifications of white quartzite

⧉ Wooden buildings

Vragaravard. Ah! how good it is to see them again; it refreshes my heart! Well, Simon, my friend, we are in the bay of Velunen now and sailing in towards Sandarro, where the waters of the Alasslan meet the sea. Yes, look! — there is the castle on its hill, and my city! At last, at last I am almost home!'

As he spoke these words, my friend's voice rose from its murmur into a paean of joy. However, though my eyes followed Avran's to the northward, I could not at first distinguish what he was seeing. Then, suddenly, I did see. South of the main mass of hills, and thus closer to us, an isolated and lower hill could be distinguished. Conical it was in shape and capped with a white topping, like a high crust of sugar on a honey bun.

As we sailed steadily closer, I realized that to be much too homely a simile. Upon the hilltop, as I now perceived, was a great castle, a castle as white and beautiful — or so it seemed to me — as the cloud castles of fairy-tale giants. I saw a cluster of tall white towers; at first I perceived three, then a fourth, but there were in fact five, the fifth hidden from our view. These were set about a tall and massive central keep of pentagonal shape. From the centre of that keep there upsprang a sixth and yet higher tower, which looked as slender as the point of a lance. From the outer towers to the summit of the central tower, five great arches soared upward, slim and graceful as the flying buttresses of a cathedral. All in all, this looked not like a mere work of fortification and defence, as did the other castles I had seen. Instead, it appeared like a crown — a crown fit to grace the head of the most beautiful of princesses.

About and below it was a patchwork of colour. Ringing the base of the castle proper, I now perceived, was a curtain wall, made not from white stone but from red. This wall was closely set with smaller towers; I could count more than ten of them and later learned that there were twenty. Nor did this complete the defensive works, for below and outside them was a whole series of isolated towers, similarly built from red stone; and below that again were more and more towers, circle upon circle of them. These lower towers were of a brown colour, darker than those about the hilltop, and in between were rings of green — bushes, surely? — improbably flecked with blue. Before the castle was a larger green space and before that, outer fortifications again of red stone at the very edge of the blue sea.

'Why are there so many towers on the hillside?' I asked Avran bewilderedly. 'Is not the one great castle enough? It looks very strong.'

He laughed. 'Well, the topmost ones *are* towers, but the rest are not! They are padin: houses. We don't build our houses to square shapes, like you English, and pack them tightly into rows along streets. Instead, we construct round dwellings, with a garden in the middle and a space between. Yet they do have a defensive purpose also, as you'll discover.'

As we sailed onward, the hill and its castle seemed to grow ever higher above us. This was not such a low hill, after all; it must rise at least three hundred feet above the sea. Nor was it so smooth as I had at first believed. Instead, it was buttressed by a series of rising ridges, some higher, some lower, each set with an ascending row of the circular padin and crowned with a stone tower just in front of the curtain wall. There were also lines of padin, though fewer of them, in the hollows between the ridges — and, yes, I could see paved roadways ascending the hill on the flanks of each ridge. Indeed this *was* a town, though utterly unlike any town I had seen.

To the east of Sandarro, a brook entered the sea, traversed some way upstream by a stone bridge; to the west was a very much larger river, too broad to be bridged. The brook to the east, Avran said, was the Ambidril; the river to the west, the Alasslan. Between their mouths, as I now perceived, there was a double row of fortifications, one a little higher on the hill atop a raised beach, the other at sea level. There were buildings in between, though I could not distinguish them clearly. When I asked Avran about them, he told me these warehouses and dwellings provided storage, accommodation and entertainment for foreign seamen and merchants, who were neither permitted to reside in Sandarro itself nor even to visit it. I was indeed to be privileged!

Steadily we sailed in toward that outer wall, very much to my bewilderment, for I could at first see neither any breaks in it nor any quays before it. Not till we were quite close did I perceive that it was interrupted in three places. Each gap was overlooked by a tower and each could readily be closed by means of great booms; these were now drawn back on to the fortified moles beneath the guardian towers but were ready for immediate use. The towers were amply manned, for I could see a number of soldiers moving about, upon and even within them.

'Ships come most often from Mentone, from Fachane or from Arcturus,' Avran commented. 'Each of those lands uses one harbour only, though our own Sandastrian vessels may enter any. The harbour for Mentone is the western one; that will be where we land. See, now, the flag on the tower!'

Indeed, a flag was being hoisted on the westernmost of the four towers guarding the harbour entrances. The colour of its field was grey, the grey of an evening sky, and on this there was displayed a golden bird of some sort, in flight beneath a crescent moon.

Its hoisting served to signal that our vessel might enter. Orders were shouted and, as the sails were trimmed, our vessel tacked, then sailed through that westernmost opening into a calm, quiet harbour in which two smaller ships were already at anchor. With more shouted orders and much activity at the ropes, our ship was brought about and drawn up alongside the quay on the west side of the harbour. There was a rattle of chains as anchors were dropped at bow and stern. We had arrived at Sandarro.

Chapter Eight

THE ROAD TO THE CASTLE

I had anticipated that the Mentonese sailors would celebrate our safe arrival with another brief religious ceremony, but not so. Presumably they did not consider the voyage ended till their ship reached Angmering.

I asked Avran about this, but he could not answer. Indeed, he confessed to knowing virtually nothing either about Angmering or even the land of Mentone itself. Truly this surprised me for, though voyages to Angmering might never be permitted, I had assumed some traveller would have brought back word of that land and city to Sandastre. All Avran knew, however, was that Mentone lay somewhere beyond the forests on the west coast of Rockall, and that Angmering must surely be large and rich.

My friend's vagueness was disquieting, for it made me again aware of how rash I had been in assuming that Lyonesse would be easily found. If the Sandastrians knew so little about a nation with which they traded regularly, then their information about other realms in this sea-girt island must truly be scanty. In journeying northward, we would be adventuring indeed!

Rather to my surprise, the quay seemed deserted. In English harbours, as I knew, men were available to unload ships at any time during daylight. Here however, as Avran told me, the longshoremen finished their duties by late afternoon and would not return till morning. The Fleming, who had come on deck again, was furious about this. It meant he could not hope to reach Brevolan tomorrow — another night on this accursed ship! However, that was his problem, not ours.

At last there was movement. A group of six men were coming out from one of the buildings fronting the quay and walking along at a leisurely rate toward the ship. From their unhurried pace they were clearly officials of some sort, but their dress was not impressive — light tunics, short-sleeved and only of knee length, dyed grass-green and belted at the waist. Their feet were booted, their heads bare, and they carried no arms.

This surprised me and I said as much to Avran. He in turn seemed surprised at my reaction.

'Why should they carry weapons? Sandastre is at peace. We have little crime here — none of your Bristol dockside murders! — and only friendly vessels are allowed into the harbour. If a criminal *did* come ashore from a ship, he would have to remain in the harbour area. We do not normally allow foreigners to enter Sandarro — only certain official guests and such true friends as yourself.' He smiled at me again and I felt a glow of renewed happiness.

One of the men on the quay — a burly man with a venerably grey beard — had, it seemed, glimpsed Avran's orange cloak. He spoke an order to one of the others, a younger man. That second man also glanced at the ship, then turned and ran back along the quay, to disappear from our view behind a building. I presumed he had gone to pass word that the Prince had returned, which seemed right and proper. I wondered what ceremonies would be arranged to greet Avran; they should be exciting!

The bearded man and his four associates were hurrying now. Soon a gangplank had been set between shore and ship and the bearded man and his colleagues were hastening up it.

The captain met them and offered the bearded man his clasped hands. The bearded man clasped his own hands about them, greeted the Mentonese with a gust of polite words that I neither comprehended nor properly heard, then pushed past him toward Avran, his face beaming.

'*Bazatié, Avran indreslef!*' were his first words. Avran had told me that '*Bazatié*' was the Sandastrian word of greeting and I distinguished my friend's name and title well enough. However, as they embraced and a torrent of sentences followed, I was unable to understand anything further. Avran greeted the other four men more briefly, then turned to introduce me to their bearded leader.

'Simon, this is Arn Beldevil, who is harbourmaster of

Sandarro. He speaks no English, I'm afraid, but I have told him you are my good friend.'

The bearded man smiled at me and held out to me his clasped hands. Mimicking the captain's response, I enclosed them in my own and returned that smile.

Indeed, Arn's was a face to smile at; strong and, though deeply wrinkled, suggesting a lifetime of contentment. His eyes were brown and gentle, yet showing both knowledge and humanity. I was not in the least surprised when Avran said: 'By the way, Arn is a priest as well as being harbourmaster. You may recall my mentioning that often our priests perform other tasks also.'

One of the harbourmaster's assistants shouldered Avran's bundle of bowstaves and would have taken his satchel also, had Avran permitted this. Following Avran's example I picked up my own satchel and cloak. After saying farewell and thanks to the captain — Avran, of course, speaking for me — we walked after Arn Beldevil down the gangplank on to the quay. So much had I enjoyed the last two days of the voyage that I was almost sorry to be leaving the ship!

As we walked along, the harbourmaster and Avran conversed in rapid phrases that were quite incomprehensible to me. Only the man with the bundle of bows followed us. Arn's other assistants had stayed on board, I presumed to arrange unloading and to see to whatever other formalities were required when a foreign ship entered Sandarro harbour.

This was my first landing in a foreign port and I expected everything to look new and strange. However, I was disappointed by the buildings which fronted the quay, very ordinary structures of wood or plaster-and-lathe, much like those of an English harbour town — Kingston-upon-Hull or Bristol. Outside one of them we stopped. After a further flurry of talk, we said farewell to the harbourmaster and his assistant, with a repetition of the clasped handshakes. Avran insisted on resuming his bundle of bows and, unaccompanied, we walked on along the quay. Between two warehouses we turned left, to follow a road up toward the outer wall of the city proper.

By then I was becoming bewildered. Surely, when the son of a ruling prince was arriving home from a long stay abroad, there should have been more fuss, more pomp and ceremony, more *notice* taken? Had Avran been telling me the truth about his status? Perhaps he was not really a prince! Yet, his manner . . . The evident excitement of Arn Beldevil on sighting him . . . Yes, I was altogether puzzled, even disconcerted.

Avran divined my thoughts and grinned at me. 'Not quite what you expect of a prince, eh, Simon? Yet as I said, my father is not a king, just an eslef; and this is Sandastre, not England. I regret, though, that you are so disappointed!'

Abashedly I blushed and, to divert his thoughts, said: 'There are no people about; I was wondering why. Surely *someone* lives here, by the docks?'

'Not in this area; it's all warehouses. There *is* a small resident population of foreign merchants and their assistants, but their houses and taverns are all at the east end, close to the Arcturus dock. The Sandarrovians who unload the ships have all returned back home long since.'

The outer wall of the city and the wall enclosing the harbour area were converging before us, as we walked along. Ahead to our left was a huge tower as big as the keep of many an English castle.

'That tower guards the mouth of the Alasslan,' Avran explained. 'There are five main towers on this outer bailey, each manned by one of the five vardai living closest to Sandarro — Avrassavard, Beldevard, Grassavard, Stormavard and Vragaravard. Each of those vardai also maintains and patrols a long section of wall, on either side of the tower. The tower is not just a place of guard, you must understand, but also a residence for the men and women of the vard when they visit Sandarro. This is Vragar Tower, the tower of Vragaravard.' He paused, then added with a wry smile: 'I came this way, rather than choosing the central or eastern gates out of the harbour area, because Grassavard watches the other two gates. I have no desire that the Grassads should learn quite yet that I've returned.'

'Are the inner towers also residences and maintained by particular vardai?'

'Yes indeed. The isolated strongpoints — the twenty detached towers that crown each of the hill ridges, guarding the roads up to the castle — and the twenty towers of the inner bailey are each looked after and lived in by the members of a particular vard. Estantesec Tower — that of my own vard — is the more easterly of the two southernmost towers of the inner bailey. Only the castle itself is under the direct control of my father, the ruling prince; and not altogether, for it contains two infirmaries, a library, schools, storehouses and much else, each with a fiercely jealous administrator. To be eslef involves much diplomacy! Fortunately, my father is a strong and astute man. For my own part, I'd hate the task!'

Again Avran had startled me. That he should regard the ruling of his land so flippantly, viewing it merely as a tiresome task; in particular, that he should state how he'd hate to be ruler — I marvelled! This was indeed a different land from my own, where so many had quarrelled so long and fought so fiercely for the opportunity to rule. Yet, even here, there were the Grassads and the Ranverems, rivals of one another and each coveting the throne; or was there indeed a throne? Presumably the ruling prince sat on *something*, but after so many surprises I was not sure even of that!

The southwestern gate of Sandarro was before us now, arched over by stone and guarded by two stone towers. The gates themselves were massive and sheathed with burnished copper. They were ajar, but a party of soldiers stood in the gap.

These were the first Rockalese soldiers I had seen at close quarters, so I gazed at them with interest. In such heat and with war not imminent, it was not to be expected that they would be wearing mail; nor, indeed, were they. Each man was wearing a padded, thigh-length jacket like the jupon of an English soldier, but much lighter and, though apparently made of some sort of hide, dyed an azure blue. Their hose were similarly dyed, but their boots were of light brown leather and of knee length, much like those of Avran. They wore no helmets but, instead, soft hats shaped to their heads, with brims hanging forward over their foreheads and curving back over their ears and the napes of their necks. At the front of these hats and on the right breast of the jupon were medallions of silver and enamel, showing a leaping silver fish on a sea-green background. (This, as I learned later, was the emblem of Vragaravard; soldiers of other vardai bore instead the emblem of their own vard, though all wore this uniform of blue.) About the waist of each man was a brown leather belt from which depended two scabbards chased in silver. That at left contained a short dagger, that at right a sword, about one cloth-yard in length and with drooping quillans so shaped as to resemble the outspread wings of a bird.

The leader of the soldiers — the serjeant, if I might so style him — was distinguished only by the fact that the medallions he bore were ringed in scarlet. Though it was quite evident that he recognized Avran, there was nothing of obsequiousness in his greeting, only an affectionate respect — a slight inclination of the head and an offering of clasped hands, which Avran seized in his own. Of the gusty exchange of phrases that followed, once again I understood nothing; yet the friendly smiles we received from the soldiers renewed my feeling of being welcome in this land.

As we walked under the stone arch I noted a heavy portcullis overhead, ready to be dropped should danger threaten. Friendly or not, this city of Sandarro was formidably defended.

Within the gate was the green space I had glimpsed from the sea — a broad area of meadowland, bright with many flowers. Beyond rose the hill of Sandarro, studded with padin and crowned by the graceful white castle, the road ahead of us curving upward toward it. Yet my attention was taken by a sight that, to me, was much more astonishing. Rushing toward us were four horned animals that I took to be deer, and on the back of the foremost there rode a girl!

I glanced at Avran and saw that his face was radiant with joy. 'It is Ilven, my sister!' he said, then called: '*Bazatié, Ilven aldrenal!*'

'*Bazatié, Avran indrenal!*' came the response; and, as her mount drew up by us, the girl slipped effortlessly from its back to the ground, to embrace Avran and pour out a torrent of words — greetings and questions, I presumed, though once again I understood nothing. Instead, I studied first the girl, then her mount.

Ilven was slim and lithe, shorter than Avran — indeed, about my own height. Her hair was of the same blazing red as his, but whereas his eyes were blue, hers were green. She was wearing a sleeveless tunic of the same shade of orange as her brother's cloak, belted about the waist and with a dagger in a silver-chased scabbard hanging at right. Her legs

92

were bare and her feet encased in soft leather shoes. She was so vivid, in dress and in movement, and her voice so musical even when I could not comprehend her words, that I found it hard to transfer my attention away from her, even for a moment.

Yet the animal she had been riding, and the others she had brought with her, deserved also of my attention. They seemed to be deer, but later I learned that they were not, for they had horns, not antlers — retained permanently, not shed and grown again annually. There were paired horns at the brow, each in the shape of a Y with symmetrically branched ends, so that each horn had four tines. In addition there were two shorter nasal horns, slim and unbranched. The animals were almost as big as horses, but their shape was slimmer than that of the cavalry and draught horses of England, perhaps more like that of the racing horses of the Saracens of which I had heard tell. Their bodies were covered with a short pelage much like that of the deer I knew, but of a pale grey colour, not brown; their breasts and bellies were white, and a narrow white stripe ran from the muzzle, up over the brow and down the centre of the neck and back to the tail. Two of the animals — the one Ilven had ridden and another — were lighter in build and bore neither bridle nor saddle; one of these was already nuzzling Avran and being caressed as Avran talked with his sister, while the other stood quietly beside Ilven. The two remaining animals were a little heavier and bore what seemed to be pack-saddles.

Suddenly I remembered that all the animals had stopped by us without instruction, the loose animals as well as the one Ilven had ridden. How had this been managed? Certainly she had not spoken to them, but had she given orders to them in some other fashion? This was indeed a day of surprises and puzzles.

However, Avran was introducing me now. 'Simon my friend, this is my sister Ilven. You will be able to converse easily with her, for she speaks your language better than I; and, as you are my friend, I hope you will be her friend also.'

Ilven was laughing at me — or perhaps, at her brother. 'Avran, how is it that one so small could twice save your life? He must be very cunning, or you very stupid! Nevertheless, Simon, I am pleased that my brother can find someone to take care of him when I am far away. Please continue doing so whenever necessary, for I value him, you see, even if he *is* stupid! Simon, I greet you with pleasure and welcome you to our land!' And she held out her clasped hands to be enclosed in mine.

Though Ilven was smiling at me, there was a serious, searching quality in her gaze, an enquiry. I perceived that her request was not made only in jest. Yes, she was teasing her brother, but also she was truly anxious about him and sincerely asking me to watch over him . . . What shade of green were her eyes, anyway? Not a sea-green, nor yet the green of an emerald; nearer to the green of a leaf in early springtime . . .

I had held on to her hands too long. She was laughing at me again as she disengaged them, but then her attention shifted to her brother.

'Avran, you'll ride back, of course. Your packs can go on a sevdru.' (So that was the name of these animals; I remembered now that Avran had said I would need to learn to ride them and to fight with some weapon — what was it? — oh yes, the sasayin.) 'However, Simon will require to ride also. He had better perch up on the other pack-saddle and you must control his mount for him.'

'Yes, of course.'

While Avran tied his bundle of bows, and our two satchels, to the back of one of the sevdru with rope from a pocket in the pack-saddle, I walked over to the second saddled animal. It was so clearly nervous of me that, though a little doubtful of those horns, I paused to stroke and scratch its muzzle and speak to it gently, as I would have done to a restless horse. To my surprise, the animal's response was immediate; it nuzzled my face and rubbed a soft cheek against mine. When I mounted, the sevdru stood perfectly still and showed no further apprehension.

Avran and Ilven exchanged glances; clearly they were as surprised as I, though they made no comment. They sprang on to the backs of their mounts, Ilven riding astride and not side-saddle in the fashion of English ladies, and soon we were following the road up toward the castle.

At the outset it was an uneasy ride for me. To be perched on a saddle designed for packs, not humans, on the back of an animal I had never seen till only minutes before, without bridle or even saddle to hold on to, when the motion of its movement was quite unlike anything I had experienced — well, it made me feel unsafe, to say the least! Ilven was riding ahead, Avran beside me; yet it was not from them that I was soon gaining confidence, but from the sure-footedness of my mount. Or was it quite that? Whatever the reason, my own apprehensions ebbed away with remarkable speed and I began to gaze about and ahead of me with great interest.

Indeed, there was much to be seen that was remarkable. If the warehouse area had disappointed me, now I could fully savour the strangeness of this new land. Why, the very grasses of the meadows were different! Their leaves were green enough, but their stems and seed-heads were more colourful than those of English grasses, being either scarlet or as yellow as ripe corn. These, then, were some of the 'flowers' I thought I had glimpsed. However, there were also true flowers in plenty, violet, red or pale blue, all of them unfamiliar to me.

Grazing among this rich pasture were many deerlike animals, heavier in build and darker in colour than the sevdru. Each had a single pair of coiled brow horns arching upward and outward like the frame of a lyre. As I learned later, such an animal was called a hasedu and was bred, not for riding, but for milk and meat, as we in England breed cows.

The sun was low in the sky now, since the summer evening was well advanced, and we threw long shadows to our right and before us as we rode. Ahead of us was the hill of Sandarro, with its many circular houses, padin, set in rows along the ridges and in the hollows. Between them, and circling the hill, were great banks of bushes flecked with blue. As our road left the meadowland and began to ascend the hill, I saw that these were roses, for both leaves and flowers resembled those of the wild roses of England. However, they were roses of a sort new to me. The thorns were much longer and wickeder than any I had seen on any English bush while the flowers were not white or pink, but of the colour of the uniforms of the Sandastrian soldiers — a bright azure blue. Moreover, those flowers were not single but massed into clusters. These bushes, with their fierce thorns, added significantly to the defences of Sandarro; but also they contributed greatly to the beauty of that strange city.

The road upon which we were riding was made from blocks of the same white stone from which the castle was constructed. These were fitted so neatly and tightly together that no grasses or weeds had found root between them. The road surface was slightly cambered and at each side were deep gutters, lined with stone and bridged over in places by slabs to provide readier access to the surrounding meadowlands. As we began to climb the hill I noticed that, whenever the road passed between one of the high blue-rose hedges, we crossed bridges formed by larger stone slabs. Later I learned that these were pivoted, so that they could be swung backward and upright. In the event of an attack, the ditch and stone wall thus formed would bar the progress of the aggressor almost as effectively as would the formidably thorny hedges.

The hill of Sandarro was indeed like a cartwheel, with the castle as hub, the hedges forming a whole concentric series of felloes and the rock ridges serving as spokes; we were now riding up between the two southwesternmost of these. There were padin not only on both ridges but also in the hollow below us. The padin were aligned parallel to the hill's circumference, each line separated from the next, lower and outer line by a rose hedge. Each padarn was set about with lawns, flowers and flowering shrubs; the Sandastrians, it was evident, were lovers of flowers.

Quite often a sevdru was to be seen standing or lying on the lawns or among the shrubs. None was tethered. One was rolling on its back like a horse, another had been garlanded with flowers by children who were still playing nearby. Those particular children were too occupied to pay any attention to us, but some others called a greeting to Ilven and received a cheerful acknowledgement.

The padin themselves were two storeys high, with roofs that were short and steeply pitched on the outward side but much broader, with a considerably gentler pitch, on the inner side. Their walls were made from large blocks of a dark reddish-brown wood, not from stone as I had thought when observing the houses from the sea. The roofs, however, had been made from planks of a different, darker wood which, when later I examined it closely, proved to have a denser grain. The doors — there were always two, one on the downslope and one on the upslope side of each padarn —

had been cut from massive slabs of a similar timber. There were no windows, just narrow slits at first-floor level. Though many doors stood ajar, I saw no adult Sandastrians and presumed they were inside at this hour, preparing for dinner.

As we continued riding up the road, I noticed that the padin on the ridges to our left and right were constructed, not of wood, but of a red sandstone, very similar in hue and texture to a stone I had seen used for buildings in Nottingham-shire. These stone structures were taller and more massive, a full four storeys. Oh yes, of course; we must be approaching the castle now and these must be the detached towers that crowned the ridges. We had climbed higher than I thought!

The road was soon swinging northward and the red curtain wall of the castle looming above us to our right. The gulley up which we were riding was overlooked both by the two isolated towers and by two towers of the castle walls. It would be a hazardous ascent indeed for an invading army.

Avran, who had been riding a little way behind me, caught me up in order to instruct me. 'The tower over on your left, Simon — yes, that one — belongs to Dernogmavard; the Dernogmes live in the valley of the Vekringa, many miles northwest of here. The isolated tower on your right belongs to Varessavard. They're a coastal vard, sailors; as much as any Sandastrian does, they love the sea. Curious taste . . . The first tower in the curtain wall is Kevess Tower. Kevessvard holds lands on our frontier with Arcturus — they're fierce fighters, they *have* to be! The tower straight ahead — the one we're riding toward at the moment — is Predaren Tower. Predaravard holds lands on our northeast coast, again uncom-fortably close to Arcturus. They're good friends of we Estan-tesecs. The tower on the further side of the gatehouse is held by Aradavard. The Aradars live in the Trantevrin Hills north of here; they're great archers, at least with our light bows! The tower beyond . . .'

At this point Ilven, who was riding ahead of us, turned and said: 'Oh Avran, surely that's enough! Poor Simon — you're trying to stuff into him too much information, he'll never remember all those names!'

I laughed. 'You're quite right, I'm afraid! Nevertheless, I do need to learn all I can. Which vard holds the gate? Your own vard — your father's soldiers?'

'Well, the five gates *are* under the direct control of our father — of the eslef — but each is manned by soldiers from the vardai holding the four towers about it. This gate, therefore, is held by men of Varessavard, Predaravard, Aradavard and Naratravard. However, Ilven is right; I mustn't overwhelm you with names. Sorry!'

'It all sounds very impressive and organized, anyway! Are any of those vardai supporters of the Grassads, or did you choose this gate to avoid the scrutiny of their friends?'

He grinned. 'You're learning swiftly, Simon! You're right, these are all men from vardai we can rely on. Now, if we'd ridden in through the *southern* gate, the Grassads would have known about it pretty swiftly. The Denesgars are certainly their allies, nor can I place my trust in the Vesprassads, for their lands march with those of Grassavard. Yes indeed, our route was selected quite carefully! Yet in truth I suppose it hardly matters. Draklin Grassad and his cohorts will learn soon enough that I'm back, anyway; and they'll recognize soon enough that you're my friend. Consequently, I fear, they'll also consider you their enemy!'

'But Avran,' broke in Ilven anxiously, 'surely they would never dare to harm you here in Sandarro — either of you?'

'I don't know. I trust not, but with the Grassads can one ever be sure?'

I laughed again, though somewhat ruefully this time. 'Well, we never leave perils wholly behind us, do we? And here, at least, I'm not being sought by the King. That's a step in the right direction!'

By this time the road — still climbing — had swung again, sharply to the northwest, so that the great gatehouse was directly ahead of us. Its gates, faced with burnished copper like those of the outer city wall, stood open. Though there were soldiers up on the battlements, there was none to bar our entry. Avran waved cheerfully to the soldiers above us and received an equally cheerful shouted response. We rode in between convergent walls, under another portcullis and over stone slabs bridging a deep gulf, with red stone arching over our heads.

Within was a green space of lawns, flowerbeds and many shrubs; ahead a grassy slope up which the road continued; and above and about us, the great walls of the Castle of

Sandarro. In the almost horizontal illumination of the setting sun they were dazzlingly white and their towering height awesome. No cloud castle, this, but a great and formidable fortress.

Chapter Nine

THE CARVEN FOREST

Within the shadow of the gate was waiting a small group of people; not soldiers, for they bore no weapons. As they moved forward to greet us, Avran and Ilven slid gracefully from their mounts. I dismounted also, though more awkwardly. Whilst they were exchanging greetings with the welcoming persons, I ruffled the neck of the sevdru I had ridden and whispered a thanks to him for bearing me so well. He turned and nuzzled me, so angling his head as to ensure that my face was in no danger from those sharp nasal horns. As I responded by stroking his muzzle, I experienced a very definite surge of mutual affection. That pleased me, but it puzzled me also.

Thus distracted, I did not immediately realize that Avran had led forward one of the group to meet me. 'Simon, this is our uncle Eldrett Estantesec. He has no English, I'm afraid, but I have told him you are my friend and he wishes nevertheless to greet you.'

'*Bazatié etreyen*, Simon!' Though not especially tall he was a massive man, with rough-hewn features and with beard and hair so short and dense as to appear like dark moss on an oak trunk. His clenched, outstretched hands were so huge that I could not properly enclose them between my own.

'Eldrett is the elder brother of our mother. He serves as — oh, as Chancellor, I suppose you'd say, to my father.'

'I am honoured to meet him,' I replied carefully. 'Please tell him that I look forward to the day when we can properly converse — when I've learned your language, that is.'

Avran translated this and the craggy features arranged themselves into what I took to be a smile. The Chancellor growled a few further amiable-sounding phrases, then Avran said: 'My father is holding a meeting of the Ruling Council.

However, since the meeting will shortly be over, Uncle Eldrett suggests we should go up and wait. We may leave our cloaks and our bundles here; they'll be taken to our rooms. Our swords, also; we'll have no need for such weapons.'

As Avran spoke, he was unbuckling his sword belt and handing it to one of the men nearby — a servant, I presumed. I followed suit though, after so many days of bearing it at my hip, the prospect of even a temporary loss of my sword made me feel uneasy. I was relieved that Avran trusted me well enough to allow me to retain my knives.

The sevdru I had ridden still stood patiently by me; there had been no attempt either to tether our beasts or lead them away. I could not resist again caressing the soft cheeks of my own former mount before leaving him. In response, he tossed his head and gave a sort of amiable snort. Then, as I turned to follow the Chancellor and Avran, all four sevdru moved quietly away, out on to the still-sunlit portion of this inner bailey where, as I now saw, other animals — all of them sevdru — were standing or feeding.

We walked up toward the castle, Avran deep in conversation with his uncle. Ilven walked beside me.

'Simon, you surprise me more and more!' she said. 'I thought — we thought you would have trouble during your ride, but you managed so well! You did not need my brother's help at all.'

'Well, I've ridden horses of course; and I was rather scared at first; but these sevdru, they're — well, they seem nice animals . . . But you used no bridles, no saddles, no stirrups. Do you always ride thus, bareback? I don't understand how you instruct your mounts what to do!'

'No, we need no accoutrements when riding casually like this. Though a soldier in war would use a saddle, stirrups also perhaps, we never need to use bridles. And, as for instructing them what to do, why should we? A sevdru is not a horse; it is more than a horse. If its rider and it are friends — if they are in sympathy — why, it *knows* what its rider wishes! Did you not feel that sympathy during your ride? Of course you did! That is why you rode so well. Truly, you surprised us! You rode not like a foreigner, an Englishman, but like a Sandastrian — like one of us!'

While I puzzled at this, she went on: 'A horse — well, I

102

understand you can ride them and, Avran tells me, even have affection for them. Yet they are like your cows, they are dull creatures — like the hasedain, which we keep primarily as a source of milk and meat. Sometimes we use hasedain as beasts of burden, but we don't *ride* them. Perhaps it may be because they are grazers, creatures of abundant food and open land, where little intelligence is needed to survive. The sevdru is a browser, a creature of the wooded hills. Several of our forest creatures have — oh, a special understanding. It is hard to explain, but — well, you'll see . . .'

Here Ilven was interrupted, for the Chancellor turned to rumble some question at her; yet she had already given me much food for thought. Yes, I *had* been aware of that special sympathy, that understanding shared with my mount; how fascinating! And, if sevdru were browsers, that explained why this inner bailey was not merely grassed, like the bailey of an English castle into which cattle might be driven for safety during an attack, but planted with so many bushes and small trees. Obviously these were to provide food for the animals!

We were climbing broad stone steps now, up the last steep rise to the castle itself. Ahead of us were yet more gates. Again they were sheathed with burnished copper, but this time they were elaborately decorated with inlaid silver, in a pattern of branches and swirling leaves that seemed to move as one looked at it, as if in a wind.

The soldiers stationed here were clad, not in blue, but in surcoats, jupons and hose of silver-grey. On the surcoats was embroidered in gold the same bird (a hawk? an eagle?) that had been depicted on the harbour flag, and beneath the same crescent moon. The eyes of the bird, whatever it was, were tinted blue and seemed curiously large. These soldiers were armed not just with swords, but also with great axes like the Lochaber axes of Scotland. They seemed relaxed, however, and attempted neither to impede nor even to question our entry.

So in we went, under yet another stone arch and into a sort of stone tunnel, about twenty yards long. I realized to my astonishment that, *within the wall* of that great pentagonal keep, we were crossing a drawbridge over a moat. Below us, a dozen or so feet down, swirled the dark waters of a river; overhead were shafts down which, at need, boiling oil or other noisome substances might be emptied upon invaders.

Soon we were over the bridge and walking out through a second arch, with a great hallway directly before us and other hallways to left and right. In the ceilings of these halls, high overhead, were massive skylights. They were set with panes of glass tinted in many different hues, green, blue, red and yellow, so that the light of the setting sun painted a shifting pattern of colour upon the white stone walls. By this hour, the lower walls might have been in deep gloom, but massive torches set in iron brackets were driving away the shadows. Between these brackets were hung great banners, each decorated with some heraldic device. I recognized, without yet identifying it, the leaping fish of the Vragars, worn as emblem by the soldiers at that first, outermost wall. Later I was to learn that each banner bore the emblem of a particular vard.

A number of people — soldiers clad in blue or silver, men and women in tunics of varied colour — were hurrying purposefully about these halls. None manifested any special interest in us, though a few exchanged amiable words as they passed by.

All this seemed very wrong to me. Surely a returning prince ought to be greeted by attendant, enthusiastic crowds and fanfares of trumpets? Such a cool reception was really rather disappointing. Only later did I comprehend that, since Avran's journey to England had not been publicized, few Sandastrians outside his family and the Ruling Council were even aware that he had been away.

Ignoring the hallways leading off to left and right we walked straight ahead, in toward the centre of the keep. Despite the height of the hallway, our passage — and that of the other people in the halls — was quite quiet and our voices evoked no echoes. Looking down, I realized that the floors were covered by thick grey matting densely woven from plant fibres of a type I had never seen hitherto. (Later I discovered it was made from a seaweed, a variety of kelp common off the southern shores of Rockall.) Not only did this silence our footsteps, but also it served to deaden other sounds. The castle was never noisy, even in its greatest chambers.

A sharp turn and we were beginning the ascent of a winding staircase — not the sort of steep, tortuous corkscrew such as ascends the towers of English castles, but one curving much more gently and with broader, shallower steps. Nevertheless it proved quite a climb, up past one floor with its great wooden door, elaborately carven and firmly closed; then on upward past one, two, three, four, five further floors and doors. By that time, Chancellor Eldrett Estantesec was breathing stertorously and even Avran and I, after the idle days on shipboard, were becoming short of breath.

It was a relief when Eldrett halted at the seventh floor. He pressed his palm and fingertips against a great circular boss on the door and, turning it, opened that door for us.

We were admitted into a corridor so luxuriously appointed as to make me realize instantly that these must be royal quarters. Such indeed was the case. Whereas the great pentagonal keep of the Castle of Sandarro fulfilled a diversity of functions, its central tower contained only the residence and reception rooms of the eslef and his family. I learned later that the spiral staircase was within the stone spine of this great tower. The short corridor into which we had now entered, like its counterparts on the six lower floors and on four further floors above us, debouched into a broader corridor circling the tower on its outer side.

However, it was not the structure of the tower that fascinated me, but its decoration; for the corridors were like a dream forest. Their floors were covered from side to side by carpets woven to represent a woodland floor, with leaves, mosses, fallen branches, patches of lichen and flowers, all in their appropriate hues. The walls were panelled with wood elaborately carven and painted to simulate the trunks, branches, leaves, flowers and fruit of a whole array of different shrubs and trees, this impression of the canopy of the forest being maintained by a carven ceiling above us. All the carving was in low relief, but it was done with such skill and artistry that one gained an impression of depth, even of distance. The leaves of the trees were sometimes tinted green, sometimes brown, sometimes golden, and they bore flowers painted in white, scarlet or blue.

I gasped in astonishment and Ilven said smilingly: 'Yes, it is indeed wonderful, Simon. These carvings were done many years back and the carpet woven long ago. Yet the woodcarvers of Berodunesse and the weavers of Ildumil are still capable of such work; the carvings can be repaired, or even replaced, at need.'

'Then those weavers and woodcarvers are craftsmen indeed! I have seen nothing to match this, even in the cathedrals of my own land or among the best work of the Flemish weavers.'

Ilven did not respond in words, but another smile told me that she was pleased. I had never seen eyes so green — or, for that matter, eyes so beautiful . . .

As we walked along the short corridor, I noticed that here and there among the carven branches were depicted birds, some of familiar shape and form, some unfamiliar; and that in the glades of the simulated forests were beasts, small or large, that were quite unknown to me. I would have liked to pause and examine these more closely, but the Chancellor and Avran, deep in talk, were keeping up a steady pace.

Soon we saw a group of men walking toward us — lords of Sandastre, by their beards and evident dignity. Almost as soon as I noticed them, Chancellor Eldrett began intoning greetings, in a voice as sonorous as the diapason of a hydraulic organ. Indeed, the meeting of the Ruling Council was over already. The representatives of the forty-five vardai were coming from the Council Chamber in an irregular, clotted and discontinuous flow, like a congregation leaving church. I found myself caught in a sea of courteous introductions to men to whom I could not properly speak — Keld Orexin, Hélu Miodren, Valatt Andracanth, Vaien Exor and many another. Indeed, there were too many names to be grasped, too many faces to be remembered — bright-eyed or sombre-eyed, with hair and beards of many lengths and shades of grey, red or brown and robes bearing many different emblems — a torrent of words and of people, or so it seemed! Eventually, leaving Avran and Ilven entrapped in a whirlpool of conversation, I edged away, out into the corridor circling the tower; for I was fascinated by the carvings and the animals they depicted.

Here, for example, was a group of sevdru, for the combination of brow-horns and nasal horns was unmistakable. So their fawns were hornless, like young deer . . . Now here was a great lithe beast, like a dread combination of wolf with tiger; did such creatures roam the forests of Rockall? No, surely not, for here was a creature certainly mythical — a unicorn, twisted horn and all. That great blue beast — almost oliphant-sized it seemed, with nasal horn, pointed brow-horns and ram's horns in combination, and with a line of spines down back and tail — must assuredly be equally mythical. What was over there? Oh, some weird kind of deer with strongly convoluted antlers. Next came carvings of some creatures like great hogs distorted by nightmare; those were too repellent to be real, I trusted, for I misliked them greatly. I drifted along from carving to carving, as fascinated as a small boy at his first fair.

The light was streaming into the carven forest in places; how was that managed? Oh yes, at intervals there were recesses in the walls on my right, leading to windows made in cruciform shape — a vertical slit and two symmetrical cross-slits — for ready defence by bowmen, I presumed.

I was so intrigued by the strange birds and beasts of wall and roof that I passed two of these windows before it occurred to me that I might gaze out. By then I had wandered about a hundred yards along the corridor, away from the group surrounding Avran. The bright, late sunshine was beguiling and no-one was near enough to notice what I did. Why should I not take a look through one of these windows? After a swift glance that ensured there were no watching eyes, I climbed three steep stone steps and edged up between the convergent walls of the recess to the window, to gaze forth with renewed wonder.

Yes, we were indeed high in the central tower of the castle. From the direction of the sun I must be looking due south. Lesser towers to my left and right were linked by soaring ribs of stone, like enormous flying buttresses, to the pinnacle of the tower by whose window I was standing. Directly below was the roof of the main keep, marged by crenellated walls and paved ways along which guardian soldiers walked. Within this walkway was a broad ribbon of glass, protected by fences, that must mark the skylights of the corridors. Closer beneath me, as I saw to my astonishment, were gardens, with trees, shrubs, flowers and stone seats. In this evening hour I could hear the stridulations of crickets and glimpse a few drifting moths, come to seek out the more aromatic blooms. A roof-top garden; what a wonderful conceit!

Looking out further, I could see the red stone curtain wall. That gatehouse must be the southern one, controlled by the Grassads' allies, which Avran had so sedulously avoided. The hill beyond dropped away too steeply for me to be able to view the padin on its slopes, but I could discern the outer wall of Sandarro. The warehouses by the harbour looked like toy houses from this height and, beyond, the sea shone like a golden shield. Far over in the hazy distance at right, the sun was sinking behind blue hills. What had Avran called them as we sailed in? Oh yes, the Bernevren Hills. It was a fascinating view, very beautiful and, to my eyes, very strange. I would have liked to linger long, drinking it in; but Avran must by now be wondering where I was! Guiltily I turned about and edged back toward the corridor.

I was about to descend the stone steps when, suddenly, I perceived two men walking toward me. They were coming from the left, from the Council Chamber, and must surely be lords. I hesitated. What would they think if they saw me, a stranger, emerging from this recess like a spy from concealment? Embarrassedly I retreated, pressing myself back against the stone wall. With any luck they would not notice me, for the sunlight streaming in from the window would deter their gaze and mask me from their view.

As the two drew closer, I saw that they were very unalike. One was a massive, florid man in a maroon tunic and cloak, leaning heavily on a gold-banded stick. He was heavy-browed and pug-nosed, with dark brown, pouchy eyes and with dark hair and beard so closely cropped as unpleasantly to suggest a fur trim to his face. On his left breast he bore in gold the emblem of a lizard with forked tongue. His associate was leaner and sandier, cloaked in dark grey. His beardless countenance seemed as if etched with a pattern of lines curving down his cheeks and about his lips. He had a facial twitch that in one moment emphasized those lines, in the next wiped them away so that, though his face was never still, his expression could not be read. His eyes, palely blue, were equally unreadable. Altogether they were a striking, yet unprepossessing pair; I was grateful that I was hidden.

Because of the bigger man's limp, their approach was slow. They were conversing in undertones and attending entirely to each other; no, they would not perceive me.

Just as they came alongside me, the big man stopped abruptly. He was looking ahead now and his face was flushing crimson with anger. He seemed to swell, like a cat on a wall that has just noticed a dog beneath it; and, since he hissed his words quite as fiercely as such a cat might have hissed, I heard them clearly: '*Ksalakass! Avran indreslef, esvrend! Ess'evrelet?*'

I risked a glance out past him. Yes, Avran was in view now; his red head was unmistakable. He and a group of the councillors had emerged into the main corridor, still deep in conversation.

The lean man was equally startled; his face twitched convulsively. '*Aldan drasselret — ievran Baroddnen ebressil!*' he said savagely. '*Vayin abran; ksalberet essnar.*' He urged his companion forward and they moved off down the corridor, toward the conversing group.

When they were fifty yards or so away from me, I hastened out from the recess into the corridor and followed them cautiously. As they joined the group, the big man called a jovial greeting to Avran. My friend's brows contracted momentarily and I was sure the greeting was not welcome, but he managed a smile and a cordial-sounding response. Then Avran looked past them, saw me and shook his head slightly. Taking the hint, I hung back and studied the wall hangings.

Within minutes the conversation had ended. The Councillors, the big man and his associate among them, headed for the staircase, only the Chancellor, Avran and Ilven remaining.

Avran smiled at me and, nodding back toward the departing group, said: 'Forgive me for any seeming discourtesy, Simon, my friend, but I was not anxious that those two should know you yet. The large man is one of whom you have already heard much — Draklin Grassad himself. His associate, and our enemy also, is Vrek Harradas; Harradavard has long supported the Grassads. Dangerous men, both of them.'

'Well, I must say they seemed to take little pleasure when they saw you were safely back. The big man — Draklin Grassad — practically spat!'

Avran grinned. 'Well, our quiet entry into Sandarro achieved something, after all. It is always a pleasure to annoy the Grassads! I would be interested to know just what he said.'

'Well, I didn't understand it, but I *did* hear it; I was looking out of a window, they didn't perceive me. It was something like this — ' and hesitantly, surely inaccurately, I did my best to reproduce the words I had heard.

All three of my auditors tensed as I did so. The Chancellor uttered a massive expletive and Ilven appeared deeply disturbed.

They exchanged a few sentences and then Avran said: 'What you heard, Simon, leaves no doubt as to the responsibility for the attacks on me. Their words, in English, would have run like this. The Grassad said: "Look there! Prince Avran, alive! Whatever happened?" and the Harradas responded: "Something must have gone wrong — those damned, incompetent Baroddans! Well, come along; we must pretend pleasure." '

He paused, then continued rather ruefully: 'And do you know, Simon, the Grassad's greeting to me was indeed so well simulated — so apparently surprised, so cordial — that it made me doubt his involvement in those attacks! Fortunate it is, indeed, that you heard their words and that, though you do not know our language, you remembered them so clearly. And fortunate also is it that they did not know they were overheard. The Grassads are vengeful and I do not wish them yet to consider you their enemy.'

Then his mischievous grin returned, driving the seriousness from his face. 'Poor Draklin, though; how he must have hated uttering those congratulations on my return! I'm sure it will quite spoil his dinner — and Vrek Harradas's, also. Well, a little indigestion should prove good for their souls!'

Chapter Ten

THE PRINCE AND THE EARL

The entrance to the Council Chamber was on the west side of the tower and inner side of the corridor. Since it was arched over by carven trees and since its doors were elaborately decorated with leaves and flowers I might have walked by unnoticing, had those doors not stood open.

The chamber within was crescentic in shape; or better, like the half of a pie with a bite — the spine of the tower — taken out of it. Its height was twice that of the corridor and its decorations similar, save that here the carven trees were vastly taller. Above the level of the corridor's ceiling, the chamber widened outward to the tower walls, so that it might be lit directly by a series of tall windows. Through these the setting sun streamed yet, filling the chamber with orange light. There were galleries in front of those windows in which spectators might sit and, on the main floor, a whole series of carven tables, with seats placed behind them which, I presumed, the Councillors had until recently been occupying. In such a setting the tables and seats seemed irrelevant and improbable, like furniture set down in a forest glade.

At the centre of the room, against the incurve of the tower's spine, was a raised dais. On it were set a table and seats in no way different from the others, save that they faced in the opposite direction. Two men were sitting there and examining a parchment, while a third hovered deferentially behind them. At our entry, both men rose and hastened beaming towards us.

The first was elderly and rather gaunt, with hair and beard that had been fox-red but were now subdued in hue by a peppering of white. Not only in the colouring of his hair but in his general aspect, he was like enough to my friend for me to be sure this was Avran's father, Prince Vindicon III Estantesec.

His face was one on which sorrow and strain had traced deep lines, without subduing either its strength or its essential good humour. His eyes were as blue as Avran's, but his gaze had a more piercing quality: such eyes could be fierce, I was sure, but now they were alight with joy. His robes were of the same silver-grey as those of the soldiers at the gate, but very elaborately embroidered with a design of flowers and leaves in green. Thus clad, he seemed a prince indeed, the woodland prince proper to this carven forest. The fashion in which he embraced my friend, and their mutual happiness in this reunion, aroused in me an instant regard for the eslef that was destined only to grow in the days that followed.

The second man was younger, slimmer and graver. He was rather pale-skinned and with hair of a much less vivid hue than that of Avran and Ilven, yet enough like them in looks for me to guess he must be their elder brother, Helburnet, Earl of Breveg. His eyes, like Avran's, were blue and his robes blue also, but of a darker hue, without embroidery; however, he wore a collar and a belt in the form of golden leaves with stems intertwined. His greeting of Avran was warm enough, but having that hint of condescension which elder brothers usually display to younger.

Belatedly and embarrassedly I realized that I must shortly be presented to these princes of the land of Sandastre, yet did not know how to behave to them. Should I bow or kneel, or was there some other courtesy that ought to be performed, of which I was not aware?

Ilven, with her quick perception, understood my embarrassment and whispered: 'Please be at ease, Simon; remember that you are our friend!'

Almost at that moment, Avran turned and said: 'Simon, my father and brother wish to greet you.'

Just those words, nothing more formal; and yet here was the ruler of this land, offering to me his clasped hands in that gesture of friendship I was coming to know. Nevertheless, as I grasped them, I did bow my head. When I straightened, I found him smiling at me in a way that made me sure the extra courtesy had been appreciated. The eslef's hands were as warm as his smile. Those of his son, the Earl of Breveg, were cooler and the smile more restrained, but I did not doubt the genuineness of that second greeting.

The third man, he who had hovered behind the two princes, now came forward to be presented; a grey-haired man in snuff-brown robes, with a humorous, twinkling glance from under bushy brows. This was Enar Servessil, scribe to the Council. Rather to my startlement he addressed me in English: 'Honoured to meet you, Master Simon, and at your service.'

After our handshake he turned away to gather the parchments from the table but, when the eslef and Avran led the way out of the chamber, I found the scribe by my side.

'I take it you do not speak our language? Then you will find matters difficult for a while. As the indreslef your companion may have told you, few here speak English. For my part, I am quick in learning new tongues and did indeed travel once to your country, many years ago. A pleasant, green land it is, but oh! what a horribly long voyage away . . . It was from me that the indreslevei Helburnet and Avran and the aldreslef Ilven learned your language; consequently you must blame their faults on my tuition.'

'But Avran and Ilven speak English very well!' I responded honestly; and, as he smiled, I asked: 'What other languages do you have at command?'

'In London I learned to speak some French at your sovereign's court, though I doubt whether it be the French of France; oh, and a little Latin. Of our Rockalese tongues, I speak also Mentonese and some Dedestan — a difficult language, that. In most of southern Rockall, our own tongue serves well; but I can comprehend, and even articulate at need, the dialects of Barodda, Salastre and western Fachane.'

'Perhaps, then, you might be generous enough to aid me in learning Sandastrian?'

'Certainly I should be happy to aid you, but I think you will find' — here he smiled again — 'that your prime tuition will come from one of my pupils. There are other matters, however, on which I might advise you; on the laws and customs of this realm, its ordering and its politics.'

I thanked him and he went on: 'You will find few echoes of England's laws and attitudes here, I'm afraid. Or rather, I should say that I find joy in those differences. Our land has been stable and well ordered for almost two thousand years, whereas yours has been torn with strife all too often.

I trust you may pardon me, therefore, if I consider our system preferable?'

We were by now walking back along the corridor. The sun's light was fading fast and the carvings made it seem that we were walking through a woodland in late evening. So many small mysteries and surprises did those carvings present to my view that, to enjoy them better, I allowed our conversation to languish.

The scribe, perceiving my eager gazings, smiled again and fell silent also. Only when we turned down the shorter corridor toward the staircase did I belatedly respond.

'I'm sorry; this castle is fascinating me so much that I am being discourteous. These carvings, these paintings are truly impressive. You Sandastrians must love your forests, to decorate your prince's palace thus.'

'Indeed, we love our whole land; its forests, its glades, its meadows, our great Lake Vanadha, our rivers and our coasts. But' — and his eyes twinkled — 'about the sea itself, most of us are less enthusiastic! Only a few vardai produce seamen — Varessavard, Eldunavard, Bernavard; and even they have stayed close to our coast in the centuries since the loss of the great fleet.'

This incident sounded so interesting that I would have liked details. However, by then we had reached the staircase and, with massive Chancellor Eldrett holding open the door for us with courteous impatience, the moment passed.

The scribe lingered behind to speak to him and our conversation was not resumed. We descended only one floor and then, as we entered upon a new corridor, its very different decorations put the matter from my mind.

In the corridors of this sixth floor, the theme was not forest, but parkland, and the effect created not so much by the skill of woodcarvers — though, to be sure, a few carven bushes stood out from the walls — as by that of artists. All the paintings I had seen in my life hitherto had been flat and, as it now seemed to me, quite unrealistic. The Sandastrian painters, in contrast, contrived to create an illusion of depth, of substantiality, in a fashion that I had never conceived possible. We seemed to be walking not along a narrow corridor, but across a broad meadow. The very matting had been dyed grass-green and had a texture like that of soft turf. The sunlight, shining almost horizontally toward us through a window at the end of the short corridor, caused our shadows to fall behind us and enhanced the sense of space. Only when we emerged into the corridor encircling the tower was the effect spoiled, not by any failure of the artists but by the pools of deep shadow between the windows, thus late in the evening with the sun so low.

Ilven was keeping step with me now. Wonderingly I said to her: 'This is surely a castle of dreams! In the keeps of our English castles, we hang only a few tapestries and weapons on our walls and the walls are almost always of stone unadorned. Never have I seen anything to approach this! Why, in such surroundings and with such a princess walking beside me, I feel like a bewitched knight in the tales of King Arthur. Mayhap I'll awaken tomorrow, to find myself chained in some dungeon. That seems the customary fate of such knights after such enchantment.'

She laughed merrily. 'I hope very much that you won't! Moreover, I assure you I have neither magic powers nor any other fey qualities. Our people have always loved the country-side. If we must live in a stone fortress, why then, we are happier if we can make it seem like a woodland or a meadow. The chambers on this floor surround the spine of the tower; they have no windows. Yet, each time we walk out from those rooms, we are able to feel free of confinement.'

The seventh floor was occupied by only two rooms, the Council Chamber and an equally large room where the Councillors dined. This sixth floor and the one below it were divided into several smaller rooms, private apartments for the eslef and his immediate family.

As Ilven finished speaking, the Chancellor hastened ponderously by us to serve again as doorman and we entered into one of those rooms. Though much smaller than the Council Chamber, this room was quite large and long. It was windowless and lit instead by torches flaring and flickering beneath flues that conducted their smoke away. The walls were panelled with light-coloured wood, polished to show the grain; the matting underfoot had been dyed a warm red.

At the room's further end, a table was being set for dinner and high-backed seats placed at either side of it. Four servants were busy completing the setting of the table. Until they were done, we stood in a group in the middle of the room. The Prince and his elder son the Earl had been talking with Avran as they walked along; now Ilven joined in, with Eldrett and the scribe listening respectfully.

Since I could not understand their words, their conversation did not hold my attention. Instead I continued to look around me. How simple this room seemed, after the elaborate decoration of the corridors! On the walls were hung only a few portraits, in positions well away from the flaming torches. I perceived with surprise that, though the latter burned so brightly, they gave out little heat — pleasantly little, for the evening was warm enough.

Soon the servants finished with their tasks and left the room. The table appointments they had set for us seemed an odd mixture of luxury and relative plainness. There were great red goblets, of a splendour I had never seen matched; as they caught the light, they glowed like rubies. Yet in contrast, the bowls and trenchers were made of wood. It was an attractive red wood, admittedly, and highly polished, while the bowls had earthenware liners; but where was the gold- or silverware that one associated with the tables of a ruler? The chairs also were of a plainness surprising in a land where woodcarving attained such heights. One — the Prince's, I presumed — was a little larger than the others and set at centre behind the table, but even so it did not seem prominent or splendid enough for a ruler. Avran's words echoed in my mind: 'An eslef is not a king.' More and more, I was perceiving the difference.

I noticed idly that, while each chair's seat bore a fur cushion, the backs of the seats were not cushioned — save one, and even then the cushion was curiously small. Abruptly I looked again; surely that cushion had shifted?

No, it was *not* a cushion! A small cat-sized animal was perched on the chair back — not a cat, though, but an animal the likes of which I had never seen. Silky grey fur, it had; a tail like the brush of a fox, but grey also . . .

Forgetting my manners, I left the group and walked over to look more closely. A round head with large ears, furred at the top but webbed beneath; neat, small legs; and, gripping the chair back, not claws, but tiny fingers. What a strange creature!

I do not think the animal heard me, for I was moving quietly and the matting underfoot was soft. Rather, it became aware of my approach by some other sense. Suddenly, without turning its body, it swivelled its head almost completely about and I found that a pair of immense brown eyes were gazing up into mine. A snub nose was raised, a small mouth puckering appealingly; what a lovable creature!

It and I gazed at one another; then, as I moved yet closer, the animal turned quickly about. With a mighty leap it was in my arms, clinging to my chest with spreading fingers. Delightedly I stroked the silken fur of its head and back, a wave of affection coursing through me. The little animal at first chattered with pleasure; then it began a low crooning quite as pleasant to hear, and quite as soothing, as the purr of a kitten.

It was only then that I realized how silent the room had fallen and that everyone was watching us. Nor had I perceived hitherto that three ladies had joined the group while I and the little animal were making our acquaintance. Blushingly I turned about and would have stammered an apology, had not Avran spoken first.

'Simon my friend, that is truly amazing; you cannot know how amazing! What you hold is a vasian. They are animals of the high forest, not rare but rarely caught and hard to rear. If a man catches a vasian young and is patient, sometimes he may succeed in rearing it. The vasian will then become his, his wholly; it will tolerate other humans, but no more than that. If its owner dies, the vasian pines away and soon dies also. Never has it been known for a vasian to transfer its affection to another — or never till now. For this animal was my second brother's. He caught it young and he reared it, for he loved animals and was very patient. As I told you on the boat, my brother was murdered — oh, three months ago. Since that time, his vasian has pined and refused food, drinking only a little water. We had expected it would die also. But now . . . Yes, Simon, it is amazing!'

Indeed, they were all eyeing me in wonderment, some exchanging quiet comments in their own language. Embarrassed and uncertain how to respond, I said nothing, continuing to stroke the quietly crooning animal that clung to me, until Avran beckoned me forward to be presented to the ladies.

One was tall, slim and grey-haired, clad like the eslef in silver-grey cloth elaborately embroidered. This was the eslevar Felguen, wife of Prince Vindicon III Estantesec and mother of Avran and Ilven. On introduction to her, I managed to kneel respectfully — this action set the vasian chattering with resentment — but to my startlement she embraced me and raised me to my feet.

'*Bazatíe etreyen*, Simon,' the eslevar said softly. Then she made some remark to Ilven that I did not understand, smiling at me the while.

Ilven was smiling also. 'My mother says that, since our brother's vasian has thus accepted you, she accepts you also — that you will have her affection, as a new son. She does not know yet that you have twice saved Avran's life. When she does, she will recognize how wise was her quick judgement.'

I blushed anew and uttered some stammering words of appreciation. The vasian meantime had climbed on to my shoulder and, with feet gripping it and a soft hand about my neck, was crooning happily into my ear. Though this was distracting, at least it freed my own hands to greet the other two ladies, the memasain Maderen asar Estantesec and Eyen asar Servessil, wives of the Chancellor and the scribe, come to join us for dinner.

The introductions over, the Prince led the way to the table. I found myself allocated the seat upon the back of which my vasian — for so I must now regard him — had been perched. Next to me at left was Ilven and at right, Avran; opposite were the Chancellor and his lady. We stood in respectful silence while the Chancellor intoned some sonorous phrases — a grace, I presumed. Then, when the Prince and Princess had seated themselves, we others seated ourselves also.

The food was all strange to me. We were brought platters of unfamiliar meats covered with aromatic sauces or heaped with vegetables of strange texture and taste. Following the example of the others, I transferred to my trencher the portions I felt I dared try, finding every item to be palatable and some even delicious. Next, a strange greenish wine was poured into our goblets by the servants. As soon as I was sure that no ritual of toasting had to be undergone, I tried it and found it slightly bitter but surprisingly refreshing.

The platters were not circulated a second time and our goblets were only twice refilled; there was none of the heavy eating and drinking one encountered at tables of the wealthy in England. With the second refilling of the goblets, dishes of fruit were successively brought round to us. There were purple berries, looking like bilberries formed in quincunx but tasting curiously nutty; globular fruit like huge orange goose-berries, tartly sweet; a heart-shaped, pear-like fruit that I did not sample; and blue berries that looked like plum-sized, miscoloured rose-hips. That indeed, as I later learned, is exactly what these were — fruits from the great rose-bushes ringing the hill of Sandarro.

Ilven pointed to them. 'Take some of those berries and offer them to your vasian,' she suggested. 'My brother used to give them to him as a special treat.'

I took a handful and offered one to the little animal, realizing again as I did so that everyone was watching. My vasian gave a crooning cry of pleasure — clearly could I sense that pleasure — and, taking it from me, ate it with the delicacy of a court lady eating a large strawberry. A second was accepted, then a third; but that, it seemed, was enough — I knew it was enough even before the gentle fingers thrust the fourth away. This restraint was wise indeed when the animal had eaten nothing for so long. After that, he settled back on my shoulder and resumed his contented crooning.

My audience exchanged phrases that seemed to echo anew their earlier surprise. Certainly, if the vasian was accepting fruit from me, he had transferred his affection to me — and so suddenly! Unprecedented, indeed! Ilven, in particular, was eyeing me with wonderment, yet her approval was also very evident.

'Tomorrow you must take him out into the garden,' she said. 'He eats principally leaves, the leaves of trees and bushes; he will find what he wants. Tonight he will sleep beside you, if you so permit. You'll find a vasian is better to have by you than any English watchdog. If danger threatens, he will awaken you without noise; while if there is no danger, his presence and watchfulness will permit you to sleep undisturbed. They are very — oh, sensitive . . . I cannot explain.'

'Thank you for your advice,' I responded sincerely. 'Yet I

have been wondering: did your brother have a name for him?'

She laughed. 'A vasian does not truly need a name, for one never needs to call it. But yes, my brother did have a name for him; he called him Mekret. In your language, *mekret* means — oh, rascal, I suppose!'

I laughed in my turn and, reaching up, gently scratched the head of the vasian. 'Well then, I think I'll name him Rascal, if he doesn't mind!' And he gave an amiable squeak, rubbing his head against mine.

By then the servants had retired from the chamber. Soon Avran and his father were deep in conversation, the Princess and the Chancellor making occasional interjections and the others listening intently. My name was several times mentioned and repeatedly there were glances my way, so that again I felt embarrassed. However, the steady humming croon of Rascal was curiously reassuring, making me feel confident that all was well and would continue to be well.

Nevertheless, it seemed an eternity before Avran addressed me. 'Our pardon, Simon, but there was much to explain and to discuss. The eslef and elslevar, my father and mother, confirm that you are welcome here in Sandarro. You must consider our land to be your home henceforward, not merely till your quest begins but for ever, if you so desire. My family feel, as I do, that our debt to you is profound.'

Avran paused, as if to better assemble his thoughts. Indeed, for a moment he seemed somewhat embarrassed; but then he smiled at me almost mischievously and resumed speaking.

'However, my father wishes for the moment to conceal, for the political reasons you understand, the full story of our adventures. Moreover, he trusts that, while you learn our language and our ways, we Sandastrians may benefit from your own knowledge of the long-bow. Thus he proposes, with your agreement, that you take on the task of instructing some of our soldiers in its use. The Council at large will be notified only that you are an expert brought from England for that purpose. So that your commands to the soldiers will be heeded, he promises that, at the next meeting of the Ruling Council, you will be appointed to the rank of centenar.'

I was rather startled by this proposal, but quite flattered. How fast I had progressed in these few days, from being merely a younger son rejected by his father as unsuited to a soldier's life, to becoming an instructor of soldiers — and appointed to high rank, at that! But Avran was speaking again.

'Lastly' — and here Avran grinned broadly — 'my father feels that your family name — Branthaite . . . Branswaite — no, even I cannot say it! — will cause too many problems of pronunciation for we Sandastrians. In view of the unprecedented occurrence of this evening, he suggests instead that, while you are among us, you should take the name Simon Vasianavar — Simon, friend of vasians. Be assured that it is a name of honour, for the vasianar are regarded with high respect, not only by we Sandastrians but also by the other peoples of southern Rockall. And it is a name much, much easier to pronounce!'

I was overwhelmed. 'Please tell the Prince that — oh, what can I say? That I am deeply honoured; that I do not merit such great courtesy, but that I shall strive to merit it.'

It was a clumsy speech, but heartfelt. Even before Avran translated, I knew by the smiles of those about me that its intent, at least, was understood.

Thus it chanced that, having left my own home far behind, I found — at least for a while — a new one that surpassed my dreams. However, I could not anticipate the perils that lay ahead. Had I done so, I might have sought the earliest ship back to England!

Chapter Eleven

THE PRINCESS AND
THE FLOWER

My awakening the next morning was slow, for indeed I had been very tired; and at first my drowsy mind could not credit the events of yesterday. Surely it had all been a dream? — the white cloud castle on the hill-top; the beautiful, russet-haired princess riding to greet us on that deerlike creature, and my own ride; the great halls and the carven forest; the kind welcome from the ruler and his consort; the little, bright-eyed animal that had accepted me so readily — no, it could only have been a dream.

Yet, as I blinked myself awake in the darkened room, I heard a steady, contented crooning. There was Rascal, perched on the pillow beside my head, gazing at me with those big eyes of his. So it *was* all true!

What had happened at the end of the dinner? Oh yes, there had been music in the firelight. The chairs had been pulled up and we had sat in a circle, each person singing in turn save for the Chancellor, who had produced a little pipe and played it with a delicacy unexpected in a man so massive. Avran had whispered brief translations of the songs to me, but of them I remembered little. Instead I recalled strange cadences and surging melodies, and in particular the voice of Ilven, sweet as a linnet in springtime.

I remembered also my embarrassment when Prince Vindicon noticed that I was drowsing and my gratitude when he used his own weariness, not mine, as excuse for ending the evening's entertainment. Avran had shown me to this room on the fifth floor — odd, to have started our visit to the castle on the seventh level and to have gone *downward* as the evening progressed! — and bade me good night. How grateful my body had been for the soft sheets and pillows, after those nights on a hard ship's deck!

123

However, I must have slept long — too long, perhaps. I had no idea of the hour since my room, on the inner side of the tower, had no windows and was quite dark. Did Sandastrians lie late in bed or were they early risers? Were my hosts by now considering me discourteous, boorish, for sleeping so long? Whatever the comfort of this bed, I must rise!

I smiled at Rascal, tweaked his ears gently, and rose with extreme care so that I would not frighten him. It was an unnecessary precaution, for his trust in me was complete; but that was a fact I did not yet fully understand.

At my movement, the door of my room opened wide and sunlight flooded in. Rascal blinked and chittered resentfully; I was dazzled also, not immediately perceiving who had entered. When I did I was surprised, for it was a boy. He was scarce an ell in height and very stocky, broad in countenance and snub-nosed, with a shock of carrot-red hair, a mass of freckles and the cheerfullest of grins. He was carrying a silver jug of water which, when he poured it into a bowl on a stand by my bedside, proved to be steaming hot. As he poured, he beamed at me.

'You slept long, not so, did you not? I wait for you to wake. While I wait, I sit and think out my English words to make sure no mistakes happen. Good morning!'

I chuckled at this strange speech and responded: 'Good morning! Well, it's most kind of you. A wash will be most refreshing and welcome.'

Without more ado, I proceeded to lave myself more thoroughly than I had done since leaving Holdworth. As I did so the vasian and the boy watched me, Rascal chittering his disapproval of such a strange activity.

When I was done, the boy produced a rough cloth with which I might dry myself, then enquired politely: 'Do you wish clean clothes in which to garb? The indreslef Avran thought yes. If so, may I fetch said clothes, that you might them wear?'

This combination of solemn courtesy and strange phraseology set me chuckling again; indeed, on that morning I felt wholly light-hearted. However, I noted that my amusement was causing the boy's smile to fade a little, so I answered hastily: 'Yes, please; that is most kind of the indreslef. I'll be happy to wear whatever he has proposed.'

The boy vanished from the room like a rabbit diving into a burrow. While he was gone, I looked around. My sword had been brought to my chamber and my satchel also; last night I had not noticed them. Good! After those nights on the ship, my own clothes were far from fresh; clean garments would be welcome.

Ah, here was the boy back again, beaming anew and with arms laden with those garments. First I donned an undershirt and briefs made of some material as fine and white as good linen, but softer and lighter. Next came a short, sleeveless jacket and hose of moss-green colour, made of the same light material; and finally, a tunic much like a cotehardie but brown in hue, not parti-coloured as English court fashion would have dictated. There were long brown boots also, much like those of Avran and of soft leather. All these garments, and the boots in particular, were so perfect a fit that I was sure my own clothes must have been examined carefully while I slept. In addition, however, I set my two belts about my shoulders and waist, for there might yet be need for my knives. Fascinating though Sandarro was, I knew also that it had its dangers.

The boy watched me wide-eyed as I dressed, but made no remark. When I was done, I smiled at him and said: 'You are looking after me excellently. What is your name?'

'My name? — yes. Truly it is Brege Estantesec, but folk call me "Brek". My father last night greeted you, I think; he is Eldrett Estantesec, Chancellor to our eslef. Since you are from England and he speaks not English, he charge me to look after you because of my good tongue!'

So this was the son of the massive Chancellor — and already so broad that surely he would grow up to be quite as huge. How fortunate that the boy was so much less solemn than the father! I decided that Brek's company would be fun, even though his English might not be quite so excellent as his father seemed to suppose.

'Well, I'm blithe to meet you, Brek. Tell me, what hour is it now? By the sunshine, it must be mid-morning at least — I fear I've slept much too long. Has the indreslef been seeking me?'

'The morning advanced indeed is; but the indreslevei in-structed me not to disturb your respected drowsings. They

125

and the aldreslef Ilven await your rising, I think, outside among the flowers, where they have food.'

'Excellent; then please conduct me to them.' I held out an arm to Rascal, who ran up it and settled on my shoulder; then I walked out into the sunshine of the corridor.

Here again the clever artists had been at work, simulating a second forest. This time, however, it was a much more open one, with bigger trees whose carven boles swelled out into the corridor and whose lowest branches appeared much higher overhead than the corridor's ceiling. As one looked toward the light, one seemed to be gazing out from the edge of the forest into a garden, with no wall between. So skilful was the depiction of flowers and grasses that only the bright sunlight showed where light was streaming in from the real garden beyond. For indeed, we were at the level of the roof-top garden that, yesterday, I had admired from above.

We walked only for a few paces along the corridor before stepping out through open doors into that garden. Only then did I appreciate how warm the day was; it matched the hottest July day I remembered. That was my first impression, but others crowded upon me. There was so much colour, more than I had known in any English garden. The flowers, massed about stone pathways, were so multifarious in form and hue as to bedazzle me. Fluttering above and among them were many butterflies, small or large, seeming like flowers that had forsaken their stems so as to weave a more intricate pattern of colour. Here and there were banks of shrubs and flowering trees, with branches bright with blossoms of orange, yellow or white. They seemed also in movement, for many small birds, green-backed but with breasts of yellow, orange or turquoise, were climbing and singing about those branches or hovering bee-like to drink nectar from the blossoms. The garden seemed athrob with the contented, quiet sound of insects and birds, as if the colour and heat had become audible; and oh the sweet scents!

I stood stock-still for some minutes, gazing about me in wonderment as I strove to absorb it all, while Rascal crooned happily and Brek waited impatiently. Then, almost bemusedly, I followed Brek to a place in the midst of the garden, where a table and some chairs had been set in the shade of a tree with flowers of a bright orange hue. Here were sitting Avran,

Ilven, and their elder brother Helburnet. The Earl of Breveg was dressed in the same dark blue robes, gold-adorned, that he had worn yesterday, but Avran was resplendent in a new orange cloak and Ilven in cornflower blue.

As they rose to greet me, Rascal leapt from my shoulders into the branches of the tree and, humming throatily, began climbing among them. The three paused in their greeting to watch him, then Ilven turned smiling eyes upon me.

'I suggested that we sit here, Simon, for vasianar delight to eat the leaves of the ebelmek. Even so, I continue to be amazed. In truth, this is a unique happening. Never, never before has a vasian survived the death of his first master and accepted another. Evidently you are a remarkable person!'

'Well, sister, if you've found a tree for the vasian to eat, I've found something better for his master.' Avran was smiling also. 'Sit down please, Simon, and have your breakfast. Here are bread, cheese and fruit. Also you must try our Sandastrian ale; it is not made from malt, as in your country, but from the fruit — the nuts — of a tree. After sleeping so long, you *have* to be hungry!'

So indeed I was. The bread was like that I'd eaten on the ship, but fresher; the cheese, made with hasedu milk, had a slightly musky odour but tasted much like a ripe Wensleydale; and the ale had a particular bitterness that made it an excellent accompaniment to the cheese. I ate with enthusiasm.

Rascal, high above my head, was equally busy. He examined each leaf with the care of a distrustful housewife choosing her watercresses, rejecting some with the disdain of such a wife who had found snails among the bunch, but plucking others and thrusting them into his mouth. More and more went in, until his cheeks were bulging.

Ilven and her brothers, who had eaten already, alternated their attention between Rascal and me, seeming to find us equally intriguing; but Brek, who had squatted down with his back against the tree trunk, concentrated his attention wholly upon me. I suspected that he was preparing in his mind some grandiose speech, by which I might shortly be amused and bemused!

After a while, Rascal ceased his investigations of the leaves. Moving deeper into the tree, he settled down on a branch and, crooning softly and drowsily, shut his eyes.

127

By then I had cleared my platter and emptied my glass. Amusedly Avran said: 'Well, if both of you are satisfied now, we may resume our discussion.'

As he spoke, Brek leapt briskly to his feet to load the crockery and the remaining food on to a tray and take them away into the castle. Avran watched him go, then continued: 'Brother Helburnet here has learned all about the happenings on the ship and your part in them. Our problem is that we'd like to know more about the late, unlamented assassins. So far as we can perceive, our only immediate prospect for doing so is by searching the possessions of the one on shipboard.'

'If only it were a Sandastrian ship!' lamented the Earl in his quiet voice. 'Then, that might be managed readily enough. However, as you are all well aware, the vessel is Mentonese; and they are always a difficult people to deal with. For our contacts with Europe, we depend greatly on them — more than we should, perhaps. How, without risking a breach of relations, can we justify a search of your late assailant's possessions? After all, he was not a passenger to Sandastre, but to Fachane. The situation is unprecedented.'

'The ship is still in the harbour, then?'

'Yes, but it will sail shortly after noon, I understand; and how, legally, can we delay it?'

I thought rapidly. 'Well, of course, you might block the harbour mouth, with one of those great booms; but to justify such action . . . Ah, I think I have it! Avran, did you not say that the assassin's clan lived in Breveg — in your brother's lands?'

'Yes, it seems he was of the Akharns. They are Baroddans, but indeed they live now within the realm of Breveg.'

'Well then, the matter is simple enough. You must inform the captain that you have received word of the presence aboard his ship of a notorious Brevegen rebel. You must ignore his protestations that the man went missing on the voyage and you must insist upon a search. Then, when you do not find him aboard, you must voice suspicions that the captain has landed him secretly in Sandarro. If you seem indignant enough and threaten — oh, to lower the boom and impound the ship, not only will the captain allow you to examine the man's possessions, but he might even suggest

128

it! And, after all, you don't need really to delay the ship's sailing for so very long — though I suspect that even a few further hours may drive our poor Fleming friend close to apoplexy!'

Avran laughed aloud. 'Excellent! Helburnet, what do you think?'

His quieter elder brother was considering the idea carefully. 'Yes, I think Simon may have found a solution for us. The man was, after all, from Breveg. In fact, if not in spirit, he was my subject and the captain will know he was Baroddan. I believe this scheme will work well.'

Having made this decision, Helburnet rose to his feet. 'I must put this excellent scheme into practice immediately. Please excuse me.' With a gesture of farewell, he turned and walked swiftly back into the castle.

'So simple an idea!' said Ilven wonderingly. 'Why could you not have thought of it, Avran? Why must my brothers be always so stupid? As I said yesterday, Avran, it is well you found this new friend. Most urgently you need *someone* to take proper charge of you!'

Avran was not in the least disturbed by these comments. 'As to that, why could not my bright little sister think of it?'

He made a face at her, then grinned at me. 'When I hear someone being really rude to me, I feel comforted, for I know that I'm home again! However, enough of these pleasantries. It's time we began formulating some plans, Simon, for there is much you must do. First of all, you'll need to learn our language. My dear sister, the worthy and entirely admirable Ilven who sits so demurely by our side, has volunteered to become your teacher.'

'Yes indeed, Simon,' she responded tartly. 'I realized I must rescue you somehow from the inept attentions of my unworthy younger brother. He has no system and no patience. If you had to rely on him, truly you would be in trouble!'

Avran grinned cheerfully. 'She's quite correct, you know. Still, I hope to teach you other skills. Riding a sevdru, for example. You began excellently, remarkably; but you will need to know more about the technique and about your mount's abilities. A sevdru can do many things that a horse cannot. And the use of weapons. You can never have used the sasayin, for example. Despite what you said on the

129

Bristol quayside, I'm sure you're an excellent swordsman, but . . .'

Here I interrupted him. 'I would that I were! Honestly, Avran, though I'm a fair archer and able to throw things, I'm terrible with the sword.'

He eyed me doubtfully, clearly believing me over-modest. 'Well, that is as may be; we'll try a few passes shortly. As for myself, I'm no bowman; though I had lessons with the long-bow, they did not carry me far. You'll need to teach *me* that; and, of course, my father is eager that you train our soldiers in its use also. You won't be able to begin that instruction till you can speak some Sandastrian but perhaps, in the meantime, you might aid me in deciding the design and arranging the manufacture of the bows and the arrows. Suitable woods must be chosen, for your English trees do not grow here, and fletchings to replace your goose feathers, for we have no geese. Moreover, you'll need to learn more about the peoples and history of this land of Rockall and the customs and laws of our own realm of Sandastre. All in all, Simon, I fear you have a busy time ahead.'

While he spoke, Ilven had been surveying me with an intent frown; evidently she was paying little heed to her brother's words. When he finished, she asked: 'Avran, why did you choose such subdued colours — such dowdy colours — for Simon's clothes? Surely you could have found him some garments of a cheerier hue?'

Almost for the first time in our acquaintance, Avran seemed embarrassed. 'Well, you see — er . . . It's like this. Simon has such a valuable talent for being unobserved — watching unobserved, hearing things while unobserved . . . I didn't want to make him conspicuous. And, er — well, I desired not to make our friendship too obvious to the Grassads and their friends, for all our sakes. Simon,' he appealed anxiously, 'you don't mind, do you? We *could* find you different clothes, you know.'

I hastened to reassure him. 'No, that's fine; I like these and they fit me excellently. Truly, I'm most grateful.'

Ilven was evidently unconvinced. 'Well, Avran, *I* think it's because you want to show off in your bright colours, without any competition! But then, Simon, if you wore what he does, you'd frighten your poor vasian away once and for all! And

130

you must not let Avran work you too hard. At the smallest encouragement, he'll be pouring out more of those complicated explanations of his; and he'll make you so confused that you'll never recollect anything!'

'Truly you make me know that I'm back, sister,' said Avran in simulated ruefulness. 'No-one else is ever quite so uncomplimentary! Well, Simon, what do you wish to do first? This evening we'll dine again with my parents, for they desire to become better acquainted with their new adoptive son. Until then, however, we are free to do just as we wish.'

I considered for a moment. 'Well, I'd like to see more of this wonderful castle of yours, so that I'll be able to find my way about it. Also I would like to have another ride on a sevdru. And — oh! there are so many new things — I want to see and do them all!'

Ilven smiled at my enthusiasm, then she said: 'Well, let us consider the castle first. Wait a moment.'

She rose from her chair and walked along a path some way, to kneel with a graceful swish of her skirts and pluck a flower from a tiny plant, a weed as I thought, thrusting up between the stone slabs. She brought the flower over to me.

'It is said that, long ago, our first prince, Selvar Dragat, was pondering how to design this stronghold. He was sitting on the grassy hill below us, where one of these little plants — we call it *estringa*, dew star — was growing. He was attracted by the flower, plucked it and examined it, thereafter building his castle to its plan. Look at the flower and you'll understand his design.'

She handed the tiny flower to me and I examined it wonderingly. In its centre was a tall stigma, silvery white in colour, arising from a five-sided stock. Out from this there drooped five anthers, each silvery white also. The five petals, however, were dark red in colour. The shape of each petal was rounded, but with four tiny symmetrical projections. The whole flower was enclosed in a cup of green sepals.

'See now,' Ilven said. 'The petals have the form of the curtain wall that Selvar Dragat built. These' — she indicated the projections — 'are the wall towers and gatehouses. Five petals; twenty projections. Five parts to the wall; twenty towers. Here' — she pointed to the anthers and stigma —

'is the castle, with its five great towers and its keep. And about and below the wall' — she pointed to the sepals — 'the great green hill of Sandarro.'

I looked carefully and with wonder at the little flower. 'But surely the fortifications are more complex than this?'

She nodded. 'Yes indeed. The outer towers and the lines of padin were constructed by later princes, for it is a law of our land that each eslef must add to, or at very least must repair, the defences of this city that is the heart of our realm. As the centuries have gone by, we have enclosed the hill in an outer city wall, built fortifications about our harbour, strengthened the bridges over the rivers, and so forth. It is a strong city now; but it needs to be strong, for there are enemies without and within our realm. I pray God that this city and we may withstand them!'

Chapter Twelve

A LESSON AND A RIDE

'If Simon desires to see more of Sandarro,' Avran suggested, 'why should we not walk out to the inner bailey, find mounts and go for a ride? Simon needs more experience in riding the sevdreyen.'

'Sevdreyen?' I echoed, a little puzzled. 'I thought you called them sevdru.'

'Aha, but that is the singular form! Several sevdreyen, one sevdru; most often we speak of the latter, since it is easiest to ride just one at a time!'

At this point Ilven broke in firmly: 'Avran, please! It is I who shall instruct Simon in our language, not you! Soon you'll be confusing him again!' Then, to me: 'But my brother is quite right. In our language, when referring to several things rather than one, the ending of the word is always changed. And he is right also, that it is time for you to begin speaking Sandastrian. While we are sitting here, let me explain some matters, to help you make that beginning.'

'Will it be difficult?' I asked apprehensively. 'I don't believe I have been granted much in the way of Pentecostal gifts. My tutor had a hard job to drum Latin into me and I encountered even more trouble when trying to learn French.'

She laughed. 'Well, our language is very different from yours, Simon. However, you'll find Sandastrian is simpler than either of those tongues, and definitely simpler than your complicated English! For one thing, there are no "the's" and "a's" to be bothered with; and for another, we have no verb "to be". Just think how much easier that is, Simon! See, now.'

The flower was still cupped in her hand. As she showed it to me again, I thought how slim that hand was and how graceful her movements.

'Now in English, Simon, you might say "Here is the flower."

133

Four words. In Sandastrian, I need say only two words, *Telen baz*, "flower here". Is that not easier?'

'I suppose so,' I said hesitantly, then asked: '*Baz* — has that anything to do with your greeting, *Bazatié*?'

'You see how Simon remembers things?' Avran commented amusedly.

'Indeed he does!' she smiled. 'I believe he's going to speak Sandastrian well, don't you? You're perfectly right, Simon; "*Bazatié*" really means "Here delight" or, as you might phrase it in English, "We're pleased to receive you here"! See again, how much simpler Sandastrian is!'

As the days passed, I was to come to agree with her. To be sure, I had my problems with pronunciation. For example, when letters are doubled in a word, they must nevertheless be sounded individually. As a beginner, I found it a hard task to pronounce separately the two Ss in 'Servessil' or the two Rs in 'Harradas'! My problems with doubled vowels were even greater. To simplify the reading of names in this account of my adventures, I shall change the Sandastrian 'ii' to 'ij', their 'ee' to 'eie' and their 'kk' to 'kc'.

In many other respects, however, the Sandastrian language is indeed simple. Pronunciation is more consistent: A is pronounced always as in 'lad', never in the lengthened form one finds in English words like 'fade', and S is never changed into a Z sound, as it is in such words as 'ease'. In learning Latin or French, one is perpetually troubled by the need to distinguish masculine, feminine and (in Latin) neuter words. In the Rockalese tongues, as in English, only animals and humans are subdivided by sex; and, for that matter, the Rockalese are more consistent than we, for they do not call ships 'she'.

The tenses of verbs are changed in simple and consistent fashion by the inserting or prefixing of an extra syllable; thus the verb *kharasar*, to build, becomes *kharaselar* in the perfect tense, *kharasamar* in the imperfect and *kharasidar* in the future, while the conditional ('might build') would be *idkharasar* and, as noted earlier, the imperative *ksakharasar*. All questions begin with the word 'Ié' (I shall write it 'Yé' for simplicity). My early troubles arose principally through the very different word order and plural forms; but at least the Rockalese are consistent in the latter, not like us with our 'mouse' and 'mice', 'house' and 'houses'!

While we sat there in the sunshine of the roof-top garden, Ilven continued my instruction by pointing to objects within our view, saying the Sandastrian names for them and making me repeat those names. I enjoyed this thoroughly and found pleasure in pleasing her by repeating them as accurately as I might; indeed, I could have sat there by her side in perfect happiness for the whole of that afternoon.

However, although Avran endured for a while this game of naming from which he had been so firmly excluded by his sister, he was becoming ever more restive. Eventually he leapt to his feet and said firmly: 'It is time I contributed also to Simon's education. We must take him out for a ride in the sunshine.'

Ilven sighed and responded: 'It's a little hot for a ride, but if you insist, big brother . . .'

She rose also and I followed suit but, as we walked back into the castle keep, down the stairs and along the corridors, Ilven continued my instruction. 'Those windows with arrow slits; one such would be *aseklin*, several would be *asekleyin*. Try it, please!' And I would repeat: '*Aseklin*; *asekleyin*.'

Yesterday, when we had entered the great corridor circling the inner wall of the keep, the sun had been setting and the torches flaring to drive away the shadows. Today there were no shadows, for the sun was almost overhead. The multi-hued windows created patches of colour in which men and women, moving about their business, seemed like fishes swimming through a rainbow. Today there were many children also, pursuing each other through the crowds with cheerful shouts, as swift and small as minnows swimming among trout.

Ilven explained that they had come out of school to go home for their midday repast. This prompted me to further questioning, and what I learned astonished me. In this land *all* children, not just those of the nobility, were given some schooling; and not just boys, but girls also. Each child was taught to read and write, to add and to measure, to compose and recite poetry, and to play musical instruments and sing. Alternate days — Mondays, Wednesdays, Fridays — were spent indoors for such instruction, by the sons of princes and commoners alike. The other three weekdays, however, were spent on practical matters and mostly outdoors. All children learned to ride and to swim; boys were taught the use of weapons and the particular skills of their father's profession, while girls were taught the domestic arts and the techniques of husbandry. Sundays were reserved for religious instruction and practice and for play.

How little education, in contrast, was received by the children of our own English villeins and bondsmen! In this, at least, the Sandastrian system seemed to me vastly better than ours. Yet I knew well that many Englishmen of my class — Uncle Hugo and cousin Hector, for example — would have decried such education as pointless and even subversive. That bondsmen and villeins should be able to read — how stupid, and how dangerous! For my part, it made me think again that my ideas fitted better in Sandastre than in England.

As we walked, I noticed once again the casualness with which my companions were treated. After all, they *were* prince and princess; yet there were no fanfares, no obeisances. Few among the crowds seemed even to recognize them and those few gave them scarcely more attention, and only a shade more respect, than any other passer-by. Indeed, this was a country *very* different from my own. Then I started; why, this *was* my country now, even if I could not yet speak its language!

We entered the tunnel, crossed the hidden moat and passed the guards, then descended the flight of stone steps into the inner bailey of the castle. Today there were no sevdreyen (I must become accustomed to that plural form!) in view; indeed, no animals of any kind were to be seen among the shrubs.

Naturally I expected some expression of exasperation or disappointment from my two companions, but there was none. Instead they simply waited, while I stood by puzzledly.

Within seconds we saw movement off to our left. Three sevdreyen were coming toward us at a rapid pace from the direction of the western tower of the castle. As they perceived us, they began to run yet faster. Soon one of the sevdreyen was nuzzling, and being petted by, Ilven, while a second was having its head scratched by Avran.

The third, however, hung back and eyed me doubtfully. This was not the sevdru I had ridden yesterday, but a much more lightly built and graceful animal whose facial stripe, only faintly marked between its nasal horns, broadened into a white circle between the brow-horns. Yesterday, of course, I had been mounted on a pack animal; this was a riding animal, as different from yesterday's as is a hunter from a shire horse. It would be correspondingly more intelligent, more nervous and potentially more responsive.

As soon as I had thought this out, I moved forward toward the sevdru, quite slowly, and extended my hands to it invitingly. Still hesitantly, it came toward me and sniffed doubtfully at my fingers. Then, as if in sudden decision, it tilted its head. For a moment I thought it would charge me — those four horns were formidable! — but no, instead it rubbed a soft cheek against my right hand and then inclined its head anew to be caressed by my left.

At these trustful gestures I felt an upwelling of confidence, even of affection — a much stronger and more immediate emotion than I had felt yesterday. As, careful of those horns, I stroked the sevdru's muzzle and scratched the white patch on its brow, I was aware that I had made a second animal friend. I realized also that Avran and Ilven were watching me intently.

'Yes indeed,' said Avran softly, as if an unspoken question had been satisfactorily answered. He exchanged glances with Ilven, then went on: 'Simon, I should tell you that your mount is a female, a "doe" as you would say it. The does of the sevdreyen are less strong, perhaps, than the males, but they are more fleet and more sensitive — more responsive to their rider. You will enjoy riding her. Try mounting her now; since you're not wearing armour, you need no saddle. Good. You have no bridle either, of course, but you can hold on to her horns if you feel insecure; she won't mind. However, it is your wish, not your touch, that will guide her.'

He mounted his own sevdru, while Ilven's beast knelt so that she could do likewise with ease. Then Avran resumed his instructing.

'You look too tense, Simon. Sit back, more upright — yes, like that — and relax! Good. Your beast's name, by the way is Vatunéast, because of her colouring; in English she'd be called Whitebrow. Very well. Now instruct Vatunéast to turn about. You can say it in English and she'll comprehend. Excellent!'

Indeed, to my amazement my mount turned right about, before I had properly uttered the instruction. Since my words must have been unfamiliar, how had she understood? Avran's comment answered me.

'You see, she responds to your thought, not to your word. Now instruct her to turn back, but *think* it, don't say it! Excellent. You see how easy it is!'

And easy it was. I had merely to decide on an action for Whitebrow to perform and lo! she was performing it — turning, kneeling, standing, throwing back her head or inclining it forward, all without my saying a word. This was magnificent, delightful! My pleasure and confidence in my mount waxed greater minute by minute, and I could sense that she was sharing my emotions.

'Come, then, let's have a ride!' said Avran. With Ilven following on her own mount and Whitebrow in third place, we rode out through the southwestern gate on to the green hill below the castle. Today, instead of taking the road toward the harbour, we rode westward, out between the Brantvut and Orrellan Towers and down the hill between the lines of padin into the broad meadowlands of the outer bailey.

Here my mount and I were put through our paces by Avran, while Ilven watched amusedly. To use terms descriptive of the gait of a horse for that of a sevdru is inappropriate, for their limbs move in different fashions and, to a rider, their motion feels entirely different. However, since there are no truly appropriate terms in English, I must do the best I can with the words at my command. So let me say that we rode first at a walk, then at a trot and finally at a gallop. At that speed I was alarmed enough to be holding tightly on to Whitebrow's horns for security, even though aware that neither Avran nor Ilven found need to do likewise. Indeed, we sped across those flowery meadows at a pace unmatched by any horse I had ever ridden, as swift and as light as the shadow of a swallow passing over the grass.

That was the limit of our exercising that day. The afternoon was so hot that I was perspiring profusely and Whitebrow's flanks heaving a little, so we were both glad to lapse to a walking pace as we returned to the castle. Avran was quite complimentary about my riding, saying that I had done as well as any Sandastrian beginner and much better than he'd expected of any Englishman! With this qualified praise I was perfectly content, especially since Ilven's words were more generous and her sweet smile heartening.

We re-entered the castle through the northwest gate, between the Menavedra and Miodren Towers. I gathered that these two vardai were in firm alliance with the ruling Estantesecs and inferred that Avran remained anxious to keep me from the attention of the Grassad party.

We left our mounts in the inner bailey. By that time, I knew that Whitebrow was truly mine. Moreover, now I could comprehend how Avran and Ilven had, without uttering any word, summoned their own mounts before the beginning of our ride. I did not understand how Whitebrow had been called, however, and I asked about this as we climbed the stone steps.

Ilven responded. Whitebrow, I learned, had been a second mount of her own which she had decided to give to me. No Sandastrian, it seemed, could summon by his thoughts any sevdru with which he had no personal bond.

I thanked the princess most sincerely for her generosity and then asked if there was any limit on distance for such calling. I knew it to operate beyond the reach of a voice, for those sevdreyen had surely been beyond earshot of us. The question seemed to surprise Avran and Ilven, as if it had not occurred to them that there *were* limits, and they conferred awhile before Avran answered me. The normal range, they thought, was less than two miles — about fifteen furlongs. Though they knew of instances when a sevdru had been summoned from farther away, this had happened either in circumstances of crisis, when the need was especially acute and the mental summons correspondingly frantic, or when the sevdru had been prepared for a summons at that time by some earlier instruction. In the months to come, I was to have good cause to remember that discussion.

'What if one's sevdru had died?' I asked.

'In that case, you would know,' Ilven answered, so firmly that I dared not pursue the question further.

We returned directly to the roof-garden and to the shade of the ebelmek, where a newly awakened Rascal greeted me with cries into which I could read both relief and reproach.

His cries animated into movement a rotund bundle beneath the same tree — Brek, who had returned to his comfortable position against its trunk and been quite as fast asleep! Before the boy had sufficiently awoken to try out his linguistic talents on me, Brek was sent away to fetch drinks and two wooden practice swords. Avran was anxious to test my little-vaunted skills.

The drinks were good; the swordplay, on my part, quite embarrassingly bad. After Avran had sent my sword spinning from my grasp for the third time, he lowered his own weapon and said: 'Simon my friend, you were entirely correct. You told me you were a poor swordsman and I did not accept your word, as I should have done. If this had been a genuine combat, I might have slain you twelve times over! Well, you *must* have instruction in this art ere you venture northward. In the perils you will face during your travels, you cannot expect to rely always on your knives or your bow.'

'I'd be delighted to learn swordsmanship properly!' I responded; and I told Ilven and he of the difficulties I'd faced in obtaining training while growing up — a story that, on the ship, I had not recounted.

'Your father was wrong,' Avran responded soberly. 'To wish to protect you — that is perfectly comprehensible. To leave you so vulnerable to any attacker — that was extremely unwise. You did well to strive to train yourself in absence of other training; yet you could not progress far enough. You *must* be able to defend yourself properly.'

'As for me,' commented Ilven pointedly and rather heatedly, 'I consider Simon *quite* able to look after himself. After all, *he* does not blunder into ambushes or remain snoring while assassins are around! A little anticipation, and there is less need for these martial arts of yours. For my part, I prefer peacemakers to warriors!'

Avran flushed red with anger, but the colour ebbed swiftly from his face and he had the grace to laugh. 'Very well, sister, I stand rebuked. Nevertheless, I believe Simon must learn to be a better swordsman.'

'So do I!' responded Ilven acidly. 'Who knows, he may have to extract you from yet more tricky situations!' But she gave me the warmest of smiles.

Avran avoided a direct reply. 'Good; we're agreed on that,

at least! So I'm afraid, Simon, that you face yet more lessons. The man to teach you this art is not I, but my own instructor, Oled Orexin. In his time, Oled was the finest swordsman in Sandastre, and perhaps in all Rockall. Tomorrow you shall meet him; but now the time for dinner is approaching. After that hot ride I'm sure, like me, you'll wish to wash before eating.'

Brek conducted me back to my room — or rather, bore me along there on the current of his talk, for a tidal wave of rehearsed speeches had been building up inside him since morning. Though many of his sentences were too convoluted for ready comprehension, I understood most of his questions — about England, its king, its wars, its wild animals and its weapons — and did my best briefly to answer them as we walked along.

This spate of words continued as he attended to my toilet and as I dressed myself in the second fresh set of clothes he found for me. Nor did it abate as, with Rascal on my shoulders, I was taken by Brek to the royal banquet room. At its door, however, he left me and scuttled away like a frightened beetle, calling over his shoulder a promise to 'serve me right in the morning'!

The company this evening was the same as yesterday's, but with one addition: the burly, bearded figure of harbourmaster Arn Beldevil. I guessed immediately that his presence related to the problem discussed under the tree; and I wondered what had happened.

It was to be some time, however, before my curiosity was satisfied. There was talk before the meal, during which many eyes were cast again upon Rascal, crooning so contentedly on my shoulder; there was a grace, said tonight by Arn in his capacity of priest; and there was an excellent repast, featuring a flavourful pie of some meat unfamiliar to me. I asked about it and gathered that it was the flesh of some small fruit-eating creature, but not even Enar Servessil, the scholarly scribe, could find an English equivalent for its name.

After the wine had circulated for the third and last time, the eslevar Felguen rose, excused herself gracefully and, taking Ilven and the wives of the Chancellor and scribe in her train, left the chamber. (Ilven, I was sure, left reluctantly.) When they had gone, the Earl of Breveg exchanged a few brief

141

words with his father and then turned to me. His rather pale face was brightened by the pleasantest of smiles.

'Your scheme worked excellently, friend Simon,' he said. 'Please forgive me if I tell the story in my own language. However, I will do so slowly, so that Avran may translate for you.'

After he had left us in the garden, Helburnet had summoned his sevdru and ridden down to the harbour, taking with him ten soldiers from his own guard. There he had found harbourmaster Arn and entrusted to him the carrying-out of my scheme, waiting the while in the harbourmaster's office.

The Mentonese ship had been on the point of sailing when the harbourmaster and soldiers hurried up the gangplank. On the harbourmaster's demand that he produce the 'Brevegen rebel', the captain responded contemptuously, brusquely denying that any such person was aboard. However, at that moment there came the sound of the lowering of the boom to block the harbour mouth; moreover, the soldiers formed a ring, hemming in the captain and drawing their swords.

Such happenings were without precedent in peaceful Sandarro! The captain lost his bluster and became nervous. Again he denied that anyone remained aboard save the Fleming, who was summoned indignant from his cabin.

Only after Arn had denied interest in that harried merchant did the captain mention the passenger who had disappeared. Arn professed to disbelieve this story, claiming instead that this 'disappearance' must have occurred not at sea, but in Sandarro harbour; that the Brevegen had been privily smuggled ashore by the Mentonese, so that he might carry through his fell designs. Indeed, the harbourmaster threatened to impound the ship and its cargo and to treat the captain and crew as collaborators with the enemies of Sandastre.

At this point the Fleming demanded to know what was happening. On learning that his own goods might be confiscated, he came close to exploding with wrath and frustration! Since Arn and his soldiers could not understand what the poor merchant was saying, he began abusing the captain instead.

Under these pressures the captain became quite frantic. He swore that he was telling the truth. Why, if the man had remained on board till they reached harbour, he would never have left his possessions behind!

Pretending to hesitate, Arn demanded to see those possessions. A sailor was sent below and returned bearing a sword, a cloak and a largish leather satchel. These were seized by the harbourmaster, but he insisted nonetheless that his soldiers should search the ship and, in particular, the Baroddan's cabin. This search was carried out slowly and thoroughly, the captain fuming and the Fleming hopping with impatience the while.

When the search was done, Arn simulated a grudging acceptance of the captain's story, sent orders for the boom to be raised and, after a moderately amicable farewell, left the ship. Chuckling, Arn added that he had never seen a ship readied for departure so promptly, nor depart so swiftly, as that vessel!

The Baroddan's possessions were taken to the harbourmaster's office for examination before the patiently waiting Helburnet. At first this proved disappointing, for the satchel seemed to contain only clothes. However, when Arn shook it, the satchel seemed over-heavy. Carefully it was re-examined and a concealed pocket was found, with a small sum in English coins secreted therein. Hence the weight; but might there be a second hidden pocket? Indeed there was; and within it was the prize of the search — a crumpled piece of paper bearing a few lines of writing in Rockalese script.

Helburnet produced this and handed it to his father. However, I gathered that the sentences were written in the Baroddan dialect, for the eslef could not read them. Instead he handed the paper to his scribe, who translated it readily into Sandastrian and then, for my benefit, into English:

You are summoned to meet with us urgently; the next stages of our campaign must be discussed. Travel to Rockall on the next available ship and make your way, directly or indirectly, to Sandarro. There we must meet on the fourth day of the first autumn moon, at the Sign of the Leaping Fish by the Arctorran harbour. *You must be with us then*; your task, if not already carried through, must be left for your colleague to perform. Destroy this after reading it.

As he concluded this second translation, Enar Servessil smiled at me and said: 'However, he ignored that last instruction, most fortunately! Simon, I congratulate you. Your scheme, so simple yet so sensible, has furnished us with information of a value beyond price.'

'It answers another question also,' broke in Avran. 'I had wondered how the assassin contrived to be on our ship. After all, Simon, I had booked my own passage only just before meeting you; the Baroddan must have arranged his before I arranged mine.'

This point had not occurred to me, but of course it was true. 'The fourth day of the first autumn month — why, that must be September, still over three weeks away!'

'Yes, but you must bear in mind that they needed to allow the late, unlamented Akharn enough time to make his way to Sandarro. After all, sailings from England to Rockall, even by Mentonese ships, are not frequent. And how convenient for us! We have ample opportunity in which to prepare to receive and, let's say, *entertain* the conspirators. They're due for a surprise!'

Chapter Thirteen

THE PATTERN OF THE DAYS

Were I to continue recounting my early adventures in Sandastre on a day-to-day basis, this story would seem endless. Moreover, it would involve much repetition, for very soon my days were organized by my friends into a fairly regular pattern. After that first day my awakenings were earlier, usually around the eighth hour of the morning. Brek was always waiting outside with hot water, and always clean garments had been set out for me; no, not an endless supply, just four jackets and tunics and an ampler quantity of undershirts and briefs. Each night, someone whisked away that day's clothes and brought fresh garments, without either awakening me or upsetting the vigilant Rascal.

Always while I washed and dressed, Brek watched and talked. He was an ever-upwelling fountain of questions about England and information about Sandastre. Since, as the days went by, Ilven saw to it that I spoke less and less English and more and more Sandastrian, my morning encounter with Brek became my prime — and, eventually, my only — chance to speak my own language. Soon I found myself becoming so accustomed to Brek's quaint phraseology that I was in danger of speaking in that fashion myself!

Then there would be breakfast, in the garden under the ebelmek tree on fine days, on wet days in a fifth-floor room close to my bedroom. The walls of that chamber were so exquisitely carven and painted with flowers, and its ceiling was of so cheerful a blue, that it seemed sunny in the gloomiest weather. Usually Avran or Ilven would be there, though often one or other would have duties that made their presence impossible at that time; and sometimes the Princess Felguen, their mother, joined us. She was always most courteous to me. As I began haltingly to speak Sandastrian, she

145

made a point of addressing me in that language, waiting patiently as I strove to frame proper responses. Never did she chide me for my mistakes, though sometimes her smiles told me that they had been amusing! Ilven was much more firm, even brusque.

'Simon, you must not be properly awake! Surely you know by now that, by saying *"Ksatevor talivar,"* you are *ordering* me to pass you your drink, not requesting me politely to do so. For courtesy, you must say *"Yé barimé tevoren talivar?"* — "Would you kindly pass me my drink?" Now try it again, properly — and then perhaps I *will* pass it!'

On weekdays after breakfast, I would have an hour or more of sword practice with swordmaster Oled Orexin. He was a tiny, white-haired man with a sparse beard whose few hairs stood out from his cheeks like the whiskers of a cat; but, unlike a cat, he had no capacity for stillness. Instead, he was as unceasingly mobile as a whirligig beetle on a pond. At our first encounter, he convinced himself quickly of my ineptitude with a sword. However, unlike Avran, he seemed in no way discomfited thereby. Indeed, Avran told me the swordmaster had professed himself glad 'to be starting from the very foundations' — no compliment, that, to my endless days of earnest exercise!

I had thought the early lessons might prove difficult for both of us when we had no common language. However, the swordmaster was so quick in comprehending my problems and so vivid in pantomiming an instruction that misunderstandings never developed. In early lessons I was taught how to employ my sword in self-defence against attacks of progressively increasing speed and subtlety. Only when I had shown signs of mastering that art was I taught how to attack; and after that, paradoxically it seemed to me, Oled Orexin proceeded to discourage me from doing anything *other* than attack! All in all, I made steady progress and the swordmaster seemed satisfied.

However, since sometimes I was permitted to watch a duel between Avran and he, I was not overwhelmed by Oled's praise. I recognized clearly that I would never equal my friend's mastery of swordsmanship, which quite matched the Orexin's own.

In the latter half of those mornings, I came into my own;

for the concern then was archery. In that art, I was the master and the others my pupils. Avran had brought from England bowstaves made of a number of different woods — of birch, ash, hornbeam, yew, blackthorn, elm, beech and auburn.* All these woods have their advocates and I am reluctant to enter into that dispute. Yet, for me, bows of elm or of yew surpass all others. The renown of yew is so great that our English kings have even forced foreign merchants to pay their import tariffs in bowstaves of that wood; yet I consider elm to be its equal, provided it be grown in the shade so that its growth rings are properly narrow. Yew is the harder wood, fine-textured and long-fibred; elm is less fine and shorter-fibred, but it bends better and has more of a spring. Maybe it is because I am not a large, heavily muscled man that I like yew less; but, whatever the reason, I prefer elm for my bows.

This might be well and good but, since none of the trees used by English bowyers was to be found growing in this warm southern land of Sandastre, we needed to find suitable substitutes. Avran commissioned two soldiers of the forest-dwelling Aradavard to procure samples of different woods for testing. Before they left, we showed them how to cut suitable pieces from the boles of young trees, with the tensile sapwood to make the back of the bow, the heartwood its belly. This is ideal, for the sapwood resists tension and the heartwood resists compression as the bow is bent and released.

The wood for arrows was more easily chosen. A tree common in the forests north of Sandarro, the ikhoras, has a wood that is heavy, close-grained and knot-free; its branches make excellent steles. For the fletchings, no goose feathers were available here since, as Avran had told me, there are no geese in southern Rockall; and, though the feathers of various land and sea birds were brought for us to try, none proved satisfactory.

In this instance I benefited from Avran's advice. It seemed that Sandastrian archers fletched their arrows not with feathers, but with stiff-fibred leaves of the slaskelest, a small plant growing at the edges of the sea, where the salt spray means that few plants can live. One picked a leaf of this plant and

* Laburnum.

ran it through one's fingers, separating the fibres. When newly picked, the leaf was as suitable as a young goose pinion for a swift shaft in still conditions and, when dried awhile, it was as stiff as an old goose feather and as effective on a windy day. The iron arrowheads used for the light Sandastrian bows were not ideal, but there was an abundant supply of them and they served well enough.

So the making of arrows could be quickly commenced but, until the two Aradars returned, we could use only the bowstaves brought from England. The arrow plates, to cover the centre of the bow and protect it from abrasion by arrows, were fashioned from the horns of hasedain, as were the tips that prevented the bowstrings from cutting into the wood. The bowstrings were made from the fibres of a flax-like plant that grows abundantly, not in Sandastre but on the windy highlands of nearby Temecula. As in England, the bowstrings were impregnated with beeswax to repel rain and dew. These Temeculan strings proved better than those of flax or linen that I had used hitherto, for they lasted much longer before fraying and in consequence, needed to be replaced much less often. A frayed and breaking string is the bane of an archer.

The staves were each cut to a length of five-and-a-half feet between nocks, so we were able to make the arrows to a length of about twenty-seven inches. These dimensions astonished the Sandastrians watching us at work, for their own bows measured no more than a yard and were quite light, used mostly for shooting birds, never in warfare. I persuaded Avran to accept the yew bow, the first to be strung, and was more than content to have the elm bow for my own weapon. These two had been already shaped by the English bowyers from whom Avran had gained instruction, but it was Avran and I who made all the other staves into bows. Thus we had eight weapons in all, ready for use — albeit of variable quality.

Avran rigged up a straw target in the castle garden and each day he and I would exercise with our bows for a while. At first we were watched by Brek, but he was so evidently eager to try his hand at archery that soon we gave him the blackthorn bow and allowed him to shoot alternately with us. Since, though small, he was so broad in the chest, he was well able to handle an eighty-pound bow. My own bow pulled at about one hundred and twenty pounds weight. Avran was heavier than me and could have managed a hundred-and-fifty-pound bow with ease, but in fact his bow pulled at the same weight as mine.

We practised each day for at least an hour and both my pupils made fair progress. However, it was as clear to me that Avran would never be an outstanding bowman as it was to him that I would never be an outstanding swordsman.

Early in the second week Ilven came to watch. After a while, she insisted on trying her hand with Brek's bow. This shocked me rather, for I had never known a woman to use a bow; but, since Avran seemed in no way discountenanced, I acquiesced. Yet Ilven had watched well. She needed little instruction in how to hold, or at what moment to loose, an arrow. Moreover, the accuracy of her shooting surprised and pleased me, as did her enthusiasm for the sport.

Thereafter, Ilven joined us at practice on most days. When I modified the ash bow for her especial use, I was surprised and deeply gratified by the warmth of her thanks. Indeed, I must confess also that I found it satisfying to be instructing her in bowmanship — not merely because it was a welcome reversal of our usual teacher-pupil relationship, but because I was coming to discover a special pleasure in being in her company. There was a quality of her voice, a grace in her movements, that made me eager to be watching her or listening to her, even though she might be saying or doing nothing in particular.

We would lunch shortly after noon, sometimes in the upper rooms of the great tower, sometimes in the messrooms where the soldiers gathered so that I could meet the men whom I would be so soon instructing.

That was the pattern of weekday mornings. On Sundays there would be a religious service, in the castle hall if it were raining, out of doors if it were not, with much music and singing of psalms or hymns in Sandastrian and a sermon which seemed to me, novice in the language that I was, mercifully short.

In the afternoons our activities were much less strictly scheduled. Very often Avran or Ilven were occupied either in performing some duty or in entertaining visiting notables from other parts of Sandastre or beyond. If both of them were thus engaged, I would take from its shelf the copybook presented to me by Ilven, a quill pen, a supply of the purple ink which the Sandastrians extracted from a shellfish abundant on their shores, and some sheets of the fine Mentonese parchment. Then I would sit in the shade of the ebelmek and, with Rascal contentedly browsing or sleeping in the branches above, I would do my inept best to read, and to reproduce on to the parchment, the elegant lines of Rockalese script.

The Rockall alphabet is quite different from ours. It is based, not upon straight lines that derive from the chisel strokes of the monument-minded Romans, but upon curves and spirals. The Rockalese have had pens and parchments at their disposal for as long as record reaches, and with a pen, of course, it is easier to draw curves than straight lines. Yes, some straight lines *are* also employed, but like the curving lines in our own alphabet, they are subsidiary. Moreover, there is no differentiation of capitals to break the line of the text. When written well the Rockalese alphabet is, to my eyes, much more attractive than ours. However, I fear I have never become truly expert as a calligrapher in any of the three alphabets I know.

Another difference to which I found it hard to accustom myself is that Rockalese sentences are written not just from left to right, like ours, but in boustrophedon arrangement. Conventionally the first line *does* read from left to right, but the second reads from right to left and thenceforward the lines alternate in direction. It is a fashion more efficient for the eye of the reader than ours, but at first it is disconcerting; I was forever finding my pen beginning a second or a fourth line on the left, as I would have done when writing English. Sometimes, when I threw down my pen in sheer exasperation, Rascal would make chittering noises at me from the tree, in shared exasperation and sympathy.

Yet there were advantages also. The southern Rockalese alphabet is simpler than ours, in that it contains fewer letters — only twenty-five against the thirty-two or so that we use.* There are no Cs, Js, Qs, Ws or Ys, nor do these exist as

* Correct in the fifteenth century!

150

separate sounds. In transliterating, though I have sometimes used a C instead of a K, the sound would be always hard, as in 'cat'; where I have written a W, a Sandastrian would use U; and where I have written a Y, the Sandastrian equivalent would be I. The letter X likewise does not exist in Sandastrian and the sound, written 'ks', survives only in a single archaic instance — the imperative prefix *ksa*, 'you must', 'we must' — a relic, presumably, from days when the men of the Empire issued all the orders! The letter H exists but is also archaic, being found only in a few verbs, the names of two vardai, certain personal names (such as Helburnet) and a very few place names — most notably Halésowan, where the great sun temple of the Empire still stands.

As I was to discover later, the X and H sounds are much more frequent in Rockall's northern languages. Moreover, the Q sound is used also, though it is always written 'kw'. As for the northern alphabet, though somewhat similar to that of the south, it is based upon straight lines like ours and, to my eyes, much less attractive. Yet, as I plied my pen beneath the ebelmek tree, I was too much bothered about present difficulties to speculate upon future ones!

Other differences proved helpful. The Sandastrians have a single letter to represent 'th', not two as we have,* pronouncing it always as in 'think' when they use it at all. However, the sound is rare enough to explain Avran's problems with my surname. Other sounds — our 'ch', the 'oo' of 'soon', the 'ee' of 'seen', and all our complex of 'ough' sounds — simply do not exist, and even 'sh' is rare.

In contrast, there are eight vowels, not five. Three of these represent three different E sounds — one for the E of 'let', one for the heavily stressed, French-style 'é' and one for a more lightly-stressed sound, like the E of the Celtic syllable 'tre'. This last is employed usually at the end of words — 'Sandastre' and 'Salastre', for example. Two other vowels represent the two different O sounds — one as in 'lot', the other as in 'old'. Furthermore, there is an additional consonant that I have transcribed as 'kh', though truly it has no English parallel. These were problems to plague me, and many were

---

* Both since lost in the reduction of the English alphabet to twenty-six letters.

my head-scratchings beneath that tree as I strove to choose the right letter E or to pronounce to myself that awkward extra consonant.

Ilven, who had been endlessly patient in teaching me the Sandastrian language, was much less so in teaching me the script. Her pen was a slender wooden cylinder to whose end had been affixed upright a slim seashell, exactly conical in shape and with so tiny a hole in its tip that the ink passed through in the steadiest of trickles. With this she wrote line upon line of beautiful script with a speed and precision that, even when writing my own English characters, I have never matched.

After each of those afternoons of wrestling with the Sandastrian alphabet, I would timorously show her the result. The atrocious blotches and pothooks I managed to produce, using a pen exactly similar to hers, quite bewildered her.

'Why, Simon, you write worse than a five-year-old!' she would storm at me. 'Are you not ashamed of yourself? And there, that's the third shell-nib you've broken in four days! Whatever do you do with them?'

I would sigh and, next day, try again. Slowly, my letters shaped themselves into a form that, if never elegant, was at least recognizable. When one day she informed me kindly that the day's copy would not make a backward Sandarrovian eight-year-old too ashamed, I was flattered, for I knew I was making progress!

If Ilven or Avran were free in the afternoon, we would summon our sevdreyen and go riding. When Avran was my companion, we would go out on to the castle hill and he would put my mount and me through our paces. Soon I was confident enough not to hold Whitebrow's horns when she was merely galloping across the meadows, yet there were enough other occasions during those early weeks when I did so!

We would ride out along one of the ridges radiating stellate from Sandarro hill, at first quite calmly and slowly; but then Avran and his mount would plunge suddenly down some declivity and Whitebrow and I perforce must follow.

At first Avran chose the gentler slopes, though taking them at increasing speed on successive days. All too soon, however, he was choosing steeper slopes, some much steeper than any horse could tackle. Always I was unwilling to show fear by turning back, so always Whitebrow and I followed; but often it was with sweating brow and pounding heart and with hands frantically clutching my mount's horns.

At the foot of such slopes, Avran would turn his sevdru and watch our descent. If he was concerned about my safety, this was never made evident. Instead he would say cheerfully: 'There now! Simple enough, wasn't it?' or some such comment; and I would be too breathless, or still too scared, to respond adequately!

Yet, of course, it *did* become easier and my confidence in Whitebrow grew steadily, though not so fast as hers in me. Thus, whilst normally she would respond to my emotions and be calm when I was calm or nervous when I was nervous, she evinced no fear during those precipitate descents. A sevdru is very sure-footed and Whitebrow knew her own abilities. Instead, her confidence helped to give *me* confidence.

This exchange of thoughts was a strange business. As the days went by, there were times when Whitebrow informed me of a danger — a concealed pit in the grass, loose stones on a slope — and I would know why she was avoiding it before even perceiving the obstacle. Similarly, my instructions to her were responded to almost at the instant my thought was framed. Soon I ceased speaking to her, for there was no need.

However, beyond that point and our sharing of emotions, the exchange of thoughts did not reach. I could not, for example, give Whitebrow a series of instructions, for she would respond only to the first. Nor did she seem ever aware of any of my thoughts that did not involve her; and, if she had any reflections of her own as we were travelling along, I was equally unaware of them. I became very fond of her indeed and very proud of our joint feats. Nevertheless, in the last analysis, our relationship was little different from one I might have had with a well-trained and sensitive dog.

Rascal was very much more intelligent and our relationship much closer. I began to comprehend his abilities one day when, on the way out to the ebelmek tree, I dropped my shell-pen somewhere among the flowers. As soon as I missed it, Rascal hopped down from my shoulder, scuttled away down the path, and returned bearing the pen proudly in his hand, crooning with joy at my surprise and pleasure.

This was the first of many occasions when he fetched me things as soon as I felt a need for them; but he made his own decisions. Normally he would not bring me anything he could not carry conveniently. Yet, should I order him (verbally or mentally) to fetch something large, he would strive valiantly to drag it along to me before I hurried penitently to his aid.

Later, I was to discover that Rascal could carry out moderately elaborate instructions. Both Avran and I were destined to benefit greatly from my friendship with the little vasian.

I am afraid I have allowed myself to get ahead of my story; but indeed, it is not easy to isolate those different concerns of my early weeks in Sandarro. To pick up my threads; if Avran were present on the afternoon rides, then I would be given plenty of brisk instruction and would have a thoroughly energetic time of it. If Ilven were my companion, however, the afternoon would be much more relaxing. She was not interested in teaching me to ride; her concerns were to make me learn her language and to enable me to understand better this land of Rockall and realm of Sandastre.

On some afternoons, Ilven and I would ride down among the padin and tour the shops and inns of Sandarro. These, like the dwellings, were round in shape and had an inner courtyard. However, they were set always in the hollows, not upon the ridges, and within the outer ring of padin that surrounded (and, potentially, defended) the foot of the hill. A single padarn might be made up of several shops; these are operated by merchants of different trades, for Sandarro has no equivalents to the streets of merchants of like trades encountered in English cities. If the padarn served as an inn, the innkeeper and his wife would live in the rooms by one entrance, the eating room and tavern would be on either side of the other entrance, and the chambers between would accommodate guests unwilling or unable to find beds in the tower of their vard.

On other days Ilven and I rode out of the city. We might leave by the northwest gate and cross the Randavren Brook, riding out to linger among the butterfly-haunted meadowlands bordering the beautiful River Alasslan or exploring the sunny glades north of the city, where herds of hasedain grazed among the trees and the trills of the herd boys' pipes mingled with the songs of the birds. Once we rode out through the north gate, to visit the hills where was quarried the red sandstone that had been used to build the towers and walls of Sandarro; and once we rode east, crossing the Ambidril, to spend a lazy afternoon on a sunny beach collecting coiled shells, little corals and starfishes.

As we talked and laughed together, my knowledge of Sandastrian grew apace and I came more and more to delight in Ilven's companionship. The days when I did not see her seemed devoid of sunshine.

In the evenings, I would dine with Prince Vindicon, his family and his guests, usually in the small chamber where I had first encountered Rascal, less often in the large banquet room next to the Council Chamber on the seventh floor. Rascal was always as welcome as I and, since it was always used in introductions, I became quickly accustomed to my new name, 'Simon Vasianavar'.

On one occasion a lady, the wife of a member of the shore-dwelling Varessavard, asked puzzledly how an Englishman came to be so familiar with a Sandastrian animal; but Avran, straight-faced, assured her that such creatures were commonly encountered in the woods of Hallamshire, from whence I came!

Always the food and wine were good; and, though I endured many prolonged and solemn postprandial speeches — never from the eslef or his family, always from the visitors — each evening ended pleasantly in music, with flutes and stringed instruments brought out and much singing. I discovered a little half-melon-shaped instrument with four strings, called an embelin, that could be tuned much like a citole and was quite as easy to play. Whenever encouraged by Ilven, I would sing one of our English ballads — of Robin Hood, of Sir Andrew Barton the pirate, of the wars in France, of witchcraft or of love — while Avran or secretary Enar Servessil translated. Whatever the reaction of the other guests, Ilven would always listen intently, her chin cupped in her hand. Sometimes, when we were out riding, she would ask me to sing one of those ballads again. I would always acquiesce but I could never persuade her to sing just for me — to my regret, for Ilven's voice always gave me especial pleasure.

As the weeks went by, I came to comprehend more and

more of the songs I was hearing during these evenings. One of Ilven's songs I loved particularly. It recalled an incident in the Esberdine War of long ago, when Sandastre's first fleet sailed forth to battle the mightier fleet of Arcturus. The fleets engaged off the island of Hasadek; that much is known, but no more, for the sea mists closed over the battle. Not a single ship from either fleet returned to harbour; indeed, no news of the fate of the ships ever came back to Sandarro or Andressellar. After that, with all its most expert sailors lost, neither country was eager again to build a fleet. So it was that the Mentonese, venturing southward, took over much of the coastal trade — and all the European trade — of southern Rockall. This was the incident to which Enar Servessil had referred in our first conversation; and it had provided an additional reason why most Sandastrians so much disliked and distrusted the sea. Ilven's song was so haunting that I strove to translate it into my own tongue. Though my translation is but a poor echo, I will set it down here:

> Remember the fleet of Sandastre
> Out from Sandarro lying.
> Remember the fleet of Sandastre
> The night-hawk banner flying
>
> > Bright were the masthead lights
> > Shining across the water.
> > Bright were the hopes of men
> > Daring to sail into danger.
>
> Remember the men of Sandastre
> With swords and with spears gleaming red.
> Remember the men of Sandastre
> Braving the sea waves dread.
>
> > Valiant was Ranverem
> > Great prince upon the water.
> > Valiant that armèd throng
> > Crowding his ships with laughter.
>
> Remember the ships of Sandastre,
> Out into Sandevrin faring.
> Remember the ships of Sandastre
> The might of Arcturus daring.

Brave were the warriors then
Never their enemies fearing.
Braver their wives ashore
Speeding the ships with cheering.

Lament ye the fleet of Sandastre
Which sailed on that distant morning.
Lament ye the fleet of Sandastre
Into the chill mists departing.

Gone are the sails so white
Gone from our quays for ever.
Vanished the flags so brave
Lost 'neath the waves for ever.

Whenever I recall that song, I seem to hear again the sweet cadences of Ilven's voice and to see the flickering torches, painting their ever-changing pattern of shadows on the walls.

Chapter Fourteen

A FLIGHT OF ARROWS

On a morning early in my third week in Sandarro, Avran set down his bow after our practice and said: 'Simon my friend, my father has besought me to request a favour from you. It seems that some of the soldiers, and some members of Council, are deriding the power of the long-bow and questioning whether there is the least need for any new method of fighting. They say: "Bows are but puny things, fit only for shooting little birds. We Sandastrians have never used bows in warfare. And what use is an arrow against a man in armour? It would merely bounce off! Why waste time on such toys?" '

'Why, Avran, you at least know the power of the long-bow — ' I began hotly; but Avran broke in: 'Yes, so I do; and my father understands it also. That is why he is asking if we might stage a demonstration, to convince the doubters of its range and its power.'

I hesitated. 'Well, it's a little early. We have so few bows yet, and all of them made of English woods. We don't know, even, whether your Sandastrian forests can furnish us with a satisfactory substitute.'

'So much the better! A truly impressive display, using a long-bow made of an ideal material, will persuade the Councillors more effectively than any feeble effort with an inferior bow.'

I laughed. 'Why, Avran, I never thought you capable of such duplicity! Very well, then, we'll put on a display. We'll make it sufficiently impressive to convince the doubters that bows can be used for more than shooting sparrows.'

'Splendid! But it must be soon, Simon. The Ruling Council meets within a few days — they assemble monthly, as you must know — and, at that next meeting, my father wishes

159

to appoint you centenar. If you have demonstrated the powers of the long-bow, that will be easy; if not, it might be harder. Shall we say in three days' time?'

I winced, but then laughed again. 'If it must be so soon, why then it must! But Avran and Brek — and you too, Ilven, if you will help us — we're going to have to work together to be ready in time. Targets must be made; we must decide on a plan for the demonstration; and all of us must practise hard!'

Avran smiled ruefully: 'Well, I can scarcely refuse, can I? Be sure I will lend you all the aid I can.'

Ilven answered rather doubtfully: 'Yes, Simon, indeed I will help; that is, if you feel it fitting that a woman should demonstrate a man's weapon.'

'Of course I do,' I answered hotly. 'You are becoming a most competent archer!' — for indeed, my doubts had been quite swept away. I was rewarded by the sweetest of smiles.

As for Brek, his smile was so huge that it seemed wider than his face as he answered in English: 'Enthralled shall I be such service to render, indubitably!'

All other activity was suspended during those three days. There were no rides or lessons for me. However, since our conversation was now largely in Sandastrian and Ilven relentless in pointing out my mistakes, in that, at least, I continued to make progress. Otherwise, from morning to evening, our concern was wholly with archery. I seemed to be running around as restlessly as a caged squirrel, seeing that straw targets were made and painted, assembling armoured saracens, making sure that our long-bows were in top condition, and either supervising the practising of my three friends or shooting at the butts myself. Before I fell exhaustedly to sleep on the eve of the Saturday demonstration, I reviewed our preparations and felt confident all must go well, if only the day be fine.

The site chosen for our performance was in the grassy meadows of the Alasslan, south and east of the Avrassan tower. There the targets and the saracens had been set up. Though the event had not been formally announced, a considerable crowd had assembled by mid-morning on the slopes above, including many blue-uniformed soldiers. Some wooden benches had been brought down from the castle on

160

the backs of sevdreyen, to provide rather spartan accommodation for the Councillors and senior officers.

Prince Vindicon and Princess Felguen arrived early, greeted me cheerfully and without formality, and introduced me to other guests. Though I had met several Councillors on the first day in the castle, their names and faces had so blurred in my mind that this second introduction was helpful.

There were two, however, to whom I had not been presented but nevertheless remembered clearly; massive Draklin Grassad, lurching along on his gold-banded stick, and lean, sandy Vrek Harradas of the face that was never still. Fortunately they arrived late, as the eslef and eslevar were settling down to watch the demonstration; so again I evaded the embarrassment of an introduction.

Avran had asked a forester of Derressdavard, an archer skilled in the use of the Sandastrian bow, to participate in the demonstration. He was invited to shoot first. He was willing enough, though he looked doubtfully at our great long-bows as he strung his own, much lighter weapon. He was allowed three arrows and asked to shoot for distance. A line had been stretched across the grass as mark. He walked up to it and, drawing his bowstring back to his cheek, loosed his first arrow.

It was a good shot with such a bow and there was a murmur of approval from the crowd. A centenar had been asked to measure the distances. When he called out that the arrow had travelled ninety paces, there was much applause. A second arrow travelled less far; but when the Derresdem loosed his third arrow, there was further applause, for that one travelled over a hundred paces.

Clearly the Prince had expected that I would demonstrate the long-bow myself, for he gestured to me to shoot next. But no, that was not my plan. Instead, I waved forward Brek.

He had attired himself for the occasion, for reasons unknown to me, in a robe of crimson that I had never seen hitherto. As he walked forward, his sandy hair and rotundity caused him to remind me of a plum bursting with ripeness. Walked, I said? Bounced, rather, for he was excited and eager, his blackthorn bow already strung and his arrow at the nock. Almost before his audience had taken heed, he drew his bow and loosed.

This time, the astonishment of the watchers was considerable. Though Brek had not allowed for an errant wind gust and his arrow had lost way, it travelled much further than that of the forester — a full one hundred and forty paces, or about one hundred and forty-five yards in my own estimation. Brek jumped with delight and I saw the craggy face of his father the Chancellor rearrange itself into a smile.

Before the excited comment had stilled, Ilven stepped lithely forward. I saw the brows of the eslef elevate in surprise, while the sudden quiet in the crowd showed their startlement. She nocked and drew, bending to her bow with a swift skill that made me proud. Unlike Brek, when she loosed she made full allowance for the gusty wind across the meadows. Her ash bow pulled at about eighty pounds, the same weight as Brek's, but her arrow travelled much further, quite one hundred and eighty paces. As she stepped back, the crowd's applause almost drowned my shout of congratulation; yet she heard it and gave me a smile that made my heart leap.

Then there was another hush as Avran came forward. Though never destined to be an accurate archer, he had great strength — more than I — and strength is everything in long-distance shooting. He was in the full glory of his orange cloak, but he threw it aside before bending and stringing his bow. Conscious of the attention of his audience and enjoying it thoroughly, he drew back the string, with the arrow nocked on to it, quite slowly. When his bow was fully bent and the tail of the arrow at his chin, Avran held the pose for several seconds, as if for a sketch, his muscles flexed and a huge grin on his face. Then he loosed.

The arrow, a flight arrow I had specially chosen to travel far, sped amply beyond the mark attained by his sister. It was a good shot indeed, over two hundred and fifty paces, or near two hundred and seventy-five yards in my judgement; and it was received by the crowd at first with incredulity, then with clamorous applause. I noticed Draklin Grassad standing stiff in amazement, while Vrek Harradas seemed quite taken aback.

The Derresdem archer was standing by me, shaking his head from side to side in wonderment. However, when I asked him to show his skills again, he was willing enough. Standing about sixty paces from one of the straw targets, he loosed three arrows in swift succession. All three clustered about the bull's eye, though none found its exact centre.

Now it was my turn. I walked twice as far from the target as he had been and took my time over my shots, for I was trying to demonstrate accuracy, not speed; that would come later. My first loosing was a little high, though close enough to the centre not to be embarrassing. On the second I over-compensated and the arrow struck the target too low. Well, third time pays for all; and indeed it did, for fortune was with me. To my pleasure, the centenar called out that I had hit the bull's eye in its exact centre.

It was a delight to receive Avran's excited embrace and a greater one when the warmly phrased congratulations of the eslef were conveyed to me. It was a pleasure also to hear further cries of wonder when the centenar shouted out the depth to which my arrows had penetrated the straw targets. However, we were not done yet!

Now the saracens were brought out, roughly carved and painted wooden figures the size of a man. On to one had been placed a coat of chain mail and on to the other, a coat of plate armour. At my request, the forester again shot first at these. He stood within twenty paces of his target, but even so the arrows glanced off both from the mail and the plate.

The Derresdem was in no way discountenanced, for he had expected this; he knew well that his arrows could not penetrate mail or armour. As he stepped aside, he unstrung his bow, for his part in the performance was done. However, he remained to watch.

I had asked Avran to shoot first; his target, the figure in chain mail. There was no need for him to stand so close as the forester had done; indeed, for our purpose of persuasion, it were better that he should stand much farther back. For this demonstration, the small Sandastrian arrowheads would not do. Fortunately Avran had brought back with him to Sandarro a pocketful of the bodkin arrowheads generally used in England, with their wickedly sharp points, lozenge-shaped heads and slim necks. We had set them on to especially heavy shafts, so all ought to be well.

Nevertheless I could perceive that Avran was more anxious about this shot. The muscle power for length was his, but his accuracy was less predictable. Moreover, I had insisted that he stand seventy paces from his target. Again Avran delayed loosing his shaft; this time, though, it was more through nervousness than any desire for dramatic effect. He loosed; but ah! he had missed, and his arrow embedded itself in the turf fifty yards beyond the saracen.

However, while the eyes of the crowd were following that arrow, he had taken a second from his quiver, nocked, drawn and loosed. This time his arrow flew true. It hit the chest of the saracen, cutting through the iron rings and burying itself deeply into the wood within.

The onlookers had been chattering at Avran's mis-shot, but they fell momentarily silent as the implications of that second shot were recognized. Then there was applause; and Avran, flushed and beaming, was receiving a second time the congratulations he merited so fully.

Now it was my turn again. Shooting to penetrate plate armour is a tricky business; the arrow can so easily glance off if one's shaft be aimed badly. I had taken the usual precaution of waxing my arrows, but did this really help or was it mere superstitious tradition? I had never served as archer in a battle, so I could not know. Well, we would see.

When I had shot earlier I had been confident, for it was a mere extension of my target practice and competitions of many years. This was different; I must not falter now! The thought of failure made me pulse with nervousness. Perversely, as if to prove myself by making my task harder, I walked past Avran's mark and took up my position a full hundred paces from the second saracen. Quickly, then, I nocked, drew and loosed, watching the arrow's flight with more anxiety than I had done ever before.

Had I allowed enough for the wind? Yes, it was travelling true; but would it penetrate the armour or just glance off? Ah! all was well. The arrow hit full in the centre of the cuirass — I could hear the *thwack* — and yes, it was through! Later I learned that it had sunk a full five inches into the wood beneath.

The clamour of applause exceeded anything before and I blushed and grinned like a girl complimented on her first pretty dress. Then, hastily, to cover my embarrassment, I busied myself preparing one last demonstration.

Three straw targets had been set up, though only two had been used hitherto. I had them brought closer together and then went back to my mark. This time I was using a full quiver of arrows, twenty-four of them. These had the smaller Sandastrian heads, but that did not matter. In the fashion of an English archer before battle, I set my arrows upright in a curving line before me, the head of each plunged into the turf. Then I took a deep breath, glanced about me, and began to shoot at the targets.

It was important to remember the rhythm. Nock the arrow, then draw it back, opening one's chest and pushing into the bow, till the thumb of one's drawing hand was at one's chin and the steel of the arrowhead touching the knuckles of one's other hand; aim for a heartbeat, then let fly. Next, with right hand following the string, seize the second arrow, to nock, draw, anchor and loose once more. Repeat; repeat; again and again, six, seven, eight times. Now change from the left to the centre target and keep up the rhythm; concentrate, Simon, concentrate! Good; sixteen shafts loosed; now for the right-hand target. Keep it up; accuracy, man, accuracy! Only four arrows to go; three now; two; ah! all loosed! As I finished, I was trembling with the exertion and scarcely conscious of the tumultuous applause.

How long had it taken? Nearly three minutes; not a very good speed really — a truly skilled archer should be able to loose more than a dozen arrows a minute — but not bad either. And my accuracy *had* been good; eight arrows in each target and several of them close to the bull's-eyes.

But Avran was seizing me, hugging me and then standing behind me to raise my arms high, as if I had been a victorious fairground fighter. There were further cheers; then Prince Vindicon rose and the onlookers fell silent as he praised Brek, Ilven, Avran and me. I do not remember all his words, but I recall that he spoke of how this demonstration had opened up new prospects for the soldiers of Sandastre. When he went on to say that I had promised to instruct them in this new way of defending their realm, there was further applause.

Afterward the people hastened down to examine with awe the targets and saracens and to mill around us, excitedly questioning us about these new super-weapons, for so they were regarded. Draklin Grassad did not seem nearly so pleased; he and Vrek Harradas left quickly, without troubling to offer any congratulations!

Yes, it was a day to remember. However, it was good afterwards to escape from the crowds and relax in the castle garden, with Rascal humming happily on my shoulder, Avran crowing with pleasure at our success and Ilven smiling at us both and trying to bring down to earth Avran's more outrageous flights of fancy.

During dinner that evening, naturally enough, the day's doings were again discussed. At one point, Avran said: 'Simon, that last demonstration was awesome! A squadron of archers, firing at that rate, could truly wreak havoc.'

'Yes indeed. Men say that, at Crécy, the English archers were firing so fast that over ten thousand arrows were discharged at the charging chivalry of France before the first knight reached our lines — and few *did* reach our lines.'

'Certainly the long-bow is a formidable weapon,' the scribe said quietly. 'Moreover, it is a great leveller. Thus equipped, the ordinary man is no longer at the mercy of the armoured knight, as the French learned so bitterly.'

Prince Vindicon had been following our talk, but saying little. Now he set down his glass and regarded Avran and me with grave approval.

'Well, my son, your inspiration and your friend's skill have undoubtedly given to Sandastre a new tool for our soldiers and hunters to use. The Ruling Council *must* approve it now. Of course, I knew the long-bow must eventually come to southern Rockall. I hear rumours that, in the great forests north of Temecula, it is being used already by settlers from your country, Simon. However, I am glad we shall have learned this skill before the Arctorrans have the long-bow, or the Baroddans; and I thank you both, from my heart.'

The eslef paused, picked up his glass again and toyed with it, then looked at me very directly.

'Yet I trust we Sandastrians will never use the long-bow to bring war upon others, as your kings have done in France, Simon. My love is of peace, not combat; and I fear that many men must die from this new weapon. Most sincerely do I trust that, in the years to come, the long-bow will strengthen we Sandastrians against aggressors, yet never make aggressors of us.'

When I went to my bed that night I was thinking of those words. Though Prince Vindicon had praised me, somehow I could no longer feel quite so proud of myself. However, Rascal sensed my equivocal mood and set out, with tricks and absurdities, to cheer me. He had me laughing again before I went to sleep and my dreams were all benign.

Chapter Fifteen

THE GATHERING IN THE INN

Our archery demonstration was staged on a Saturday. Late on the evening of that day — too late for Prince Vindicon to entertain them — a delegation from Mentór in Breveg arrived on an Arctorran coastal vessel. They were come to summon Helburnet back to his earldom where, they reported, trouble from Baroddan rebels was mounting.

Among the delegation was a priest; and that gentleman was courteously invited to preach the Sunday morning sermon. He was not an attractive person — large and flabby, with a pimply skin and lips pursed as if in perpetual disapproval of some improper story. The style in Brevegen services, it seemed, was for much longer sermons than were usual in Sandastre. Moreover, his address to us, as we stood in sultry heat on a green slope of Sandarro Hill, was delivered in a plummy, portentous voice I found excruciatingly monotonous. Several times I yawned, though contriving to conceal this discourtesy behind a hand; and indeed, I came perilously close to falling asleep on my feet.

The delegation's arrival, and the news it brought, meant that Prince Vindicon and his family were embroiled in meetings and receptions; even Brek had been called into service. Thus I faced a solitary afternoon. However, after the excitements of yesterday and the tedium of the morning, my lassitude was so overwhelming that I desired neither activity nor company. Instead I betook myself into the shade of the ebelmek without even my copybook and, with Rascal melodiously crooning in the branches above, fell swiftly and deeply asleep.

Yet, after a while, my sleep became troubled. Into a tranquil dream there burst an alarm note, a trumpeting of warning:

'Wake up, wake up! Danger threatens — danger! Wake up!'
And so I did; but it came close to being my last awakening.

I was lying on my left side, on grassy ground in the deep
shade of the tree. I opened my eyes to see advancing upon
me an entire stranger, a dark-haired, weaselly man in servant's
livery. A raised dagger gleamed in his right hand. As I
twitched awake, he grinned with fierce delight and leapt
toward me, crying: '*Ksavakhass, zakhetrid!*' — 'Die, foreigner!'

My heart seemed to contract with fear, for truly I thought
my last hour was upon me. Though I groped for a knife, I
could not hope to draw and throw in time.

At that moment Rascal, hissing like an angry adder, dropped
upon my attacker from the tree. Full on to the man's shoulders
he fell and clung instantly to his head, the vasian's little
fingers closing over his eyes.

With a shriek of amazed fear, the assassin dropped his
dagger and groped frantically upward with both hands,
striving to dislodge this creature that had leapt upon him.
Staggering backward, he caught his heel against a paving
stone and fell heavily. As he rolled over, Rascal leapt clear
and scampered away.

By that time I was on my feet, a throwing-knife in my
hand. Yet, despite his fall, the man moved too fast for me.
In one convulsive movement he had regained his own feet
and was running away.

Readily might I have killed him, but I could not slay a
man already in flight, whatever his intentions had been. My
attempt to disable him failed, for the thrown knife merely
twitched his sleeve. At least it startled him, for I heard his
'Aargh!' of fright; but that was all. Before I could start in
pursuit, he vanished from my view into the castle.

Rascal scampered to me and, running up me, clung about
my neck, making whimpering cries like an anxious mother
animal. I stroked and made much of him, for unquestionably
he had saved my life. Only when he had calmed and was
crooning with pleasure did I go to retrieve my knife and try
to alert the guard. Eventually my inadequate Sandastrian
phrases urged him into action. However, though the castle
was searched, the dark-haired man could not be found.

Yet I was able to describe my assailant accurately enough
for identification. He had arrived in the train of one of the

170

Brevegen guests, the priest himself as it proved. The livery had been stolen from a castle servant, who had been knocked unconscious and hidden in a pantry only a few minutes before the murder attempt.

When he learned of the incident, Avran was deeply disturbed. What concerned him especially was that the man had known, not only where to find me in a garden he could never have visited, but also that I would be alone. Only the guards on the tower could have known both these facts. There had been a change of guards shortly after my arrival under the ebelmek; one of the six retiring soldiers must have betrayed me, but which? All seemed loyal. As a precaution, all six were dismissed from duty in the castle.

'I am angry that this happened,' said Avran grimly, 'and I am profoundly grateful that your vasian was there to warn you and to save you. Nevertheless, you should feel flattered! It means that our enemies now consider you a person to be reckoned with — a danger to their interests.'

'It's a compliment I could have done without,' I said ruefully. 'Was it the Grassads again, think you?'

He shook his head. 'No, this time I think we must blame the Baroddan rebels exclusively. It was a hastily conceived attempt and clumsily executed; Draklin Grassad would have been less precipitate, more subtle. Moreover, I believe Draklin and his cronies are enough Sandastrians at heart to want us to have the long-bow, whereas those Baroddans certainly will *not* wish it.'

'Clumsily executed or not, it came close to succeeding — too close for my comfort!' I responded uneasily. 'Rascal did not wake me soon enough. If he had not leapt upon the man, I'd have been dead.'

'It is remarkable that he alerted you at all!' Avran responded reprovingly. 'A vasian is essentially a nocturnal creature; he is a good guard at night and would have warned you of the assassin long before he came near you. In the daytime, though, the vasianar are drowsy and much less aware of dangers. Yes, Simon, you were very fortunate indeed.'

I sighed and nodded. 'Yes, I was fortunate. Yet can we foresee a time when we'll be free from the threat of such attacks?'

My friend laughed shortly. 'One is never altogether safe;

this world is an unsafe place. Yet mayhap we'll root out this nest of rebels shortly. It is tomorrow that they plan to meet and I am hoping nothing has happened — the Akharn's absence, for example — to scare them off. I believe all will be well, for they cannot have learned what occurred on the Mentonese ship; it left here too swiftly and was not calling at Mentór.'

He fell silent for a while and I was silent also. Then suddenly Avran grinned. 'Well, today's incident has one asset, at least. After this, my sister can no longer claim I am the only one ever to be caught napping!'

Prince Vindicon and his family were engaged with their guests that evening and not anxious to advertise just how high I stood in their favour. Consequently, instead of dining with them, I had been invited to dine privately with Enar Servessil and his wife Eyen, both of whom, by now, I had come to know well and respect highly.

This was a new experience for me, and made doubly novel because the Servessils did not live in the castle. Their quarters were on the uppermost floor of the stone tower of Servessavard, standing beyond the castle walls on the highest southeast ridge of Sandarro Hill. Only just above our heads, guards were keeping incessant watch from the ramparts; one could hear their feet as they patrolled, but not so loudly as to be distracting. From the two arrowslit windows of the chamber in which we dined, one could view the city and harbour walls and the valley of the little River Ambidril, hazy now in the waning of the sun.

The chamber was quite small and its furnishings plain. Moreover, I was astonished to learn that Eyen asar Servessil had herself prepared our excellent meal. It was still hard for me to comprehend the simplicity with which so many of the most powerful — and, I presumed, most wealthy — Sandastrians lived. No English noble would willingly have endured such quarters, nor would any English chatelaine have contemplated soiling her dainty hands with kitchen tasks. I felt privileged to be thus honoured and, paradoxically perhaps, was made instantly to feel at home.

Whilst Avran and I had been on the Mentonese ship, I had gained a little knowledge concerning the Baroddans, enough to satisfy me for a while. However, now that I had

172

come so close to falling victim to a Baroddan dagger, I felt I ought to know more. When that excellent meal was finished and we were relaxing in the torch-glow, Enar gave me the opportunity for asking questions by expressing again his horror concerning that attempt on me. After dismissing that matter I asked why, when Prince Helburnet's rule was so benign, was it so bitterly resented?

Enar seemed happy enough to respond at length, I think because the question was so much in the forefront of his own thoughts. The history of that region of southwest Rockall, I learned, had always been turbulent. Originally there had been several earldoms west of Fachane and east of Sandastre. Three of these — Skayarock in the western Helbevin Hills, Vassaretta in the valley of the River Badayin and Breveg in the Brevegen Hills — were made up of peoples much like the Fachnese; red-haired, fiery and emotional, capable of strong loyalties and yet too unstable to be reliable allies. However, there were four other realms also — Mentór, centred on the city of that name in the valley of the Sekheyin; Aldagard and Denniffey to the north, in the eastern Helbevin Hills; and Darrinnett, north of Lake Vanadha — whose people were of different character, black-haired and fierce, persistent and unforgiving.

Between these seven small realms there had been centuries of war. At first Skayarock expanded, gobbling up Vassaretta and Denniffey. Then that realm fell apart and a resurgent Denniffey swallowed up Darrinnett. Next, armies from the Temeculan realm of Elvenost conquered all those states in an empire that proved only short-lived. After that, warriors from the Sandastrian vard of Ranverem seized the earldom of Mentór, conquered Aldagard and the three Fachnese earldoms, and forged for themselves a new, upstart kingdom they called Barodda.

Upon my asking when that had happened, the scribe responded casually: 'Oh, relatively recently — just twelve hundred years or so ago.' The memories of Sandastrians were indeed long!

The rule of the Ranverems in Barodda had endured for over three hundred years and that vard had settled the coastal lands south of the city of Mentór. Yet ultimately its rule had been overthrown. In the centuries that followed,

173

four Baroddan families — the Akharns, the Okhunars, the Khatains and the Salasslens — had struggled for the crown, each again and again holding it for a few decades and then losing it after some brief, bloody struggle.

After such a history of instability and violence, it is scarcely surprising that, when the Sandastrians and Fachnese together had overthrown King Saiondar II of evil memory, the peace they brought was welcomed by many. The true Brevegens, the families of Fachnese connection, were strong supporters of the new regime; so also were many Baroddan families, most notably the Okhunars and Salasslens. Other Baroddans, however, still longed for the days when power was held in their own hands, however perilously. There was continual unrest in the north of the new earldom, where the Akharns and Khatains were forever stirring up trouble.

Yes, it was a complex history; but it made me understand that, whilst some of his subjects might hate Earl Helburnet and the Sandastrians, many others were deeply grateful that the years of bitter internecine feuding were over.

That recounting of history took up most of the evening and it was late when, having said my farewells, I rode back to the castle. Who would be at the inn next day, I wondered? Baroddans for sure; Akharns or Khatains, most likely. But would Draklin Grassad venture to show himself — or even Vrek Harradas? Well, we would see.

The harbourside inn whose sign was a leaping fish was a two-storeyed building that looked very European to my eyes. It had a spacious cellar at water level into which casks of wine or barrels of ale could be rolled up a tunnel from moored vessels. The public rooms were at quay level; above them was a series of smaller rooms, available for hiring by the motley denizens of the waterfront for private parties. Close by were the Strangers' Houses, where sailors found amusement and visiting merchants dwelt. The inn and the Strangers' Houses were owned and staffed by Sandastrians, but the occupation was not an honoured one and persons working there stood low in the regard of the worthier citizens of Sandarro.

The proprietor of the inn was one Kesvar biek Neriss.

His name requires some explanation. In Sandastre, crime is rare but — as everywhere — it did occur sometimes. A minor offence is punished by a short spell of labour at some unattractive task — cleaning out the drains of the padin on Sandarro Hill, for example, or labouring at the docks — and that would be all. A more major crime means, not only a longer spell of punitive labour, but also expulsion from the family clan for a period. Until the elders of the vard considered his punishment sufficiently prolonged or his subsequent conduct sufficiently meritorious, the criminal must work somewhere well away from the clan lands and must bear the stigma of a differenced name — biek Vendahl, biek Dasnar. (If this seems harsh I should note that, at reinstatement, the undifferenced clan name is resumed, the record of the crime expunged and the ex-criminal welcomed back like a returning Prodigal Son.) A truly serious crime — malicious injury, deliberate arson, treachery or premeditated murder — might mean prolonged confinement on the tiny prison island of Yezadek, banishment, or even execution. In the latter case, the name of the criminal is expunged from all national or family records, with the intent that both the crime and its perpetrator be entirely forgotten.

What crime it was that Kesvar biek Neriss had committed, I never learned; however, it had caused him to be sent far from the lands of his vard and to labour long and uncongenially in the docks. Scribe Enar Servessil had investigated the innkeeper's background thoroughly; it transpired that he had been reasonably honest since his punishment and was very eager to return to the northern forests. The covert offer of reinstatement in his vard *seemed* to have made him willing to aid us; but was he truly to be trusted? That remained to be ascertained.

The chamber reserved by the conspirators for this meeting was on the second floor. That was convenient for, unbeknown to them, there was a storage loft in the roof above, beneath the steeply pitching wooden tiles. Though the note found in Asd Akharn's satchel had specified no time for the meeting, the innkeeper had revealed to Servessil's agents that it would take place late in the afternoon, before the inn filled with sailors anxious for their evening carouse.

We entered the inn considerably earlier, by way of a rowboat and the tunnel. Indeed, we participated in the delivery of wine casks from an 'Arctorran' coastal vessel — actually a small Sandastrian ship skilfully disguised. After twelve 'labourers' had repeatedly gone up and down the tunnel in a deliberately confusing sequence, we were pretty sure no bystander could be aware that four remained within!

I was one of those four and glad, after the sweaty labour in the tunnel, of the chance to wash in the innkeeper's kitchen before taking up vigil in the loft. The innkeeper, a harried-looking man with a surprised moustache, and his massive, muscular wife were at that time alone in the inn, their servants having been sent away on 'urgent' errands. The two welcomed us obsequiously and escorted us to the upper room.

Up a ladder we went and through a trap door; not a long climb, for the meeting room was not lofty. Sacking was laid thick on the floor of the loft to muffle our movements and a plank displaced to ensure easy watching. Then, with the trap door back in place and the ladder taken away, we settled down to wait.

Avran was with me, of course, and scribe Enar Servessil armed with parchment and charcoal sticks for note-taking. The fourth was a person unfamiliar to me hitherto; Etban Dernogme, vardaf (elected chief) of Dernogmavard, a man of unimpeachable integrity whom Avran had enlisted as in-dependent witness to the proceedings. He was an elderly man with fierce eyebrows, an upswept white moustache and direct, piercing blue eyes. His vard, I gathered, was aligned neither with the Estantesecs nor with the Grassads, so that all members of the Ruling Council would heed his words. Evidently he felt himself to be present in a judicial capacity for, after a courteous response to his introduction to me, he fell resolutely silent.

Deliberately we had arrived well ahead of the conspirators. Consequently, we had to wait for what seemed an interminable time in silence and idleness before, at last, we heard voices below.

The innkeeper was ushering up into the chamber three men. None was familiar to me, but Enar Servessil recognized and identified them to us in a whisper. Two were Baroddan merchants who travelled often to Sandarro; the third, a stocky fellow with curiously blank half-moon-shaped eyes, was a Sandastrian thief whose family clan, Exoravard, had long since disowned him. These three conversed in undertones; clearly they were waiting for the arrival of others.

There came a heavy step on the stairs and, to my great surprise, who should appear but the bulky Baroddan priest, whose verbosity had so tried my patience! I heard Avran's indrawn breath and Enar's softly murmured comment: 'So the Salasslens are in the plot! I thought they, at least, were our friends.'

Following the priest furtively, nervously, was another whom I recognized, the weaselly man who had tried so recently to murder me; and behind him came a sixth man whom Enar identified as the captain of the Arctorran ship.

The priest was clearly important in the conspiracy, for he was greeted with respect. Yet still they waited; the company was not yet complete.

Two more arrivals followed. The next was a sandy, pale-skinned man with a fixed smile who, it seemed, was of Bredennavard, a clan firmly allied to the Grassads. Close upon his heels came a tall, lean fellow with prominent eyes of the palest blue, oddly combined with long, dark hair and beard. His cold gaze travelled all about the chamber before he responded to his fellow conspirators' greetings; and I shivered, for I sensed that here was a killer.

Avran stiffened beside me. 'Khass Khatain! Long have we sought him,' he whispered. 'How comes he to Sandarro?'

Clearly these two were, like the priest, important in the plot, for great deference was shown to them by most of those below us. Yet the weaselly man tried hard to efface himself in a corner and, when Khass Khatain at last spotted him, he cringed away. And with just cause, for the Baroddan leapt upon him, slapped him hard across the face and poured at him a stream of abuse.

Avran chuckled quietly. 'Well, well! It seems the Khatain knows of the attempt on you yesterday, Simon, and is not pleased that it failed!' But then he fell silent, for someone else was entering the chamber.

I drew in my breath sharply and Atban Dernogme, crouched opposite me, seemed to stiffen and bristle like a hound scenting a wild boar. As for Avran, he was nodding slowly. His whisper seemed more to himself than to we others: 'Vrek Harradas! We need doubt no longer.'

Chapter Sixteen

THE FIGHT IN THE UPPER ROOM

It was evident that the Harradas regarded himself as the leader of the group below us, for he nodded only the most perfunctory of greetings to his fellow conspirators before seating himself at the head of the table. At his gesture the others sat down also. Khass Khatain made a great show of deference in ushering the priest to the seat at the table's foot; yet, peering down through the crack, I saw the sardonic amusement in his eyes and was sure it *was* only a show.

As soon as all were seated, Vrek Harradas began to speak. I was able to follow much of what he said; and afterwards, the scribe filled in the gaps for me.

'We have little time, brothers,' he began, 'so I trust you will forgive me if I lead our discussions. You all can understand Sandastrian, I take it? Good; for, to my shame, I have difficulty in comprehending your rich and ancient Baroddan dialect.'

He said this in a tone of such infinite condescension that I was surprised to note the gratification with which his auditors received the speech. I think this amused him, but that ever-mobile face defied any reading of expressions.

'I regret also to have to expose you to dangers by calling this meeting here in Sandarro,' he continued with perfunctory solicitude. 'However, I am so closely watched by the spies of that cursed puppet of the Estantesecs, Enar Servessil' — Enar smiled — 'that it would have been yet more dangerous to try to meet you elsewhere; and a meeting of leaders was vitally necessary. The culmination of our schemes is in sight and we must arrange the final stages with care. Yes, I *will* have some wine; thank you.'

As Vrek Harradas drank, his pale blue eyes examined each of his fellow conspirators in turn, steadily, as if assessing their reliability. Khass Khatain and the captain seemed merely amused, but the priest and the others were uneasy under that gaze and the weaselly assassin shrank away from it. When the Harradas had drained his goblet, he resumed his speech.

'Have you received tidings yet, I must ask, as to what happened to the two colleagues we sent to England? Of course, we summoned back only Asd Akharn, instructing the other — what was his name? — oh yes, Kuakh Kerslen, to try to carry through the assassination of that accursed Prince Avran. You have heard nothing? Strange! I was assured the message had been delivered. Yet, had he received it, Akharn surely would have been here with us. They must have missed both message and quarry, for that stupid young prince is no match for two men so able!' (At this point, Avran grinned and I could not resist a responsive smile.) 'Well, no doubt they'll be reporting shortly.

'Otherwise our schemes go well. Since last we met, the second stage of our plan has been carried out, as you all know; and now we must plot the third. Thanks to our reverend colleague here' — he inclined his head to the fat priest, who smirked in self-satisfaction — 'the so-styled Earl of Breveg will shortly be hastening back to Mentór. There he must be dealt with swiftly. Now, my *dear* Sakhar Salasslen, perhaps you might briefly summarize the situation and your plans? Are your Baroddans well primed for an uprising? How will you proceed?'

The priest pursed his lips importantly and responded, in the overripe-plum tones of which I had already heard too much: 'Aha, sir, truly I may say that you may rely on me! My cousin, who styles himself leader of our clan, unfortunately has been a consistent supporter of you Sandastrian usurpers of our realm; and many others hold ideas that are similarly misguided. However, we have worked out a pretty scheme to smash that support.'

He paused, gazing around him in overweening self-satisfaction, and took a swig of wine before proceeding: 'My cousin has a small son, on whom he dotes. When the accursed Helburnet sets out from Mentór on his planned northward tour — the poor fool yet hopes to seduce the hearts of our Baroddans to his cause! — the boy will disappear. Later his corpse will be found by some — ah — innocent person in the cellar of a house in which the prince has stayed. Naturally we will provide adequate — ah — evidence that the prince's followers did the killing. After that, what more simple than to arrange an attack on Prince Helburnet by a justly enraged mob? During that attack, you may be assured, the prince will die!'

'But will the Salasslens believe Helburnet arranged the killing? Will your cousin believe it?'

The priest smiled maliciously. 'I doubt it! I doubt it! But what will it matter? The prince will be dead by then and so also will my cousin's heir! What more natural than that I, the head of the second branch of our family, should become the leader of the Salasslens? And, of course, you may trust me!' He sat back, slapping his paunch complacently.

Vrek Harradas eyed him and nodded, his face twitching into, and away from, a smile. 'Naturally we trust you! After all' — he coughed — 'do we not plan to make you Earl of Breveg after the Estantesecs are rooted out? And ultimately, I doubt not, King of Barodda, when your lost northern realms are recovered from the Fachnese. Your country could have no worthier leader!'

Was that praise or was it sarcasm? Whatever it was, it caused the priest to swell with gratification. However, I saw that Khass Khatain was casting his eyes ceilingward and seemed amused. If the priest did gain the throne of Barodda, I doubted whether he would retain it long!

'Yet we must be sure that the accursed Helburnet does die,' Vrek Harradas continued. 'Whatever transpired in Bristol we do not know, yet it is clear that a unique opportunity was lost. Moreover, I hear that another attempt was bungled yesterday. What can you tell me about that, Kain Bredennar?'

The smile fixed on the lips of the sandy-haired man gave him an air of complete confidence. 'Well, now, I did my part properly. My cousin in the castle guard informed me that the English archer would be alone and vulnerable to attack; and I passed the word to our colleague Yohin Akharn here.' He indicated the weaselly man. 'However, it seems he was frightened away by some small creature — a vasian, was it?'

At this, the assassin yelped in protest and began to frame excuses. Vrek Harradas's cold eyes silenced him.

'But, cousin Bredennar,' he asked in superficially velvety tones which yet did not conceal the iron of anger beneath, 'what made you decide on this attempt? You did not consult me; nor do I recall authorizing you to take initiative, either in this regard or, for that matter, in any other.'

The fixed smile did not even flicker, yet the sandy-haired man was clearly nervous. 'Our friend Khatain — our other Baroddan friends — they seemed to think the Englishman's weapon a danger to them. They asked —'

Vrek Harradas broke in again: 'And are Baroddan interests paramount in this matter, cousin? I did not know that!'

His tone was a withering blast, yet swiftly it became again a honeyed breeze. 'After all, gentlemen, our strength is that we work together, is it not? Come now! Such instant initiatives are foolish, except in a crisis; and this was not a crisis. Cousin Bredennar' — his tone became bleak again — 'I must discuss this matter further with you, afterwards. Perhaps you are not quite experienced enough for this committee; perhaps you should be superseded . . . Ah well, that can wait till later. Back to business, gentlemen! Remember that our twin aims, to restore the realm of Barodda and to set the Grassads on the throne of Sandastre, must be carried through together if either is to be attained. Tell me, reverend cousin, how the killing of Prince Helburnet will be assured?'

He had addressed his question to the priest, but it was Khass Khatain who responded. He thrust back his chair and set his feet on the table.

'You have no need for anxiety, cousin.' His tone mocked that of Harradas. 'I will see to it myself. These Akharns may be unreliable, but you can trust we of Khatain! When I was instructed to undertake the assassination of Prince Brandar Estantesec just a few short months ago, did I not carry it through? Why, it was I myself who cut his throat, while he lay sleeping! Be assured I am more than a match for any Estantesec!'

As the discussion between the conspirators was progressing, the anger of my three colleagues in the loft had been mounting. Etban Dernogme was spearshaft stiff and pale with contained emotion, while the scribe, though steadily taking notes, was far from calm, as his twitching cheek muscles revealed.

As for Avran, he was scarlet and so swelling with fury that I had been fearing an explosion was imminent. With this revelation and taunt, it came. Avran jumped forward, seized and threw aside the trap door in a single dynamic gesture, and leapt down on to the floor of the room below. He landed on his feet, swung about and drew his sword in one continuous flow of movement, to confront the Baroddan.

'So you say you're a match for any Estantesec!' he spat. 'We'll see! Get to your feet, murderer. This is the time of payment!'

The shock of Avran's arrival into their midst seemed momentarily to have benumbed the conspirators, but all of them were on their feet quickly. Khass Khatain had gone white; he backed away from Avran and seemed to reach for his sword reluctantly. Others were much swifter in drawing their weapons. Soon Avran was ringed by blades.

Before they could attack him, the situation had changed. Sword already in hand, Etban Dernogme dropped down onto the table, the wine flagon and goblets toppling and falling at his impact. In a moment he was standing on the floor, an old war-dog bristling for a fight. Enar Servessil produced a whistle and blew it loudly, then leapt down on to the table and to the floor. Swiftly the three swordsmen formed an outward-facing triangle at the centre of the room.

For my part, I was too unconfident of my abilities in swordsmanship to join them. Instead I remained looking down from the loft, throwing-knife in hand, with no-one paying me any heed.

The scene was one to remember. The priest, pasty-faced, had backed into a corner and was so evidently terrified that I knew he would pose no threat, while Kain Bredennar was sidling toward the stairway, intent only on escape. Four of the other conspirators — the two Baroddan merchants, the Arctorran sea-captain and Vrek Harradas — were already engaged in swordplay with Etban Dernogme and the scribe. The remaining two, the weaselly man and the Sandastrian thief, bore no swords but had drawn their daggers. The thief was merely toying with his and watching the fight, but Yohin Akharn had dropped to the floor and was crawling toward Avran under the screen of the benches.

As for Avran, his attention was concentrated wholly upon the murderer. Khass Khatain seemed also unaware that anyone else was in the chamber. His face was yellow now and his eyes fixed upon Avran, with the appalled concentration of a man in a nightmare. As Avran's sword thrust out, he made a defensive motion that seemed almost involuntary. The clash of the swords roused him; he took a deep breath and abruptly came fully alive. Soon the two were embroiled in a combat whose ferocity and skill — for these were swordsmen of equal calibre — I had never seen equalled.

So fascinatedly was I watching this that I forgot about the weaselly man for a few moments. Suddenly I saw him beneath me, sneaking up behind Avran with dagger at the ready. For a second time I might have killed him with a thrown knife. Indeed, almost I did so; but then I remembered Rascal and, instead, leapt down upon him.

My weight, of course, was much greater than the vasian's had been. Yohin Akharn gave a whistling scream of exhaled breath and fright combined, as I landed upon his back; then he was flat on the floor beneath me, winded and, in fighting terms, finished.

As I scrambled to my feet, the thief biek Exor hurled himself upon me. Fortunately my knife was still in my hand and I hurled it up at him with an underarm flick. It buried in his chest. Clutching vainly at the hilt, he collapsed backward and died.

By then, one of the Baroddan merchants was coughing out his life on the floor and the second had been wounded and disarmed. The scribe was engaged with the sea-captain, evidently a skilful swordsman, and Etban Dernogme was battling it out with Vrek Harradas. However, soldiers were now pounding up the stairs, a dozen or more of them. The sea-captain, distracted by their coming, was disarmed by an adroit stroke of Enar's sword and the Harradas, with a grimace, put up his own sword in surrender.

Khass Khatain and Avran, however, were still locked in a duel of such speed and sheer aggressiveness that neither seemed aware of the events about them. Suddenly I cried out, for I feared disaster had struck my friend. The wine flagon had fallen from the table and rolled some distance. Avran, avoiding a sword-thrust, stumbled upon it, staggered backward and fell helplessly. Khass Khatain gave a crow of delight and leapt upon him.

However, the Baroddan was not watching his own footing. The flagon had been sent spinning and was copiously discharging its residual contents. I am not sure whether Khass Khatain's foot caught it or whether the spilt wine caused his foot to slip. In any event, he lost balance and plunged forward.

I do not think Avran even thrust at him; I believe that the Khatain impaled himself on Avran's sword, finding the fate he had earned by chance rather than by Avran's skill. Whatever the cause, Khass Khatain was dead before the soldiers seized and lifted his body off that of my fallen friend.

Avran stood up and drew out his sword from the Baroddan's body. He spoke as if to himself. 'Oh brother Brandar, I would that I had scotched this snake ere ever he brought about your death! Yet now he is dead also and you may rest easier in your grave.' He breathed deeply and sighed, then turned and smiled at me. 'Well, Simon my friend, that was brisk while it lasted. It has been an afternoon to remember.'

'It has indeed,' I responded. My voice was unsteady, for I was only beginning to recover from the excitement and my anxiety concerning my friend.

Avran wiped his sword on the cloth covering the table, then sheathed it. At last noticing that harbourmaster Beldevil was with the soldiers, he smiled and said: 'Ah, hello, Arn! You arrived in good time to take away these traitorous scoundrels. I suggest you remove them through the tunnel to the ship, for we don't want this affair to be noised abroad yet. Can we trust in the silence of your men? Oh yes' — noticing they wore medallions of a leaping fish or of a silver tree — 'I see they are all of Vragaravard or Avrassavard — excellently chosen! Good; then would you please remove these miserable traitors?'

So it was that the six captives — Vrek Harradas, Yohin Akharn, the fat priest Sakhar Salasslen, the captain, the surviving Baroddan merchant and Kain Bredennar, captured as he tried to flee — were hurried covertly from the inn. The corpses of the three dead conspirators were also removed, discreetly in barrels that were weighted and thrown overboard when the ship was well out to sea.

Because the fight had occurred in an upstairs room, it had attracted no attention. Moreover, since Arn Beldevil's soldiers were no greater in number than the regular patrol of the docks, their leaving attracted no more notice than had their arriving. Any bystanders must have dismissed both happenings as either a precautionary visit to the inn or a false alarm.

As for the four of us who had shared the vigil, we remained in the inn, at first to wash and then to drink wine with the innkeeper and his wife. The couple were ecstatic at the thought of returning to Nerissvard, the fat wife jigging with joy and whirling her laughing husband round in a happy dance. With honours ahead, the prospect of keeping silence for a few more days troubled them not at all.

The emotions of the four of us were more complex. Etban Dernogme, though grimly satisfied by his part in the apprehension of the conspirators, was still simmering with fury at the treachery of his fellow vardaf. Enar Servessil was wrapped in thought about the implications of what we had heard and the complexities to come, while I was suffering a reaction from the tensions and dangers just past. As for Avran, he seemed in the shadow of recollection of his dead brother. Thus, though we sympathized with their celebration, we could not share in it fully.

It was only when we were riding up toward the castle, on sevdreyen procured for us by the harbourmaster, that Avran seemed to come to himself. He urged his mount alongside mine and observed cheerfully: 'Well, Simon, whatever may happen next, we've ensured an anxious few days for Draklin Grassad. Indeed, I believe this will finish him. My, what a pleasure that will be!'

Chapter Seventeen

THE RULING COUNCIL MEETS

During the three days that ensued before the meeting of the Dakhvardavat (the Ruling Council), the story of the events in the inn did not leak out. However, it was known soon that Vrek Harradas and the Brevegen priest were missing and that some other lesser figures, mostly Baroddans, had vanished. What had happened? Had there been a plot of some kind? Surely these men could not have been arrested; but where had they gone? The inns of Sandarro and the corridors of the castle were abuzz with rumours.

In the meantime, the six former conspirators had been taken to the prison island of Yezadek. There, on the suggestion of Enar Servessil, they were kept apart and questioned separately.

It did not take long for fuller details of the plot to be elucidated. Kain Bredennar was all too ready to tell what he knew, for Vrek Harradas's cold remarks had convinced him that, even should the Grassad faction seize the throne — an unlikely event now — his own days were numbered. One consequence of his revelations was the arrest of the soldier, another Bredennar, who had betrayed me.

Also very ready to talk was the weaselly would-be assassin, Yohin Akharn, eager to save his skin at any cost to others. Through twice sparing his life, I had secured for us much information. The promise of a small sum in gold and passage to England on a Mentonese ship elicited from him a whole mass of details concerning the names of the Brevegen plotters and the locations of their meeting places and stores of arms and armour.

During those days, I resumed my studies and exercises. Indeed, each of us tried to behave as if all was normal, affecting surprise at the rumours and puzzlement at the disappearances. Not even during family dinners with the eslef and eslevar were the developments discussed. Since we were each agog with curiosity as to what would happen next, this was all pretty frustrating for Avran, Ilven and me. You may be sure that, on the day the Ruling Council met, we were seated early in the spectators' gallery! Nor were we alone, for many others had come in the hope of hearing answers to the questions of those few days.

Since the lands of the vardai were scattered throughout Sandastre and, for many, the ride to Sandarro was a long one, a vardaf often would send some representative to meetings of the Ruling Council at which no important business was anticipated. Not so today. With the exception of the leaders of Lednavard, whom I learned was very sick, and of Harradavard, all the vardavai were in their seats; and, indeed, even Lednavard had sent a representative. Avran pointed out to me the head of Bredennavard, an elderly and ineffectual-looking man; and, of course, I needed no aid to recognize the vardaf of Grassavard!

Again Draklin Grassad arrived late. He stumped to the centre of the chamber and gazed about him belligerently, as if in aggressive quest for Vrek Harradas, before going to his seat.

As soon as the vardaf of Andravard, who was also a priest, had intoned the prayer that conventionally began each meeting of the Ruling Council, one of the vardavai rose to his feet seeking Prince Vindicon's permission to ask a question. No, it was not Draklin Grassad but the leader of Densgavard, a massive red-bearded man with broad shoulders. Even before Avran whispered to me that the Denesgars were allies of the Grassads I had guessed it, for by now I was familiar with the Grassad habit of ensuring their arrows were shot by others. The question was predictable: Could the Prince please inform them of the whereabouts of their colleague, the vardaf of Harradavard?

'Yes indeed,' responded the Prince. 'Most regretfully I must report that he and others are under arrest for their part in a conspiracy to overthrow this realm of Sandastre.'

There was a stricken silence, then hubbub. When the scribe had pounded on his table with a gavel to restore order, the Denesgar leapt again to his feet: 'May we have

details of this conspiracy? And, in view of the known align-
ments in this Council, is there — ah — any independent
witness to it?'

The Prince gazed fiercely at the vardaf. 'That second
question is unacceptable and insulting. You will please withdraw
it.'

Evidently the Denesgar realized he had said too much, for
he mumbled an apology and sat down quickly. Nevertheless,
as I reflected amusedly, the Prince had arranged that both
questions could be answered effectively! He was speaking
again. 'In answer to your first question, I shall call successively
on the vardaf of Dernogmavard and upon our scribe. Etban
Dernogme, please address us!'

His moustache bristling, the Dernogme rose to his feet
and unrolled the parchment scroll upon which, in that upper
chamber, he had made notes. His exposition was long and,
to its auditors, sensational. He began by telling of the two
attempted assassinations of Avran, in Bristol and on the boat,
and of the finding of details of the meeting in the dead
assassin's satchel. (I stole a glance at Draklin Grassad and
saw his heave of anger.) Etban then described the assembling
of the conspirators and read out their names.

At this, hubbub broke out again. Though this was quickly
stilled as the vardaf continued speaking, it was to a mounting
background of excited comment on floor and in gallery that
he recounted in detail what we had seen and heard.

When Etban repeated the aims of the conspiracy as expressed
by Vrek Harradas — 'to restore the realm of Barodda and
to set the Grassads on the throne of Sandastre' — there was
uproar! Angry vardavai were pounding on the tables and
shouting their fury at this treachery. Draklin Grassad seemed
to shrink in his seat and his principal followers — the vardavai
of Bredennavard, Densgavard, Vespravard, Goretsavard and
Marexavard — were readily identifiable by their embarrassment
and confusion.

It was long ere Enar Servessil's gavel-thumping restored
order, but then the remainder of the account — the story
of the fight and of the arrest of the surviving conspirators
— was heard out in comparative silence.

The scribe, called upon next, spoke very briefly. He
endorsed Etban Dernogme's statements and revealed that

'two of the prisoners' — names left unspecified — had provided full enough details of the plot to enable its extirpation.

As he sat down, all our eyes turned upon Draklin Grassad. The Prince waited awhile, then said gently: 'Perhaps the vardaf of Grassavard would care to comment upon these revelations?'

The man seemed to have aged. He rose fumblingly, clinging to his cane as if to a lifeline, and stood silent awhile, as if fighting for words or for breath. Yet I know this was in part an act, for his eyes, under those heavy brows, were ranging the chamber calculatingly. At last the Grassad spoke, in a sort of stricken gasp.

'My Lord — my colleagues of this Council — what can I say? Only that I was entirely ignorant of this . . . this terrible conspiracy . . . and I am appalled by it. I have friends — I know I have friends — who have been eager, unduly eager as I now recognize, to see justice done to we Grassads, but this . . . this wicked plotting with the enemies of Sandastre . . . I am horrified, truly horrified. Though, as I assure you, I am quite innocent of any involvement in this — this foul plot, yet I feel I must resign herewith from the Ruling Council.'

His impromptu speech was a startling *tour de force*; and it went well, for the hum of comment that followed was hushed and respectful. I am sure Draklin Grassad not merely hoped, but actually expected, that he would be asked to withdraw his resignation. However, that was not to be. Etban Dernogme was on his feet again and craving permission to speak.

'My Lord, it is true that the name of our colleague of Grassad is not among those revealed to us. Yet I find in the list those of Hebek Grassad, Darolayn Grassad, Avabek Grassad and Yakiyn Grassad, all of them high in the ranks of his advisers; and, as we all know, Vrek Harradas was his close friend.'

He paused, allowing another ripple of comment to die away; then proceeded: 'I think it proper, in the interests of his vard, that our colleague's resignation be accepted and that his vard be required to appoint a successor who, shall we say, is less tainted with suspicion.'

There was a rumble of approval, and he went on: 'Since three names from Bredennavard, all of them senior and among the advisers to its vardaf, are listed, perhaps that vard might also be asked to reconsider its representation in this Council? I propose further that Vrek Harradas be expelled forthwith from this Council and that, for his treachery, his life shall be forfeit!'

Such a roar of acclamation followed this speech that its endorsement by the Council was immediately evident. When the Prince requested other comments, none came save that of the vardaf of Bredennavard who, pale with confusion and embarrassment, tended his own resignation.

When the vote on Etban's three motions was taken, all the other vardavai, even those who had hitherto supported Draklin Grassad, rose to endorse them. At that point, the vardaf of Bredennavard scuttled from the chamber; but Draklin Grassad, defeated at last, stumbled out slowly.

Then Prince Vindicon spoke again: 'Since we have now three vardai unrepresented on this Council and since action must be taken urgently to eradicate this conspiracy, I do not propose to proceed with other business today. However, I would like immediately to thank several persons. The former keeper of the Leaping Fish Inn, Kesvar Neriss, and his lady will, I understand, be returning soon to their northern home; and I believe a generous grant of land will be made to them?'

The vardaf of Nerissvard having concurred enthusiastically, the eslef went on: 'Our colleagues Enar Servessil and Etban Dernogme, our harbourmaster Arn Beldevil and my son, the indreslef Avran, already stood high in our regard and now stand yet higher. However, I would like especially to honour our English guest, Simon Vasianavar. Already we were respecting him for his skill with the long-bow and his promise of tuition to our soldiers. Now I can acknowledge publicly that, not only has he twice preserved the life of my son, but also the stability of this realm. Through the powers you have vested in me, fellow Councillors, I proclaim him centenar of our army and free citizen of Sandastre. Simon, please rise!'

I did so, red to the ears with embarrassment and with Avran pummelling my back in his usual excessive enthusiasm.

191

As they cheered me, I became aware that Rascal, who had been perched forgotten on my shoulder, was leaping up and down and squeaking with joy.

The conspiracy had deep roots and many of them yet remained to be dug out. Twenty Sandastrians were identified as being involved in greater or lesser degree and punishment was meted out to them in proportion. Kain Bredennar, henceforward Kain biek Bredennar, saved his own life through his confession; yet he did not escape lengthy imprisonment on Yezadek, where twelve others were, for varying terms, his companions. Six were adjudged small fry in this shoal of plotters and, under differenced names, served out their terms cleansing drains or labouring on the quays.

The situation of Vrek Harradas was more complicated. That he was one of the leaders in the conspiracy, we knew; that he was its actual leader, we did not believe. From the words I had overheard in the castle, we knew well the identity of its true instigator. Yet my unsupported evidence was not enough to bring the Grassad to trial. I had repeated words spoken in a language that I did not understand; could anyone, myself included, be absolutely sure that I had done so accurately? The Estantesecs and Enar Servessil might so believe, but any moderately astute advocate could have convinced any court into laughing away such evidence. The Baroddan conspirators had made contact solely with the three Sandastrians present at the meeting. Only if Vrek Harradas could be persuaded to give evidence against him might Draklin Grassad be brought to trial. Since the Harradas had been sentenced to death already, there seemed little likelihood that he would turn informant.

To the surprise of everyone, however, there came news from Yezadek that Vrek did wish to testify at the next meeting of the Ruling Council. Would this be the breakthrough that was needed? Might he be seeking to save himself from execution by divulging the name of the conspiracy's true leader?

If the Harradas had been brought from Yezadek by ship directly to Sandarro, the deepest taproot of the conspiracy might indeed have been unearthed. Unfortunately, the

Sandastrians' dislike of the sea betrayed them, for it caused them to prefer, so far as possible, to use land routes. Consequently the Harradas was taken instead on a small sailing vessel to Denbranad, on the larger neighbouring island of Denbradek. There his escort and he were transferred to a second, equally small vessel for the longer passage to the port of Ildumil, where a strong escort of mounted soldiers awaited the prisoner.

In the middle of its crossing of the Denbredin Channel the little sailing ship encountered, and fled before, a much larger and swifter vessel bearing the forbidden red flag of Barodda. Within sight of Ildumil, the fleeing vessel was caught and boarded. The soldiers of the escort were heavily outnumbered and surrendered after a brief fight. Vrek Harradas was released and taken aboard the Baroddan pirate ship. As it sailed away southward he was glimpsed last at its stern, waving a derisory farewell to his former captors.

On board that vessel, as was later realized, there had escaped several of the Baroddan leaders of the conspiracy. They did not return to Breveg and their destination was long to remain unknown. Arcturus, presently at peace with Sandastre but eternally its enemy, was an obvious refuge; moreover an Arctorran, the sea-captain, had been among the conspirators. Yet Enar's spies assured him that the fugitives had not gone to Andressellar. Indeed, they could not be traced to any of the Arctorran ports.

The sea-captain himself, together with the three principal Baroddan conspirators arrested at the Leaping Fish, was destined for long incarceration in the prison of Yezadek. (Unlike we English, the Rockalese are remarkably reluctant to impose sentences of execution. Moreover, they regard prolonged imprisonment as a punishment worse than death and, even though their prisons are much pleasanter places than ours, I believe they are right. Normally only incurably violent criminals and the dangerously insane are executed.) Yohin Akharn, clutching his Judas gold, departed on the first Mentonese vessel to England and was heard of no more.

Over a hundred other Baroddans were arrested, but those remaining in Breveg were all minor figures in the plot. Moreover, the Sandastrians respected them as being men and women loyal to their country, however unworthy of such loyalty that country might be. Thus Earl Helburnet dealt with them gently. Each was given the choice between imprisonment or the swearing of an oath never again to take up arms against the government of Breveg. Only six diehards chose the first alternative; the others all duly pledged their word and were released immediately.

When one remembers that Earl Helburnet's own beloved brother had been a victim of the plot, his clemency was, to my mind, remarkable. Yet it had its effect. Thenceforward his rule was more universally welcomed in Breveg and, even in the north, his troubles subsided.

Draklin Grassad, though the true leader of the conspiracy, could not be brought to trial for his crimes. Yet perhaps he was punished enough; for another man was vardaf of Grassavard in his stead, the support of the other vardai had been forfeited and his personal influence was gone. Grassavard was no longer a power in the land and Draklin Grassad retired from Sandarro, to pass his days in bitter obscurity.

Chapter Eighteen

A Conversation on a Hilltop

During the week following the exposure of the conspiracy, the two Aradars returned from the forests, bringing with them two hasedu-loads of potential bowstaves cut from many different trees. Most proved unsuitable. Some of the woods were so hard and heavy that they had no flexibility at all; others were too short-fibred and entirely too flexible. Yet three or four proved satisfactory and one stave just about ideal. It had been cut from the bole of a daranek, quite a small tree common in the forest glades of south Sandastre, with a leaf the shape of a fleur-de-lys and yellow berries so sour that the juice of one would curdle a pint of milk. Soon bowyers were brought from Basselt and fletchers from Meteletza — each Sandastrian town and region had its own special craft — to make long-bows and arrows for the newly formed corps of archers I was to train.

Since I was now wearing the silver-grey surcoat of a soldier of the castle and bearing, about the emblem thereon, the gold circle of a centenar, I found myself in authority over men much older than myself. It might have been an uneasy authority, but for the amiability and friendliness so natural to Sandastrians.

One of my first recruits was Avalar Derresdem, the Sandastrian archer who had contested with us. He was eager to master this new sort of bow and was a welcome recruit, for he was resourceful and merry. Yet, to my surprise, he had more difficulties than my other pupils, for he had to unlearn techniques mastered over many years. For the first time, I understood why Oled Orexin had been pleased that I knew so little about swordsmanship!

Once those initial difficulties were past, however, the Derresdem became an excellent archer with the long-bow and proved of great assistance to me in teaching his fellow Sandastrian soldiers. Each day, my corps of recruits spent some hours in standing with bowstaves held at arm's length. Avalar Derresdem's songs and jokes enlivened those tiresome times of passive exercise. So entirely good-humoured was he that even his teasing of a soldier who mis-shot would set not only the other trainee archers, but the culprit himself, laughing.

My own training in swordsmanship and in sevdru-riding continued; and soon Avran decided it was time for me to learn to use the sayasin also. Truly this was a weapon special to Rockall! Between the two brow-horns of one's mount, one tied a broad ribbon. This was made, not of cloth, but of congealed sap trapped from a tree, the meremek, that grew locally in the high forests of eastern Sandastre. Such trees were greatly prized and carefully tended. Dranbarsedd, the fortress town of Menavedravard, was the centre of their culture; and there also were made the V-shaped wooden darts, sasialin, which were shot from the sasayin. Into the leading edge of the dart — the tip of the V — was set a strip of metal sharpened to a razor-like edge. The darts were set into a series of overlapping pockets in a strip of leather fastened harness-like about the shoulders of one's mount.

While riding along, a dart was taken out from its pocket by the left hand and set in place before and about the elastic strip, its point foremost and its ends enclosing the strip itself. The two ends of the dart were then grasped by the right hand and drawn toward one's body, thus pulling back and stretching the ribbon of gum. Since the wood of the dart was quite flexible, its two ends closed together as one pulled, which made it easier to increase the tension. The sasayin thus functioned like a horizontal bow and, when loosed, the dart travelled almost with the speed and force of an arrow.*

At short range the sasayin could be quite a formidable weapon, for the forward edge of a sasial was quite as sharp

* The sasayin is better understood if compared with a boy's catapult of the present day. The horns of the sevdru correspond to the Y-frame and the elastic ribbon to the rubber. Indeed, the sap of the meremek hardens into a material very like rubber, a substance unknown in the Europe of Simon's time.

as the point of an arrow. Though its penetrating power was less, such a dart could readily disable or kill man or beast. In warfare, the sevdreyen wore an armour of light chain mail over their trunks and upper limbs and a head armour of chain or plate, to protect them against these weapons. Their riders would be armoured also and would bear a small concave shield on each forearm, to protect themselves and their mounts against such missiles. Even so, at close quarters, the sasial might be travelling with sufficient force to cut through chain mail.

It was exciting to practise with this new weapon, riding swiftly forward and loosing my darts, according to Avran's shouted orders, at targets set above, below, or to the side. Oddly enough, the tension on her horns prior to loosing the dart disturbed Whitebrow not at all; sevdru horns must be quite insensitive, at least at their bases. Greatly did I enjoy myself and soon I was Avran's equal at this new martial art. However, when he shot edgeless sasialin at me, I was much less adroit than he in blocking them with my arm shields.

As autumn advanced and night fell ever earlier, I began to participate also in the royal sport of Sandastre. Like all gentlemen's sons in England, I had been trained in falconry; and, whilst out on rides with Avran and Ilven, several times had I seen falconers training and flying falcons in the meadows or short-winged hawks in the forest glades on sunny days. Now, however, I was initiated into a style of falconry quite new to me.

In Rockall there are no owls. Instead, there are hawks which fly only in the dim light of dusk and dawn — large-eyed and soft-pinioned birds, not so noiseless in flight as owls but much swifter. Though nighthawks will prey on any unwary small creature that they espy among the undergrowth, their prime quarry is sought and caught in the air — bats.

As with day-flying birds of prey, there are several sizes and types of nighthawks. Smaller adult nighthawks and the eyasses of larger breeds are carried by a falconer on foot and loosed at the little insectivorous flittermice, for sport and to provide the birds with food. At full growth, however, the larger nighthawks are flown from sevdru-back, their quarry the large leaf- and fruit-eating bats that haunt the forests and glades of southern Rockall. These bats not only provide good sport but also furnish a very tasty meat. It was their meat, indeed, that I had eaten on my second night in the castle of Sandarro; the Sandastrians preferred it to all other.

We would set out from the castle just before twilight, in groups of no more than four, each with his nighthawk on his gloved wrist. When the black shape of a bat was glimpsed against the sky, one of us would loose his hawk at it. The back and wing tips of each bird were painted with a luminous substance, culled from a fungus growing in forest humus; thus, as the nighthawk flew, one could discern its weaving path through the darkness of the trees, even if one could no longer see the flickering flight of the quarry it was pursuing.

We followed our hawk, riding at breakneck speed through the dark forest, ducking beneath branches and trusting in the surefootedness of our mounts. Not only was there danger of being knocked from one's sevdru by a bough or of one's mount stumbling in the darkness, but also there was the risk of coming unawares upon some fell beast. (As by now I had learned, most of the animals depicted in the carven forests were not legendary after all, but very real.) All in all, such a pursuit through the dark forest brought a heart-pounding exhilaration unmatched in any other sport I had tried.

Sometimes the quarry would be caught. Very often, though, the pursuit was in vain, the bat eluding its pursuer by dodging among the tree branches. Usually one's nighthawk could be called back successfully, but sometimes its frustration would make it angry. Then one would have to wait or search patiently among the trees till it tired of freedom and returned to the fist.

There are four principal nighthawks considered of first class for hunting. The brown-flecked bird of the high plains of Temecula, the black hawk of the great forests and the creamy-grey hawk of Fachane each have their advocates, but for me one nighthawk surpassed all others; the silver-plumaged, blue-eyed nighthawk of Sandastre. This was the bird that, long since, the Sandastrian princes had adopted as their emblem, depicting it on their shields, surcoats and badges in soaring flight against a night-blue sky under a crescent moon. After seeing the speed and skill of this hawk in its pursuit of its elusive quarry, well could I understand why they had chosen this device!

Indeed, the nighthawk was an emblem popular among the Sandastrian vardai. The Mentlidds bore as their charge the brown Fachnese nighthawk, in flight upon a silver field; the Orexins, Goretsads and Denesgars had chosen the black nighthawk with its red eyes, respectively volant on a golden field, displayed on a silver field, and perched on a red field; and the Vissavants bore the silver nighthawk perched against a black field. Because the Indrens held the high honour of having been the earliest gard, they proudly bore the silver nighthawk in soaring flight; but on a field that was red, not night-blue, and without a crescent moon.

By now I was coming to read these blazons, and those of the other vardai, with the same ease that I could read the coats-of-arms of English families. I would recognize with pleasure, by the yellow-flowering estelen tree on its silver field, a member of my friends' vard the Estantesecs or, by a golden axe on a checkered field, their loyal supporters the Menavedras. In contrast, if I saw the golden forked-tongued lizard on a blue field of the Grassads or the sable bat in flight on a silver field that symbolized Harradavard, I knew well that I must be cautious!

I was becoming familiar also with the customs and habits of the Sandastrians, guided in this by Ilven's careful instruction and by day-to-day experience. From Enar Servessil I learned much concerning the history and ordering of his land and something also of the lands about it — of Temecula, long the ally of Sandastre; of Arcturus, its enemy — passive or active — for an even longer time; of Salastre, a realm so turbulent and disunited that rarely did it pose any threat to its neighbours; of the volatile Fachnese, passionate friends of Sandastre at some times, passionate enemies at others; and of the mysterious, idol-worshipping Dedestans, who had such small traffic with their neighbours. These were the principal southern realms, though others had come into being or vanished as the centuries rolled by. The home of the Mentonese merchants lay far to the north, Enar knew not where; and, as Avran had admitted on the ship, surprisingly little was known about it or them.

Beyond the hills of southern Rockall and north of Sandastre and Fachane, there were vast grasslands drained by a great river, the Werenthin. These were the home of the Montrions, also called the Montariotans, a group of nomadic warrior clans with whom the Sandastrians had only an intermittent commerce and no friendship. Eastward, these grasslands turned into open parklands where many sevdreyen grazed — the twin realms of Antomalata and Sapandella, too concerned with their own quarrels and with resisting Montrion incursions to involve themselves much in the affairs of their southern neighbours. Nowhere in the hills, the grasslands or the parklands would I find Lyonesse; of that, at least, Enar was sure.

Beyond these open lands, however, there were great forests which, until comparatively recently, had been little explored or populated. To these regions, during recent centuries, had come many of my countrymen, building castles in the forest glades and carving out fiefdoms or little kingdoms at will. Enar knew the names of only a few of these little realms — Dellorain, Orelney, Atelone, Dakalet — and it seemed likely enough that Lyonesse might be another.

To these forests, then, must I travel if I hoped to find my father and brother. It might not be so great a journey as Avran had expected, but assuredly it would be as perilous as he had predicted. Few travellers from southern Rockall had ever passed beyond the great plains.

As the weeks slipped by, as the skill of my archers grew apace and as my own skill with the sword and sasayin waxed, I began to realize uneasily that the time for setting forth on my journey was drawing closer. I knew I was becoming daily better equipped for it. Though some words and phrases still confounded me, I could get along well enough in Sandastrian and my confidence in sevdru-riding was considerable. My problem was that I was feeling an increasing disinclination to set forth. Sandarro was the home of the best friends I had ever made and, now that the threat of the Grassads was removed, I could imagine no happier land in which to live. Then also, bulking ever more prominently in my thoughts, there was Ilven.

Since I had taken on the task of training the bowmen, our archery practices together had become fewer and our outings rarer. Only on a few Sunday afternoons did we sally forth on sevdru-back together, and then usually in the company of Avran also. He was my friend yet, on those excursions, somehow his company was not altogether welcome to me . . .

200

Then came a succession of rainy weeks, with archery exercises carried out in sodden cloaks and serious problems keeping our bowstrings dry. In such conditions, long rides would have been absurd and I saw Ilven only in the evenings.

Suddenly I realized that Christmas, and the turn of the year, was almost upon us. My trainee archers included men from most of the vardai of Sandastre. All wished to return home for this season, the most joyous in the Christian year.

A testing of their ability was organized in which, to my pleasure, Avalar Derresdem won highest honours and Brek distinguished himself also. Then we put on an archery display for the Ruling Council, on a windy day of fitful rain with only a meagre crowd of other spectators; and after that, abruptly, I found myself with free time again.

Already Avran had gone off with a troop of soldiers, planning to journey up the valley of the Vekringa to Basselt, fortress town of Naratravard. There he would be meeting — indeed, by now might already have met — his brother, who was travelling back across the Baroddan Hills to join the celebrations in Sandarro. Enar Servessil was gone to Beroduness upon some unspecified errand; and, apart from my daily sword practice with Oled Orexin, I had little to occupy me.

Thus was I especially delighted when, on a bright morning with the residual drops of yesterday's rain still sparkling on the bushes, Ilven proposed that we embark upon a day's outing. Our cloaks, a satchel of food and a flask of berry wine were obtained and tied to the saddle of a pack-sevdru. Then, with Ilven on her mount Telesslen ('Gentle One') and I straddling Whitebrow, we rode out through the north gate.

Over the Randavren brook we went and out into the parklands beyond, where hasedain grazed and herd boys watched. The climate of this land was so mild that no living tree or bush ever shed its leaves wholly. However, each year, when the second flowering season was ending, the leaves of particular branches would turn colour, producing brown or yellow hues among the green, brown or red among the gold (for many Rockalese trees have yellow foliage). All the trees and bushes seemed athrob and atrill with small birds. Butterflies were flying still — swallowtails striped in

201

scarlet and black, birdwings iridescent in silver and orange, and tiny blues, each searching out the few remaining blossoms. Great red dragonflies soared high over the watermeadows and crickets chirped amid the grass. Even in December, this land of Sandastre was as colourful and alive as England in high July.

I did not enquire of Ilven our destination, not simply because I was accustomed to her leading our excursions but rather because, wherever she chose to go, her very presence would give me pleasure in that place. It was an unceasing joy for me to behold her — the torrent of auburn hair that flowed down to her shoulders; the beauty of her eyes, green always but constantly changing in hue, according to light and mood; her lips, always so ready for smiles or for laughter; and the graceful slimness of her as she rode along so carelessly, so confidently.

During our earlier rides, Ilven had felt it necessary to be didactic, challenging me to identify trees, birds or flowers whose names she had already taught me or furnishing me with the names of those new to me. On this day, however, she seemed content that we should ride along in companionable silence.

From our direction at setting forth, I had guessed we might be heading again for 'Beldelven Hill' — or so I named it to myself, for it formed part of the lands of the Beldevils and the hill had indeed been delven into, to furnish stone for the walls and towers of Sandarro. (Its real name was Tas Beldevain.) However, after following our earlier road for much of the morning, we left it before reaching the quarries and took instead a narrower, steeper track.

The whole hill was the shape of a great cottage loaf, its flanks of red sandstone, its crust of white quartzite. An English bridle path would have wound up the steep southern side of such a hill in circuitous curves. For sevdreyen, no such favours of routing were necessary.

We rode straight upward, relying upon the nimble-footedness of our mounts. Steeper and steeper became the slope, so much so that, ere its end, I was clinging unashamedly to Whitebrow's horns and, despite my confidence in her, afraid that she and Telesslen must fall backward at any moment. However, that danger passed, the slope slackened and, laughing rather breathlessly as our tension eased, Ilven and I found ourselves on the crest of the hill.

There was little soil here and only a grassy heathland covered the broad hilltop. We turned our mounts about and gazed southward. Over to our right, the stream of the Alasslan was hidden by the trees, but we could see the azure-blue waters of its estuary and, more distantly, the wave-wrinkled bay into which it opened. Beyond was the green wall of the Bernevren Hills. South of us, the hasedain in the parklands below were reduced to ants and their great horns to mere antennae, while the mighty castle of Sandarro, seen thus from above and far away, was no more impressive than a child's toy. Farther away on the southern horizon, Ilven told me, the great island of Hasadek might sometimes be seen; but, though our eyes strove to penetrate the shimmering blue distances, we could not glimpse it.

Since the days of summer heat were so long past, our viewpoint might have been too cool a place had there been any wind; but the day was still and the sunshine delightful. Now we had reached it, the hilltop was almost as flat as a table. We rode relaxedly onward for a few miles to its northern edge, where the slope fell away quite as steeply as that up which we had ridden. Almost north of us ran the broad valley of the Alasslan; the line of the Bernevren Hills, to our left now, was broken only where the Alasslan's tributary stream, the Vekringa, flowed in from the northwest. To our right an undulating mass of high land — the Trantevrin and Sandastrian Hills — closed the horizon. The whole landscape was a harmony of gentle hues, green with touches of brown and yellow and an occasional splash of scarlet where some tree had taken autumnal fire.

'Ilven, I like your land of Sandastre,' I commented. 'It is so warm and so kind, with none of the harshness of my own moorlands.'

'Yes, it is a beautiful land,' she responded, smiling at me in a fashion that caught at my heart. 'Must you leave it so soon? Must you leave it ever?'

'I must seek my father and my brother,' I answered shortly.

'Do they expect you, then? How *can* they expect you, when they have not sent you clear word even of how to find them?'

'No, they do not expect me; but I have vowed to myself that I shall seek them out, and seek them out I must.'

'I do not understand why.' She was looking at me with green eyes clouded and brows furrowed in puzzlement. 'After all, it is they who left you, not you who left them. Can you not forget them and stay here? My father values your services highly; we all — well, we all like you . . .'

'Believe me, I'm tempted to stay here; but, if you had lost your father and lost Avran, would *you* not wish to seek them? Moreover' — I hesitated, then went on — 'you see, my father thought me still a child. He loved me, but he thought me less than my brother. His last message to me — it gave me his blessing, and yet it was a challenge also. I feel I must respond to it, to — oh, to prove myself, I suppose. But Avran — there's really no reason for Avran to go with me, you know. He should stay here with his family — with you.'

'If you go, then Avran will go also,' she stated flatly; then firmly she changed the subject. 'I'm hungry. Let us dismount and have our food.'

The tussocky grass had quite dried in the sun and the hilltop would have been a pleasant place anyway. With Ilven beside me, it was idyllic. Though I ate and drank well, I remember nothing of that repast, yet so exactly do I remember Ilven on that day that I could sketch the very pattern of the silver-thread embroidery adorning her green riding tunic and could repeat all the trivialities of our talk. However, I will content myself with a retelling of its latter part.

When the remains of our meal had been stored away into the pack, I had thought Ilven might wish to begin the return ride; but no, she seated herself again on the grass and said to me: 'Well, Simon, you are speaking Sandastrian quite freely now. In general you've learned our language well; but you make a few mistakes still. When my mother and the other ladies left the meal last night, you spoke of them as *edre*, "they": the word should have been *ekre*.'

'No, I don't really understand the difference,' I admitted.

'Oh come, Simon; surely you know by now that *ste* means "me" and *este* means "we"? And that *dre* means "he" and *edre* means "they", when you're talking of a group of men? Well then, if *kre* means "she", then *ekre* must mean a group of women! You can use *edre* for a mixed group, but not for a gathering of ladies only; it's quite offensive!'

Her mischievous grin took the sting from this reproof and I smiled in response. 'I stand corrected! I'll remember in future. But there was another thing last night that left me puzzled. Enar's wife is called Eyen asar Servessil and the Chancellor's is Maderen asar Estantesec; but there are other wives who are called something different. That young man from Trantevar, for example; his wife was called Dorren atar Derresdem. Why the difference? Does it depend on which part of Sandastre one comes from?'

She laughed. 'Oh no, no, Simon! It's much simpler than that. When a woman and a man decide to marry here, they don't really know if it will work, do they? How *can* they know, until they have lived together? So our marriages are arranged in two stages. For five years, a marriage is — oh, provisional, I suppose. Up to that time, a couple can separate without disgrace to either, and any children are accepted into their mother's vard. A first-stage wife is called *menatar* and she takes her husband's name provisionally — atar Derresdem, atar Estantesec. When five years have passed, they must decide definitely how much they love each other. If they elect to stay together — and remember, the wife chooses also! — then she becomes *memasar*, a second-stage, permanent wife — asar Derresdem, asar Estantesec. If her husband dies during the first five years, she resumes her maiden name; if afterwards his widow, unless she marries again, is called *pirasar* and continues to use his name, asar Derresdem or asar Estantesec. It is all very logical, you know!'

Ilven perceived by my expression that I found this rather shocking, so she went on: 'Consider all the trouble your European kings have when their marriages don't prove a success! All those tiresome legal arguments alleging it never *was* a marriage, all those petitions to the Pope for nullification! How stupid, when it can be done so much more simply!'

I had to agree with this argument, but now I was puzzled by something else. 'When you say that a man loves his wife, you use the verb *verissven*; yet, if you were to say you loved your brother or father, you use *delessven*. Why is that?'

She looked at me very directly as she replied. There was

something special about the smile on her lips, something special about the set of her head, some new look in her eyes that set my heart tumbling over within me.

'Why, your English language is so clumsy! Those are quite different emotions, after all. If I were to say that I loved my sevdru Telesslen, I would use *zalassven*, for that is one sort of love, the love one feels for an animal. If I use *delessven*, it is to express a respectful love, as one feels for a parent, an uncle, a brother. If I use *verissven*, why then that is a passionate love, the love of a man for a woman or of a woman for a man. It is the love I feel for you, Simon — and, I think, you feel for me. Do you not?'

There could be only one answer. My heart seemed to be bursting from my body, bursting up into my throat, into my head. I took her into my arms and there, on the green hilltop, we poured out to each other the words of our love.

That was a time of great joy; and yet I was troubled also. 'But Ilven, how can this be? How can you want me so? After all, your family — your father . . . You are aldreslef of Sandastre and I, merely an English traveller to your land. If we declare our love, will not your father be angry? Will he not wish to end our relationship — wish to expel me from his realm, even? Surely he could not accept me as — well, as a proper husband for the princess, his daughter?'

Still cradled in my arms, she smiled up at me. 'Oh Simon, you are stupid! Can you not realize that an eslef is not a king, nor even a prince in your European sense? He is — oh, the custodian of the land, if you like. He does not have some special sort of blood, such as your English kings claim. He is crowned, yes; but he is not anointed with any divine oil!'

She paused, looking up at me with those adorably bright, moist eyes, then said: 'And, Simon, do you not remember how, on your first night here, my mother the eslevar accepted you as her son? I think she guessed, even then, what I felt already about you; and, as for Avran, he has long known it. No, you need have no fears. My father respects you, my mother and brother both are fond of you, Simon Branthwaite, Simon Vasianavar! This is your land also, if you wish to make it so.'

'Oh Ilven, you know that I do! Yet — what about my father and brother? What about my journey?'

'Why, of course you must go — you and Avran. But oh, Simon' — she clung to me almost fiercely — 'come back! Come back safely!'

Chapter Nineteen

THE SETTING FORTH

In Sandastre, an engagement to marry involves none of the tiresome preliminaries — the seeking of a father's approval, the setting of a wedding portion, the legal arrangements — that would be requisite in England. On our return to the castle that evening, Ilven took me to her parents' private parlour and, in my presence, quietly told them of the plighting of our troth.

Prince Vindicon and Princess Felguen received this intimation with smiles that told me they were not in the least surprised and not at all disapproving — this to my great relief, despite Ilven's reassurances. Moreover, Prince Vindicon's words were heartening, initially at least.

'Simon, even before you arrived in our land, your actions had merited my profound gratitude. Since that time, you have given us even greater cause for gratitude. Already we regard you as a son and, naturally, we welcome this news.'

He took Ilven's right hand and placed it into mine, a gesture of committal that moved us both. Yet his next words surprised me.

'However, Simon, you should know that Avran has told us of your quest, and that he plans to travel with you on that quest. It grieves me that you must go, but I comprehend your reasons and I honour them. I think it fitting, also, that Avran should go with you, even though his doing so will double our anxieties. Beyond doubt, your journey will be hazardous. Most sincerely do I trust that the two of you will surmount all the hazards you encounter, that you will discover the land you seek, and that you will return from it safely and swiftly.'

He paused, then went on more gravely: 'Yet it seems to me only proper, Simon, that your betrothal to our daughter should not be announced *until* you return. At that time, not only can we celebrate the completion of your quest but also we can install you into the position and circumstances that you merit. Until that time, both actions would be premature.' His further thought — that I might not return — was no less evident for being left unspoken.

At her father's words, Ilven turned perfectly white; clearly she had not expected this. That she could exhibit the quickly-flaring temper that went so often with red hair, I had scarcely realized hitherto; but now she seized my hand and, the colour returning to her cheeks, glared at her father the eslef.

'This is unjust and unkind!' she said fiercely. 'Father, it is only Simon that I love or can ever love. Why *must* we wait? Surely this delay is needless? Why can we not — '

I interrupted her. 'Ilven, dearest, I think you are wrong and your father right. So long as I live, nothing shall keep me from returning to you. Yet supposing I do not return? You should not be tied to me irrevocably.'

She snorted indignantly. 'I would not be, anyway! Simon, have I not explained to you only today that our Sandastrian marriages — '

Again I interrupted her. 'Yes, I understand that. Nevertheless, much though it will grieve me, I am prepared to wait for you and I hope you will wait for me.'

This silenced Ilven and, indeed, deflated her; she gazed at me so piteously as to wring my heart. However, I turned again to Prince Vindicon, bowed my head and said: 'I am honoured by your words, my father and my prince, and I accept the condition you have pronounced.'

The eslef stepped forward and laid his hand on my shoulder. 'I knew already that you can be courageous; I am glad you have fortitude also. You are yet young and, given fortune, you will have many years of joy to come.'

Thus did I accept a hard condition. As I knew well, Ilven had expected that we would marry before I set forth on my quest; and she was deeply upset that this would not happen. Under such circumstances, I believe my response was the only one possible. Yet Ilven was sobbing in her mother's arms and proved hard indeed to console. Nor did she come ever to agree that her father's decision, and my acceptance of it, had been right.

*   *   *

Christmas in Sandarro began memorably. Avran returned with Helburnet on its eve, to be welcomed by a dinner at which many of the lords of Sandastre were present. After the repast, and after attiring ourselves appropriately, we joined the castle servants in the great hallway. The vardavai mingled with the soldiers, cooks and butlers with a freedom and amiability that still astonished my English eyes. Walking and jostling cheerfully together, we set forth down the passage out of the castle. As we emerged from the southern gate, the torches in the castle were progressively extinguished and the lights in the towers and padin about and below us were dimmed.

We walked down the hill in the bright moonlight, to find its lower slopes thronged with people — all the people of the city, save those too lame or too infirm to come forth, those who were tending them, and the guards of the castle and city walls. Many folk had brought instruments and struck up tunes, we adults clustering about them and singing or listening, whilst the children ran from group to group in frantic endeavour to hear and see all. Below us, the harbour area was quite dark, the waters beyond coruscating with moon-tipped waves. Above us, the great castle seemed an artefact of silver and enchantment.

As midnight approached, the songs ended and the small groups combined into larger ones centred upon priests, each of whom told the story of the events of the first Christmas to those about him. The children were tiring by then and some, wrapped in blankets their parents had brought, lay sound asleep on the grass already. When the telling was done, there were prayers; and then, with the musicians playing again, we sang more carols to keep at bay our own drowsiness. Long shall I remember that night, sitting there in the darkness, with Ilven by my side and in my embrace.

Suddenly there was a bright spark high above us — a flare lit by a soldier who, high on the soaring central tower of the castle, had glimpsed the first glimmer of dawn on the far eastern horizon. Other sparks danced outward and downward, as soldiers ran with torches down its soaring buttresses to light flares about the five lesser towers. Next, a ring of lights spread about the whole top of the hill, as soldiers on each of the towers of the curtain wall lit their own fires.

211

Soon the whole great castle above us was shimmering in light, to honour this dawn of Christmas Day.

There was a shout of joy as everyone about us leapt to their feet; and of course Ilven and I rose also. As flares progressively were lit on each of the detached outer towers and on those of the city wall below and about us, the whole concourse of people joined, for the first time, in a single swelling carol, 'Light of a World's New Day' — the song of gladness with which the people of Sandastre always welcome Christmas morn.

All the children were awake again now and humming with excitement. After the carol and the blessing that followed it, they ran about and among us with new vigour as we trudged back up the hill, to padarn, tower or castle keep, for the feasts that ended this night of vigil. And then Sandarro fell quiet again as, despite the sunshine of late morning, most of its people slept.

However, Christmas in Sandastre is a celebration of one day, not of twelve as in England. Between Christmas and New Year, Avran and I began the preparations for our journey. Although life had seemed tranquil since the exposure of the conspiracy, we knew well that there were still Baroddans unreconciled and Grassad supporters unappeased. Once in the wilds, we would be infinitely more vulnerable to an attack. Thus, though our departure could not be concealed, it seemed best that our aims and our plans should remain secret.

Accordingly, though no formal announcement was made, the word was quietly spread by Enar Servessil's agents that Prince Avran soon would be travelling as ambassador to Temecula and that the English centenar Simon Vasianavar would be accompanying him. A troop of soldiers was in fact mustered for just such a journey.

Indeed, for a time Avran and I did consider travelling via Temecula. From our studies of Enar's maps, it was evident that the trade route which followed the Siskeven River to its headwaters, traversed the Sandastrian Hills and descended the valley of the Pardeter to Irrelat in Temecula would afford the easiest beginning to our journey. Moreover, it would allow us to avoid the grasslands where the Montrion tribes roved, passing instead through the much more civilized parklands of Antomalata into the great forests where, we presumed, Lyonesse lay hidden.

Two factors decided us against travelling that way. Firstly, it would mean that Avran would feel impelled, for courtesy's sake, to visit his father's friend the King of Temecula in his capital, Stavrasard — and Stavrasard not only lay well off our route but was, for a Sandastrian prince, dangerously close to the border of Arcturus. Secondly, there were rumours of renewed war between Antomalata and the neighbouring principality of Sapandella. No, that pathway would not serve.

There were two principal alternatives. One was to take a western route, following the valley of the Alasslan to its headwaters near the castle of Dassan, then crossing the Helbevin Hills west of Lake Vanadha into Darrinnett and thence venturing into the grasslands. However, here again there were problems. Anciently Darrinnett had been an independent realm; its people longed to restore that independence. Though of Baroddan kinship, they had been reluctant subjects even of the King of Barodda; now they were yet more reluctant subjects of the King of Fachane. According to Enar's spies, Darrinnett was simmering with rebellion and was presently a most unsafe region to traverse. That way seemed also excluded.

The third route was the one upon which, provisionally at least, we had decided. Initially we would follow the valley of the Siskeven, as if toward Temecula, thus giving verisimilitude to the rumours Enar had fostered so industriously. However, at some point thereafter we would quietly leave the company, who would indeed go onward to Temecula. Instead, Avran and I would traverse the Trantevrin Hills to Argray, then follow the east shore of Lake Vanadha into the lands of Estantevard, which straddle Sandastre's northern frontier. There we would need to discover a route northward toward the great plains, through the cluster of little realms that lay between Darrinnett and Temecula. Though this route surely would have its hazards, they were less evident.

I was in the most uncertain of moods, torn between a deep reluctance to leave Ilven and an eagerness to begin my journey quickly, so that I might hope to return to her sooner. Avran, in contrast, had no such equivocal feelings. For him the downfall of the Grassad cause, though eminently desirable, nevertheless had deprived his life of something of its savour; unlike me, he was eager for this new adventure. Thus it was he that decreed our departure date and time — the forenoon of the first day of the Year of Our Lord 1404 (in England, January the First; in Sandastre, Avbalet Ava).

The company of soldiers we were to join numbered only twenty, for this was an escort — or the semblance of one — and not a war party. Although nominally under Avran's command, its true leader was centenar Berim Andracanth, a solid and grizzled warrior who, since he could be trusted with any secret, had been taken into our counsels.

All the soldiers were mounted on sevdreyen, as indeed were Avran and I. However, I would not ride Whitebrow and Avran would leave behind his sevdru Gedreylen ('Brave One'), for those were beasts too obviously valuable to be ridden by the ordinary soldiers that, after leaving the party, we would be pretending to be.

We had tried out our new mounts in the days since Christmas and had established the necessary personal links with them. Avran seemed pleased enough with his sevdru, Zembelen ('Dark One') and I was sufficiently content with Rokh ('Warrior'), even though he could never match White-brow in his skills or my affections.

A more difficult problem was Rascal. For the moment, and for many days to come, he would travel with me; but when we passed beyond the southern hills into the grasslands, what then? There might be no suitable food in the grasslands; for indeed, the vasian was very selective about what he would or would not consume.

I had gone to great lengths to try to make Rascal friendly with Ilven. He was prepared at least to be tolerant of her, even sitting on her shoulder on occasion, provided always that I was close by. Yet the vasianar are single-hearted creatures. If I instructed him to return to her — supposing he could find his way back to Sandarro — would he obey? If he did return, would he thereafter feed normally or would he, in my absence, refuse to eat and go into a second decline? I was so fond of him by then that such problems disturbed

214

me deeply; but they were problems for the future and might, for the moment, be set aside.

All too soon, or so it seemed to me, the time of our setting forth was upon us. That first morning of a new year had brought an advance guard of cirrus clouds from the southwest. While we lunched on the viands traditional to that day, massy cumulus clouds built up, driving away the sun and subduing the colours of the early-winter landscape. In consequence, when we rode forth, even the white castle behind us — for naturally, we were leaving through Sandarro's north gate — seemed dingily grey. As we left the castle, with a doleful Brek waving frantic goodbyes, I felt the first spattering of raindrops.

Already I had said my painful private farewell to Ilven, but she had ridden with her father out to the gate, to utter a formal farewell — an action that simultaneously caused me gladness and a renewal of grief.

Soon the final moment of parting was upon us. The eslef gave a farewell clasped handshake to Avran and then to me, saying quietly: 'Believe me that I shall be praying for the safe return of both my sons, the old and the new' — words that touched my heart.

To Ilven I could find little to say, much though my heart reached out to her. However, as we took each other's hands for the last time, she whispered: 'Come back to me, Simon; come back quickly. And bring Avran back safely.'

My beloved was smiling bravely enough, but I saw the tears she was striving to conceal and found it hard to relinquish our handclasp.

As Avran and I turned and rode out through the gate to join the waiting soldiers, the rain commenced in earnest. When I had left Holdworth, it had been in such weather but, though I had been saying farewell to my home, my heart had been high. Since then I had found a new home. The leaving of it brought only anguish.

GLOSSARY OF SANDASTRIAN WORDS

All Sandastrian words are defined where first used in this account. However, for the convenience of any reader who finds them hard to remember, they are here brought together for ready reference.

A **abrar**, *v.* to come

alberar, *v.* to pretend

aldrenal (*pl.* **aldrenalei**), *n.* sister

aldreslef (*pl.* **aldreslevei**), *n.* princess of secondary status

Arktorran, *adj.* or *n.* Arctorran (Arcturan) 1. of, or pertaining to, **Arktoros** (Arcturus); 2. an inhabitant of that land

asar, *conj.* placed between personal name and husband's surname of a second-stage wife

aseklin (*pl.* **asekleyin**), *n.* arrowslit window of a fortification or castle

aspadarn (*pl.* **aspadin**), *n.* component unit of a **padarn**, *q.v.*

astre (*pl.* **astrei**), *n.* land, nation

atar, *conj.* placed between personal name and husband's surname of a first-stage wife

atra, *n.* or *adj.* southwest

ava, *n.* or *adj.* one (numeral); first

avar, *suff.* friend of, ally of

Avbalet, *n.* January

B **baeldis**, *n.* or *adj.* east

barimé, *adv.* 'Yé barimé . . .?'—'Would you please . . .?'

Baroddnen, *adj.* or *n.* Baroddan 1. of, or pertaining to, Barodda; 2. an inhabitant of that land

baz, *adv.* here

bazatié, *n.* greeting: welcome (literally 'We're pleased to receive you.')

biek, *conj.* placed between personal name and surname of a convicted criminal

D **dakheslef** (*pl.* **dakheslevei**), *n.* king

dakheslevat (*pl.* **dakheslevatai**), *n.* kingdom

dakhvardavat, *n.* Ruling Council of Sandastre

217

daranek (*pl.* **daranekai**), *n.* deciduous tree with leaves of fleur-de-lys shape and sour yellow berries: wood used for bowmaking

delessvar, *v.* to love respectfully, as a parent or friend

drassrar, *v.* to go wrong

dre, *pron.* he

E **ebelmek** (*pl.* **ebelmekai**), *n.* deciduous tree with flowers of bright orange hue

ebra, *n.* or *adj.* northwest

ebressil, *adj.* incompetent, inept

edre, *pron.* they (used for males or mixed sex groups)

ekre, *pron.* they (used for females only)

embelin (*pl.* **embeleyin**), *n.* musical instrument of half-melon shape with four strings (*cf.* citole)

eslef (*pl.* **eslevei**), *n.* ruling prince

eslevar (*pl.* **eslevarei**), *n.* consort of ruling prince

essnar (*pl.* **essnarei**), *n.* pleasure, enjoyment

este, *pron.* we

estelen (*pl.* **estelnai**), *n.* yellow-flowering deciduous tree of northern Sandastre: the symbol of Estantegard

estringa (*pl.* **estringanai**), *n.* 'dew star', wildflower whose shape suggested the plan for Sandarro Castle

etreyen, *adj.* hearty, cordial

evragar, *n.* shining coppery-red metal (orichalcum of the ancients)

evrar, *v.* to happen, occur

éast, *adj.* white

F **Fakhhayin**, *n.* Fachane

Fakhniis, *adj.* or *n.* Fachnese 1. of, or pertaining to, Fachane; 2. an inhabitant of that land

faraslef (*pl.* **faraslevei**), *n.* earl

faraslevat (*pl.* **faraslevatai**), *n.* earldom

felbra, *n.* or *adj.* southeast

G **gard** (*pl.* **gardai**), *n.* ruling family (of Sandastre)

H **hasedu** (*pl.* **hasedain**), *n.* heavy antelope-like herbivore; pelage dark brown; having two spiralling, lyre-shaped horns. Used as a beast of burden and source of meat and milk throughout Rockall; by the Montariotans, used also for riding.

I **id**, *pref.* conditional prefix to verb ('might')

ié, *pref.* 'would you . . .?'

ievran, *adj.* accursed, damned

ikhoras (*pl.* **ikhoranai**), *n.* tree whose branches are used for arrow-making

indrenal (*pl.* **indrenalei**), *n.* brother

indreslef (*pl.* **indreslevei**), *n.* prince of secondary rank

K **kharasef** (*pl.* **kharasevei**), *n.* builder

kharasar, *v.* to build

kre, *pron.* she

ksa, *pref.* imperative prefix

L **lakassar**, *v.* to look, gaze

M **marnis**, *n.* or *adj.* south

mekret (*pl.* **mekreyet**), *n.* rascal

memasar (*pl.* **memasain**), *n.* second-stage wife

menatar (*pl.* **menatain**), *n.* first-stage wife

Mentoniis, *n.* or *adj.* Mentonese 1. of, or pertaining to, Mentone; 2. an inhabitant of that land

meremek (*pl.* **meremekai**), *n.* deciduous tree of high forests, whose sap congeals to form an elastic, rubber-like substance

N **nendra**, *n.* or *adj.* northeast

P **padarn** (*pl.* **padin**), *n.* circular house

pirasar (*pl.* **pirasain**), *n.* widow

R **Rokalnen**, *adj.* or *n.* Rockalese 1. of, or pertaining to, Rockall; 2. an inhabitant of that island

rokh (*pl.* **rokhei**), *n.* warrior

S **salis**, *n.* or *adj.* north

Sandastren, *adj.* or *n.* Sandastrian 1. of, or pertaining to, Sandastre; 2. an inhabitant of that land; 3. the language spoken in Sandastre and adjacent lands

sasayin (*pl.* **sasayinar**), *n.* catapult-like weapon set between the brow-horns of a **sevdru**

sasialin (*pl.* **sasialinar**), *n.* the dart propelled from a **sasayin**

sevdru (*pl.* **sevdreyen**), *n.* antelope-like herbivore having two for-wardly-directed nasal horns and two brow-horns, branching twice symmetrically in Y-fashion so that each horn has four tines; pelage grey, with white underparts and central white line down neck and back; used as a mount and capable of simple telepathic exchanges with its rider.

slaskelest (*pl.* **slaskelestai**), *n.* small salt-tolerant plant with stiff, fibrous leaves used for fletching arrows

T **talivar** (*pl.* **talivarei**), *n.* drink

talivarar, *v.* to drink

tas (*pl.* **tasar**), *n.* hill

telen (*pl.* **teleyin**), *n.* (any) flower

telessil, *adj.* gentle

telesslen (*pl.* **telesselain**), *n.* a gentle person (usually female)

tevorar, *v.* to pass to, or hand over, to someone

U **ustres**, *n.* or *adj.* west

V **vaien** (**vayen**), *adj.* along (as in 'come along')

vakhast, *n.* ejaculation of surprise ('My goodness!')

vandolayakh!, *v.* 'I surrender!'

varas (*pl.* **varasei**), *n.* dried and spiced meat

vard (*pl.* **vardai**), *n.* family-clan

vardaf (*pl.* **vardavai**), *n.* chief of a family-clan

vasian (*pl.* **vasianar**), *n.* small, tarsier-like arboreal primate of southern Rockall, large-eyed and with grey pelage; capable of moderately extensive telepathic interchanges with its owner; very faithful

vatun (*pl.* **vatayin**), *n.* brow

verissvar, *v.* to love passionately one of the opposite sex

Y **yé**, SEE **ié**

Z **zakhretid** (*pl.* **zakhretidai**), *n.* foreigner (used in aggressive, dero-gatory sense)

zalassvar, *v.* to be fond of an animal

zembel, *adj.* dark in hue